OF GUNS, REVENGE AND HOPE

D. LAWRENCE-YOUNG

Copyright © David Lawrence-Young
Jerusalem 2011/5771

All rights reserved. No part of this publication may be translated, reproduced, stored in a retrieval system or transmitted, in any form or by any means, electronic, mechanical, photocopying, recording or otherwise, without express written permission from the publishers.

Cover Design and Typesetting by S. Kim Glassman

ISBN: 978-965-229-533-0

1 3 5 7 9 8 6 4 2

Gefen Publishing House, Ltd.
6 Hatzvi Street
Jerusalem 94386, Israel
972-2-538-0247
orders@gefenpublishing.com

Gefen Books
11 Edison Place
Springfield, NJ 07081, USA
1-800-477-5257
orders@gefenpublishing.com

www.gefenpublishing.com

Printed in Israel   *Send for our free catalogue*

To my wife, Beverley Stock,
who has had to live with the heroes
in this book for over a year,
and also to Marion Lupu,
my ever-meticulous and patient editor.

Also to my life-long friend,
Malcolm (Mac) J. MacCarthy of Sunderland, UK
who gave me the idea of writing this book
and then followed this up by supplying me with
some important source material and background information.

Although based on historical events, this is a work of fiction.

No character or event in this book, with the exception of historical persons, is real, and any resemblance to real persons is unintentional. All dialogue in this work is the product of the author's imagination, including that of real-life historical or public figures.

Other Books by the Same Author

by David L. Young
Tolpuddle:
A Novel

Gunpowder, Treason & Plot:
A Novel

Of Plots & Passions:
A Thousand Years of Devious Deeds

Communicating in English (ed.)

by D. Lawrence-Young
Marlowe:
Soul'd to the Devil

Will Shakespeare: Where Was He?
A Novel

Of Guns & Mules*

*Also published by Gefen Publishing House

Contents

PART ONE: OF GUNS

Chapter One: Tel Aviv, Summer 1940 3
Chapter Two: From Civilian to Soldier 15
Chapter Three: From Tel Aviv to Tobruk 29
Chapter Four: To Derna and Back 49
Chapter Five: Tobruk under Siege 61
Chapter Six: Cairo and Tel Aviv 73
Chapter Seven: Qena 87
Chapter Eight: Pushing the Germans West 103
Chapter Nine: Tripoli and Malta 115
Chapter Ten: Italy 129
Chapter Eleven: Foggia 141
Chapter Twelve: Finally – The Jewish Brigade! 151
Chapter Thirteen: Into Battle at Last! 161
Chapter Fourteen: Offensives on the Front Lines ... 177
Chapter Fifteen: Tragedy at Mount Ghebbio 199

PART TWO: REVENGE

Chapter Sixteen: Revenge Is Mine 219
Chapter Seventeen: Further Acts of Revenge 239

PART THREE: HOPE

Chapter Eighteen: From Tarvisio to Belgium 251
Chapter Nineteen: Belgium, Tamar and Home 267

Afterword 277
Acknowledgments 285
Bibliography 287
About the Author 289

PART ONE

OF GUNS

CHAPTER ONE
Tel Aviv, Summer 1940

Did you ever read the book about my *abba*, my dad, David Levi? It was called *Of Guns and Mules* and was all about the times when he was a soldier in the ZMC during the Great War, or the First World War, as they call it now. What's the ZMC? That's the Zion Mule Corps, a unit of Jewish soldiers in the British army that fought at Gallipoli, in the west of Turkey.

"Why did you call it *Of Guns and Mules*?" I asked when I was younger. "What did mules have to do with the war? Didn't the British army have trucks?"

"Of course it did, but not on the Gallipoli Peninsula. It was too steep and rocky to use them there, so we used mules for transportation."

"Transporting what? Guns? Ammo?"

"Yes, and food and water and other supplies. We used to take this stuff to the men up on the heights and then bring the wounded back down with us to the hospitals and first-aid tents down on the beach."

My father also told me about their commander, a one-armed ex-Russian officer called Joseph Trumpeldor. Later I learned that he had been killed soon after the war ended while defending Tel Hai in the Galilee. Some Arabs had gotten into the outpost he was guarding and in the firefight that followed he and seven others were killed.

And he told me that when the campaign at Gallipoli was over, the British broke up the ZMC. The men refused to fight in Ireland and told their officers they had volunteered to fight the Turks. As a result they were transferred to England and later became the core of the newly formed Jewish Legion. This unit became part of General Allenby's forces, which pushed the Turks out of Palestine toward the end of the war in 1918. My father took part in the fighting near the Dead Sea, at Umm Es Shert and Es Salt.

Ah yes, if you read this book, you'll also learn that my *abba* had a girlfriend called Yehudit. She had been at school with him in Tel Aviv and after the war they got married so she became my *imma*, my mom. They had three kids. The first was me, and later the twins, Dina and Rachel, came along. This meant I was the big brother, and to be honest, I am big. I'm tall, nearly six feet, skinny (but with muscles in the right places) and I have a mass of dark brown wavy hair on top – too much hair, my mother says. I have a suntanned face and dark brown eyes.

I don't like school or reading very much; I prefer using my hands for working with tools and pieces of machinery. Instead of doing boring exercises in algebra or writing essays, I prefer helping my neighbor repair his old Harley-Davidson motorcycle. It's big, black and shiny and has a 1000-cc engine. He pretends that he knows how to deal with it and calls me over "just to show me." But to tell you the truth, I know much more about mechanics than he does – but I don't tell him that. Every so often he lets me ride it around the block where we live in Tel Aviv and I love feeling the wind blowing through my hair while I'm controlling this noisy mechanical monster. My mother doesn't like this business at all and keeps telling me that one day I'll get killed riding up and down Ben-Yehuda Street the way I do. But she knows she can't stop me. After all, my eighteenth birthday was a few months ago so I'm not a kid anymore. My father just smiles and says, "Just ride carefully, son, and keep your eyes open for the cops."

By the way, I forgot to tell you. My proper name is Benjamin Levi and I'm named after a friend of dad's who was killed in 1915 at Gallipoli. Everyone – everyone, that is, except my mother when she's annoyed with me, and my Hebrew teacher, Mr. Grossman – calls me Benny. And if we're talking about school, my best friend there is Danny Schwartz. This is kind of strange because Danny is the exact opposite of me. But they say opposites attract. He is quiet, of average height, wears thick glasses and loves school. I'm telling you, he really loves it. When I'm outside playing football, he'll be sitting in the school library reading a history book or some other book on biblical commentaries. And this he calls fun! I've never seen him with dirty hands and he can't tell the difference between a half-inch wrench and a screwdriver, but we're still the best of friends. I think what I really like about him is that he is honest and reliable, and if I need any help or advice, I go to him first. He's also a little more *frum*, religious, than I am, and when he leaves school he wants to study Bible and philosophy at the Hebrew University in Jerusalem.

"Danny," I say to him. "What do you see in the Bible? It's just a collection of old stories from way back when."

"You're wrong, Benny. Behind all these 'old stories,' as you call them, there's a whole world of ideas and philosophy."

"Oh, yeah? Like what?"

"You know the *Akedah*?" he asked, looking at me through his thick glasses.

"When God commands Abraham to sacrifice his son, Isaac?"

"That's it. Well, it's not just a story of an old man about to kill his son because God told him to. It's also about the question of sacrificing the things you love best, even your children, for an idea, for something spiritual."

"But, Danny, killing your son? Wasn't that a little too much?"

"Well, it never came to that in the end, did it? It was just a test."

"Some test," I said, but nevertheless I thought about what Danny had said. I knew he didn't say such things out of the blue.

So this was the situation at the beginning of the forties, in 1940, to be exact, when this story begins. Here we are, two eighteen-year-olds in Tel Aviv, living in British Mandatory Palestine, during the war – the one that started in 1939 when the Germans invaded Poland. Now, although you may think this was an exciting period, it wasn't for us. We, that is, Danny and I and lots of our friends in school, thought that the world was leaving us behind. My mother wouldn't let me join the British army and insisted that I, unlike Moishe Unterman, a noisy kid in my class, couldn't leave school until I had finished my studies.

"A man without an education will end up as a road sweeper," my mother constantly predicted. "You wouldn't want that, now, would you?"

"No," I'd say. "But look at Sammy Greenfeld. He's running his father's shop on Allenby Street. He left school early and *he's* always got money in his pocket."

"Ha! You call *that* a living? Selling buttons and zippers? No, my son, you will finish your schooling and then go to university or technical college and learn something useful. Now get on with your homework."

But of course, none of this prevented us from watching the British army's recruitment march, which took place in downtown Tel Aviv. This happened soon after the Nazis invaded Poland in September 1939 and the British decided they needed a strong force in the Middle East. This was especially so in Egypt as the Brits, who were in charge of Mandatory Palestine, had to protect the Suez Canal so that their supplies of Middle East oil as well as their route to India would be safe.

The parade was really impressive. Hundreds of people were there to watch as rows and rows of soldiers, both men and women, marched down Ben-Yehuda Street in their best uniforms. They were all carrying rifles – all of them, that is, except those who were playing drums and trumpets and other instruments. At the head of the parade there were some smartly dressed officers as well as other soldiers who were carrying huge banners that said, "Men and women! Join the army! Sign up to protect your country!"

After the parade was over I sat in a café on Gordon Street with Danny, his sister Shoshana, and Sarah, her best friend.

"It's strange, isn't it?" said Sarah. "There's a war going on in Europe and the Germans have invaded Poland and Czechoslovakia and taken over Austria. Britain has declared war on Germany and yet here we are, sitting in a café in Tel Aviv as though nothing unusual were going on."

"Well, it's not our fight," declared Shoshana. "Our fight is with the Arabs and the British Mandate. We want an independent Jewish state and they don't want us to have one."

"You're wrong, Shoshi," I said, ordering another coffee. "It is our war in a way, even though it is taking place over in Europe."

"How? Why?"

"Because there are millions of Jews in Poland, Austria and Czechoslovakia and the other countries the Nazis have overrun, and if you believe what Hitler wrote in that book of his – "

"*Mein Kampf*?"

"Yes, well, they're going to be in for a terrible time. I know my father is very worried about some of his family over there and he's trying to persuade them to leave. That is, if it's not too late."

"And then where will they go?" asked Danny.

"They can come here, or go to America."

"But the Americans are making problems. You know they're talking about immigration quotas?"

"That's right," Sarah added. "And then there was that incident with the ship, the *St. Louis*, the one that sailed at first to Cuba and then to America. The Americans refused to let some nine hundred German Jews land, and sent them back to Europe."

"So, in other words, this is the only place that Jews can escape to?"

"Yes, Shoshi. That is, of course, if the Brits will let them in," I said.

"Well, I doubt that very much, at least not since they brought out that White Paper of theirs that says they'll allow only fifteen thousand refugees to come here per year for the next five years."

"But what can we do about it?" Danny asked, his normally placid face looking agitated for a change. "It's not fair. It looks as though the Germans are about to overrun all of Europe and make the Jews there suffer, and all we do is sit here in Tel Aviv drinking coffee and discussing the situation as though we were talking about the Bible or some other subject in school."

"You're right, Danny," his sister said. "But what can we do? We're only school kids."

"Well, I know what I'm going to do," I said. "As soon as I can, I'm going to join the British army. Then at least I'll feel as though I'm doing something positive."

"But the Brits are against us as well," Shoshana said, wiping some cake crumbs off her face. "You know, with that White Paper restricting immigration."

"That's right – but you remember what Ben-Gurion said? 'We'll fight the White Paper as if there's no war and –'"

"'We'll fight the war as if there was no White Paper,'" Danny finished off.

And that is exactly what happened. For the next few days I had some tearful and noisy arguments with my parents, especially with my mother, but in the end we came to a compromise. We decided that, first of all, I would finish my schooling in the summer, and only after that could I go and join the British army.

The British army and the Jewish authorities had agreed that when the war started in September 1939, the Jews in Palestine would be allowed to volunteer for the army, and eventually over thirty thousand did so. For political reasons, the Brits wanted the Arabs to volunteer as well but only a few of them did.

I think my father was very proud that I had made that decision, but was unwilling to say so in front of my mother. A few days later, while we were walking along the seafront one Shabbat afternoon, he told me that although he was worried about what might happen to me in the army, he felt proud that his son had decided to do his part for the Jewish people.

"Of course," he explained, "it was easier in my time. Then, at the beginning of the Great War, I was forcibly exiled from Palestine to Egypt by the Turks. There I volunteered to join the Zion Mule Corps and my parents couldn't do a thing about that." He smiled as he remembered the times he had spent with his friends then. "Ah, yes, they were really special. They were the sort of friends you make for life. You know, friends you can really count on."

"I know that, *Abba*. You keep telling us about Nathan and Jacob and what you did in the ZMC and afterward in the Jewish Legion."

"OK, son, fair enough. But don't tell your mom how proud I am of you or she'll kill me. She'll say *I* gave you the idea and then I'll never hear the end of it."

"It's too late. She knows already. You never were any good at hiding your feelings," I laughed. "But you know what?" I said as we were about to turn for home, "I think that *Imma* is proud of me as well, she just won't admit it. Yesterday I overheard her saying to Mrs. Cohen upstairs that she also wants me to 'do my part,' as you said. But she hopes that I'll be doing something safe – like being a mechanic in the army. Of course, she'd really like me to be a doctor or lawyer but you know that's not going to happen. I don't have the brains for that," I said, tapping the side of my head. "You, of all people, should know that my brains are in my hands: I can fix things like *Imma's* vacuum cleaner and help you with the car."

He nodded in agreement.

"Now take Danny," I continued. "He's the one with brains. Always reading stuff, and not garbage either. Last week when I asked if he wanted to join some of us in a ball game he said no. He said he'd gotten into this great book about Spinoza and philosophy. Me? I didn't even understand the title of the book he was reading."

And if I'd had any doubts about joining the army, they were swept away when toward the end of the school year France fell to the Germans and the Italian air force bombed the oil refineries in Haifa. They also killed over one hundred people and wounded even more when they dropped a few bombs on my hometown of Tel Aviv.

"You see," I said to my mother on the night after the "all clear" sounded. "We have to *do* something. We can't just wait here like sitting ducks. I know you'd prefer me not to sign up but I feel I have to. It's just the right thing to do. And anyway," I added, half smiling, "you know what I'll be like if I don't join up – the worst pain in the neck the world has ever seen."

Despite her worries, I saw my mother nod her head in agreement and my father smile quietly. They both knew their oldest child and they realized that they didn't really have much choice. Once I was determined to do something, I would do it. They remembered when I was a kid and wanted to buy a bicycle. We couldn't afford it then, so I began to do all sorts of odd jobs around the neighborhood and saved up enough money, and a few months later bought a second-hand, red and slightly rusty bicycle.

My parents also realized that since the Nazis had conquered most of France and their Italian allies had bombed us here at home, the thought that Palestine somehow would not be involved in this war was a vain hope. And so, day after day, the British army recruiting stations were now full of young and not-so-young men signing up.

It was therefore no surprise when at the beginning of July 1940, I found myself lining up with two of my best friends, Danny and Yossi, at the nearest recruiting station.

Danny told us that his mother had tried to stop him, even though his sister was on his side.

"She asked, 'Daniel, what will I do without you?'" he recounted as we waited in line. "'You are the man of the family now that your father's dead – God forbid, if anything happens to you… What will I do then?'"

"'Don't worry,' I told her. 'You know me. They'll take one look at me and my glasses and make me a clerk. I'll probably spend the war sitting in an office downtown counting rifles or bullets, so don't you worry. And besides, I can't just sit here at home doing nothing knowing that Benny and Yossi have joined up.'"

"Did that convince her?" I asked.

"No. She started going on about my studies. You know, about studying at Hebrew University one day."

"I told her that joining the army didn't cancel that out; it just postponed it. I still want to study philosophy, but I guess I'll just start my studies a little later, that's all."

As a result, on that sunny July morning the three of us stood in line outside the recruiting station wondering what the future held in store for us. I admitted – but only to myself – that despite my outward show of bravado, I was scared of being seriously wounded. But I suppose all soldiers have that feeling, and even if they serve for many years they will not admit that to anyone.

And it's strange, but even though I didn't like school much, especially subjects like Bible and literature, as I was standing in line that day, I couldn't help but remember the scene in Shakespeare's *Henry V* when on the night before the battle of Agincourt one of the soldiers talks about "a heavy reckoning to make, when all those legs and arms and heads, chopped off in a battle, shall join together at the latter day and cry all, 'We died at such a place.'

I certainly hoped that nothing like that would happen to me or my friends.

CHAPTER TWO
From Civilian to Soldier

I was now at the front of the line. After a few minutes the red-capped military policeman in his sharply pressed uniform waved me into the long, low building covered with recruiting posters. Stepping in from the bright sunlight outside, it took me a few moments to get used to the somewhat gloomy room. Suddenly a voice called out, "Over here, son," and I found myself facing a recruiting officer. Like the redcap outside, he was wearing a well-pressed uniform and looked very efficient. He was sitting on the other side of a long trestle table piled high with forms and rubber stamps. A small box to his right held items such as pen nibs, a bottle of ink and some loose rubber bands. Pinned on the wall behind him was a large Union Jack flag next to a smaller picture of King George VI. The officer smiled, pointed to a chair and asked me to take a seat.

"So you want to join the king's army?" he began.

"Yes, sir."

"Then I'll ask you a few questions and after that you'll sign this form at the bottom. Is that understood?"

"Yes, sir."

He then asked me what I later learned were routine questions, about my name, age, family, address and health, and whether I was a British subject, had a vaccination record and had any special skills.

"I'm very good with my hands, sir. I'm good at repairing things like car engines, sewing machines and all kinds of machinery, sir."

He wrote this down and then looked up.

"Do you know how to drive a car or a motorcycle?"

"Yes, sir, but only unofficially. I don't have my license yet."

He smiled. "I see, and I don't suppose you are married, are you?"

"No, sir."

"Tell me, Mr. Benny Levi," he said, reading my name at the top of the form. "How is it you speak such good English?"

"My grandfather was American, sir, from New York. We also speak a lot of English at home. I can speak English as well as I can speak Hebrew, sir, and I also know a lot of words in Arabic."

He smiled. "The swear words?"

"Yes, sir. There aren't many swear words in Hebrew. If people want to swear here, sir, they usually do it in Arabic or Yiddish."

"Yes, I've learned that since I've been serving here. But let's get on. I can see there's quite a queue of people outside and I want to get finished today. So, sign here," he said, pushing the form over and showing me where to sign.

"So, Mr. Levi, you are free to go now. You'll be hearing from us very soon," and he indicated to the redcap by the door to send the next person in.

"Is that it?" I asked, surprised that it was all over so quickly.

"Yes. What did you expect? That I'd give you a rifle or a tank? But don't you worry," he added. "I promise you we'll be in touch with you very soon. The army needs healthy fellows like you, especially with your mechanical skills."

"That's right, sir," said Danny, who was now sitting in my place. "Benny will fix your trucks and I'll read the instruction manuals."

"Excuse me, young man," the officer said. "But in the British army we don't have any, er, what did you call them? Trucks. Here in the British army we use lorries."

"Lorries?"

"Yes, and if we allow you to fix them, that's what you'll call them."

"Yes, sir," we both replied together.

"I see you two know each other."

"Yes, sir," I said. "We're good friends. We've known each other for a long time, in fact since we were both in kindergarten."

"Will we be able to serve together?" Danny asked.

"I'll note it down but I cannot promise anything." And I saw him scribble something on the bottom of my form and also on the one he was preparing for Danny.

"And sir, would it be OK if our friend, Yossi Ivri – he's being interviewed at the next table – also serves with us, sir? He was also in kindergarten and school with us. The three of us are kind of like the three musketeers."

"And," Danny added, "Yossi is also very good at fixing engines and things. If you put us all in the same unit, sir, you'll never have a dead truck, er, lorry, sir, in the British army." The officer smiled at Danny's enthusiasm and wrote something else down on our forms.

Ten minutes later, the three of us were standing in the shade of a large tree at the far end of the courtyard.

"Huh! That was a little disappointing," I said.

"Well, what did you expect," Danny asked, echoing the officer's words, "that he'd give you a rifle or a white horse or something like that?"

"No, but he didn't ask us if we knew how to use guns or…"

"Polish our boots," Yossi laughed.

Danny smiled and looked at us. "Well, my friends, we're just going to have to be patient, that's all. My uncle Ezra who served in the Great War told me that the British army is famous for its bureaucracy and paperwork."

"I know," I added. "We've just seen an example of it."

"Don't be like that, Benny. From what I've read in the papers they'll be needing us pretty soon."

Yossi nodded his head in agreement. "Danny's right. Now let's buy an *artik* at that kiosk over there. I need a popsicle to cool me down."

My friends' predictions were right about the army needing us soon. Three days later the three of us were back at the base standing in line again. This time, however, we were lined up in front of a long shed marked "Stores – Entrance to Authorised Personnel Only. By Order."

"Whose order?" I whispered to Danny.

He shrugged his shoulders. "I don't know. I guess the army writes that on everything. Now shhh. There's an officer coming this way."

"He's not an officer. I think he's a sergeant major. Look at the stripes and crown on his sleeve."

"Well, whatever he is, let's see what he wants from us."

His voice boomed out. "You three, have you filled out all the forms in the office over there?" he asked, pointing to where we had been three days earlier.

"Yes, sir."

"Right then. Let's get you kitted up," he said, and we followed him into the long shed – by order.

The next hour passed in a whirl as, in addition to being measured (more or less) for uniforms, we were also issued with – and had to sign for – boots, belts, pouches, helmets, blankets, two sizes of packs, mess tins, cutlery, can openers, mugs and all other sorts of equipment that we had never dreamed about. Then, with our arms full and our backs loaded, we had to try to organize all this equipment into some sort of order if we were to remain at all mobile and at least look like soldiers.

"And that's not all, lads," the quartermaster smiled as we signed for the equipment. He watched us struggle under our loads. "I recommend you buy a compass and a torch as well."

"A *torch*?"

"Yes, Danny," I said. "Torch is the British word for flashlight."

"I see we're going to have to learn a new language in the army," said Yossi, picking up his mug and mess tin for the third time.

"And, lads," the quartermaster called out as we staggered in the direction of the door. "If what I hear is right about the place they're sending you, don't forget to buy yourselves some cream against mosquitoes and sandflies. And by the way, if you think you're loaded down now, just wait till they give you your rifles and all the gear that goes with them. Then my lads, you'll know you're in the king's army."

"As if we didn't know," muttered Yossi, picking up his mug once again.

Outside we found a place in the shade and put all the smaller things in our backpacks – that is, our haversacks – and made ourselves as comfortable as we could.

"Do we have to put our uniforms on now?" asked Danny.

"I guess so. Look around and see what the others are doing."

We looked out over the parade ground and saw the other new recruits changing from civilian clothes to army uniforms. Some were in various stages of civilian undress, buttoning up their new khaki shirts and trousers, and others were busy threading their unfamiliar and awkward webbing belts through the loops in their pouches. A few recruits were already wearing their new black and shiny boots, but most still had them laced together and slung over their shoulders.

I asked Yossi what size his shirt was.

"Large. What's yours?"

"Medium. Let's swap, OK?"

"Do either of you have a larger beret than mine?" asked Yossi. "This one looks like a *kippah* on my head."

Neither of us did. "See if you can switch with someone else after the parade."

"Benny, how do we lace our boots? Crisscross on the outside or on the inside?"

"Don't know. Look at the officer's shoes when we go on parade."

"When's that?"

"In about five minutes, so let's get moving."

And so, although we now looked like soldiers making our way over to the parade ground, the truth was that we were all as green as grass and clearly had a lot to learn about the British army.

Five minutes later, we joined the rest of the recruits standing three-deep in a large hollow square. Two majors and a captain were standing in the center, their uniforms immaculate and sharply pressed, their boots highly polished. My uniform was new and my boots were clean but I still felt scruffy in comparison to those officers. Even their regimental badges and other insignia and belt buckles shone in the bright morning sunlight. Spaced along in front of our lines and standing between us and the officers were several sergeants. They were trying to make some sort of order out of our lines in the way that sheepdogs deal with unruly flocks.

The sergeants called for silence in the ranks and the oldest-looking officer, a red-faced man with an impressive mustache and beady eyes, made a short speech. He told us how important it was that we had volunteered to serve and defend our country and then he added a few words about the fine traditions of the British army. Then he stepped back as the other major said a few more words about the regiment. And then we took the oath, our right hands held high.

We swore to be faithful and bear true allegiance to the king and defend him from his enemies. We swore to observe and obey all of His Majesty's generals and officers and all those who were set over us.

Although I felt rather cynical about this part of the oath, picturing King George VI sitting on his throne in Buckingham Palace in London while Danny, Yossi and I were defending him, I must admit that this swearing-in ceremony was pretty impressive. When it came to parades and traditions, I whispered to Danny, you couldn't fault the British.

After being dismissed we were told to go home and report back at the base on the following morning at seven o'clock.

"Seven o'clock? I'm still asleep then," muttered Yossi.

"Well, lad, you're in the army now," said a sergeant who had overheard him. "Just make sure you're back here at seven. And when we say seven, it means seven, and not one minute later. I know we're in the Middle East but, for the army, seven is seven. Don't forget."

We felt proud, if not a little self-conscious in our new uniforms as we walked home. And we made sure that we were back on the parade ground well before seven the following morning.

"Danny, what happened when you got home? Did your mother start up again about you leaving her?"

"Of course, but now I think she's gotten used to the idea. And you know, even though she won't admit it, I think she's really proud that I've signed up. She said I reminded her of my dad when he was serving in the Jewish Legion."

"Funny you should say that. My mom said the same thing. So I guess we're carrying out some sort of tradition. But shhh, we've got to get into threes like yesterday."

We did so and were then divided up into small groups to learn about the rifles we were to be issued with.

"Now listen, men, and listen carefully," our instructor began, running his knobbly fingers along the barrel of his rifle. "This 'ere is the British army's favorite rifle – the bolt-action magazine-fed Lee Enfield three-oh-three. It was first used by this army in 1895 and since then the Aussie, the Indian, the Canadian and the South African armies have decided to use it as well."

"Wow!" I whispered to Yossi. "That means this rifle is almost fifty years old."

"That's right," Danny whispered from behind me. "It's been around since Queen Victoria was on the throne."

"Trust you to know that," I said, and turned to hear what the instructor was saying.

"Now, this beauty's proper name is the Short Magazine Lee-Enfield, the SMLE, but some jokers call it 'Smelly.' But I don't want to hear any of you lot call it that. If you 'ave some respect for this rifle," he added, caressing it lovingly, "then it will serve you well. Now look 'ere. This rifle has a magazine which 'olds ten rounds of ten bullets, loaded from the top. Each bullet has a 7.62 diameter."

"Seven point six two what?" Danny asked. He had to know everything.

"Millimeters. And if you want some more figures, 'ere goes. This rifle weighs nearly nine pounds and is just over forty-four inches long from the butt to the end of the muzzle – the barrel alone is twenty-five inches. It has an effective range of 550 yards and a maximum range of two thousand yards. Now," the instructor continued, picking up a bayonet, "You can make this rifle even more deadly if you add this 'ere bayonet to it. See, it clips on 'ere. This bayonet is the standard British type: sword-edged, 17.2 inches long and weighs just over one pound. Let's 'ope you never have to use it. Is everybody happy now? Have you got enough figures?"

A few of us nodded, and the instructor then took us over to the firing range. He fired ten rounds at a target and then pointed out how the rifle automatically ejected the used rounds. One of them fell near Danny, who picked up. He dropped it immediately.

"It's hot," he said. "I never thought of that."

"Of course it is," I said, showing off my knowledge and firing-range experience. "It was full of gunpowder that just exploded!"

"Ah, so that's what fires it," Danny said, blowing on his fingers. "Now I understand."

We returned to the firing range after a short break, and for the first time we fired real rifles with real bullets. I was used to using my air gun, but this was a completely different feeling. We were all sore on our right shoulders where the end of the stock recoiled, jamming the butt back into the tops of our arms. Of course we all claimed that it didn't hurt at all. By the time we finished firing off our magazines, my ears were ringing. I couldn't help imagining what it would be like in a battle, with thousands of men firing their rifles at the same time. And this, of course, would be in addition to the sounds of shells exploding all over the place.

During our time on the range Yossi was the best shot as he scored half a dozen bullseyes. Danny and I tied for second place. Apart from aiming and shooting, we also learned how to load the magazines, what to do if a bullet jammed in the chamber or magazine, how to remove the bolt and how to keep the rifle clean.

After we finished at the range we were lined up and we held out our rifles for inspection. The instructor and two sergeants moved down the lines and inspected every rifle for cleanliness. When I handed mine over, the instructor returned it. "You 'orrible little man!" he bellowed at me. "Just look inside that rifle barrel of yours! What have you got in there? Footballs?"

"Footballs, sir?"

"Yes," he continued bellowing. "Look at those great big black spots inside. Now clean it properly."

I could see Yossi grinning. His rifle was spotless. Not a "football" in sight.

Our weapons and general training continued for six weeks. During this time, apart from improving our marksmanship, we went on route marches, learned how to salute and to march in formation and were taught basic signaling and communication skills. We also peeled mountains of potatoes – "spud-bashing" in British army slang – and learned how to use our bayonets. This we did by charging huge, pillow-like sacks stuffed with straw and yelling bloodcurdling noises at the same time.

In addition, we had to attend lectures on personal hygiene and the history and traditions of the regiment, as well as the basic geography of North Africa where we'd be sent once our basic training was over. On the lighter side, we also learned the words of several popular army songs such as "Lily Marlene," "Kiss Me Goodnight, Sergeant Major" and "Bless 'em All." The last one was my favorite, and I really liked it when all of us would sit around the campfire in the evenings and blast out the chorus:

> Bless 'em all, bless 'em all.
> The long and the short and the tall.
> You'll get no promotion this side of the ocean,
> So cheer up my lads, bless 'em all.

Yossi would accompany our somewhat raucous singing with his accordion.

It was also during this period that Danny, Yossi and I volunteered to become drivers. This meant that our original spic and span uniforms looked pretty well worn, as the greatest and most useful skills we learned during those six weeks were how to drive a British army Bedford lorry and how to look after its six-liter engine. This was a real workhorse of a vehicle. It had a manual gearbox and a collapsible windshield, and the front cab had side doors and was covered with a canvas roof with Perspex side screens. These squat and ugly lorries were easy to identify, as they had high crash bars in front of the radiators for general protection.

When we told our friends that we had volunteered to become drivers they told us that we would never have any rest or free time from that moment on. This did not bother us, as we felt we were learning useful skills that would serve us later in life. This was especially true for me. For a long time I had dreamed of owning a large repair workshop in Tel Aviv bearing an impressive "Benny's Motor Repairs" sign outside. I also hoped that being a driver would get me out of the long route marches that the army seemed to like. Sometimes I was lucky, sometimes I wasn't. But when I wasn't out marching all over the hills, I had to undergo courses on how to deal with all sorts of mechanical problems such as blocked carburetors, dirty oil and air filters, leaking radiators and faulty spark plugs. We also learned about the vehicles' electrical systems and how to change lightbulbs and deal with jammed starter motors. Of course we also practiced changing tires and adjusting noisy tappets. We also learned how to speak the King's English and say "spanners" instead of "wrenches," "petrol" instead of "gas" and "gear stick" instead of "gear shift."

One of our instructors, a burly Scotsman from Glasgow who, despite his name of McPhee, was known as "Scotty" or "Jock," insisted that we learn to strip down various engine parts in semi-darkness. "You're no' gonna have lights on all o'er the desert, now, are you?" he would say. By the time our vehicle maintenance and repair course was over, I must admit there was not much about lorry engines I did not know. In his bookish way, Danny would always consult the instruction manuals first, but Yossi and I would base our knowledge on previous experience and intuition. However, the results would be the same: clean, sweetly running engines and greasy hands and overalls.

While we were on our training course, we heard that the British had decided to separate their new Arab units from the Jewish units. There had been too much tension between the two groups to make such joint units a working proposition. In the meantime, however, we saw a steady stream of new recruits pass through our camp; most of them were Jewish. Very few Arabs signed up, and the officers assigned to be in charge of them had a very easy time. Later they were transferred over to work with the growing number of Jewish recruits.

This six-week training period passed very quickly. We worked hard, learned a great deal, got cut hands and blistered feet and, all in all, felt that we were doing a good job. One Thursday morning, toward the end of the training period, Danny told me that Captain Wellesley Aron, a Jewish officer in the British army, would be inspecting us on our next parade, after which we would be considered full-fledged soldiers.

"You mean we've been playacting up to now?" I asked.

"No, Benny, of course not. But tomorrow we are going to have a big passing-out parade and then we'll be told where we're going to be sent."

"And King George will come and check if my boots are highly polished and if I have any more footballs in my rifle," I said, remembering how I'd been punished for having had a dirty rifle and scuffed boots at the last inspection parade.

"Of course," smirked Yossi. "And Queen Elizabeth will bring some of those quaint English tea cakes here as well."

"All right, you two. That's enough," Danny said. "Now let's get ready for this parade. I'm going to check out Betty."

"Betty?" Yossi and I said as one. "Since when do you have a girlfriend?"

"Betty's not a girl. Betty's the name of my lorry. Betty the Bedford."

Perfect was the best word to describe the parade that was held the following day. There was not a cloud in the sky, there were no footballs in my rifle and my boots, like little round mirrors, reflected the sun. Our uniforms were immaculate, and the lorries were all found to be in perfect working condition. As we stood there in a hollow square formation, Captain Aron surveyed us from his wooden platform and gave a short patriotic speech which ended "*Chazak v'ematz*, be strong and of good courage," and "*Hashem oz l'amo yiten, Hashem yivarech et amo bashalom*, the Lord will give strength unto his people, the Lord will bless his people with peace."

Unfortunately Captain Aron's prayer for peace would not be answered, as the Nazi war machine was gathering strength. The persecution of our fellow Jews in Europe and North Africa was on the rise. In the meantime, the Germans were bombing London, and their Italian allies were advancing on several fronts in Africa.

The response in Palestine to all this was to join the army, and by the end of the year there were over nine thousand Palestinians serving in the British army, most of them Jews. Danny, Yossi and I felt proud that we were among the first to have taken this fateful step.

CHAPTER THREE
From Tel Aviv to Tobruk

Officially, we were now fully trained soldiers, but the fact was that we were still very inexperienced or, as one brawny sergeant called us, "wet behind the ears." This lack of experience also led to many cases of misunderstanding between us raw recruits and several of our junior commanders – the British corporals and sergeants – as they did not speak any Hebrew. This led to orders not being carried out properly or sometimes not being obeyed at all.

Although Danny and I with our American backgrounds had no problems with this and, in fact, often acted as unofficial translators, we could see that our unit's morale was falling. One day there was an argument between an English sergeant and one of our men, Yochanan Goldwasser, over the word "oil." The sergeant had meant "engine oil" and Yochanan had thought he was talking about cooking oil.

"You think I'm going to fill my engine with olive oil?" Sergeant Jackson barked.

"But I thought you meant – "

"You're not here to think! Just bring me two gallons of what I ordered. Now move!"

Incidents of this kind happened all the time and the men in my unit, the men who had joined up with such high hopes and expectations, were now feeling very low.

"I'm telling you," complained Avner Goldstein one day. "I joined the army to fight the Germans, not to sit around here polishing wing mirrors and sorting out piles of nuts and bolts."

"I agree," Yossi added. "I've just spent two hours sorting out spanners and screwdrivers into different sizes and then putting them in special toolboxes. I've really had enough of this."

"And I wanted a day's leave to go to my cousin's son's *brit* in Tel Aviv," skinny Yigal added. "And when I asked the sergeant for a pass, he laughed and said there were enough Brits here and we didn't need any more."

"Very funny," said Danny. "But at least he could pun in both English and Hebrew."

Yigal and I were not so impressed.

Eventually the unit's morale sunk so low that Captain Aron decided to call for a special parade. He addressed us in Hebrew. Apart from referring to a few breaches of discipline, he told us that from now on the unit would be run in accordance with the traditions of dignity and self-respect, and that Hebrew would be the official language of our unit – that is, as far as was practical. As he was talking, I could see the men straighten their backs and pull back their shoulders.

From that day on, our morale improved. I guess the captain also had a few words with some of the more aggressive British junior officers and NCOs (non-commissioned officers). Now the men took pride in their work, slacking came to a halt and only a few of us were punished for looking sloppy or for turning up late.

In our spare time we laid out a flowerbed and planted it with blue and white flowers to form a *Magen David*, a Star of David. We also spelled out our unit's name and number below in small white painted stones.

In the meantime, the Jewish Soldiers' Welfare Committee in Tel Aviv donated a Hebrew typewriter, so all our notices appeared in both English and Hebrew. We also established the tradition of having a Friday night service, a tradition that was to continue when we all served abroad in North Africa and Europe.

When we received the typewriter, we also received a pair of silver candlesticks and a box of prayer books. All of this reinforced the feeling that we were not merely a part of the British army, but a Jewish part. And as for the Palestinian aspect, we sang Hebrew songs in our free time or while we were working on the greasy engines of our lorries.

I remember one day while I was singing and cleaning the carburetor on a three-ton Bedford, one of the British lance corporals tapped me on the shoulder.

"'Ere, man, is that one of your Jewish songs you're singing?"

"Yes."

"And is that the same Jewish what they wrote the Bible in?"

I took a break for a few minutes to explain to him that the "Jewish" of the Bible was more or less the same "Jewish" that he heard us using, except that the language had been adapted and modernized since biblical times. He walked away looking very impressed with his new knowledge.

However, although we were now feeling better and the relations between the Jewish soldiers and the British officers had improved, we were all very impatient to be sent to the front in North Africa where we knew the action was taking place.

Luckily our feelings of frustration would not last for too long. At the beginning of December 1940 almost the entire company was given the order to proceed to Egypt. The only ones who remained behind were those who had to train the new recruits who were arriving daily at the Sarafend training camp. Fortunately Danny, Yossi and I were chosen to be sent to Egypt.

"I guess that means another parade," I said to Danny when I saw him sitting on a toolbox cleaning his rifle.

"Of course. Don't you know the Brits love military parades? So go and get yourself ready. We're due on the parade ground at two o'clock. Dov Hos and some other important bigwigs from the Jewish Agency will be there as well."

"Dov Hos? The guy who was in the Jewish Legion in the Great War?"

"That's right. Now let me finish cleaning my rifle, and make sure yours is clean as well."

I saluted my friend. "Yes, sir." He ignored me and continued looking for footballs in the barrel of his rifle.

Despite my naturally cynical attitude toward parades and the British love of "spit and polish," this particular parade was very impressive. Dov Hos, who, with his glasses, neat hair and dark, pinstriped suit looked more like a bank clerk than a past war hero, described the pride that he and the Jewish population of Palestine felt about our units and the fact that shortly we were to take an active part in the fight against the Germans and their allies. Then a Jewish Agency official, whose name I have forgotten, described how the Nazis were persecuting the Jews in the countries they had overrun. "It is up to you to put a halt to this as soon as possible," he declared, throwing his arms up into the air. "This man, Hitler, *y'mach shemo*, may his name be erased, must be blotted out in the same way that Amalek was in the Bible. You soldiers, you Jewish soldiers, must do all you can to bring an end to this state-organized anti-Semitism. We must all stand up and be counted. We fought Haman in the past, we survived the medieval blood libels and the Cossack massacres, now we must stand shoulder to shoulder and defeat this Hitler and his Nazi forces. You men," he said, swinging his arms around, "are being given a chance to defend the Jewish nation. Do it, and do it well. *Chazak v'ematz*, be strong and of good courage."

The unit's colors were then paraded and Major Babcock gave another short but rousing speech. Of course, none of us could have known then that within a few days Dov Hos would die in a tragic car crash. We heard about it over the radio only when we were driving south toward the Egyptian border.

Just as we were about to leave the parade ground, a few men remained standing at alert and began singing "Hatikvah (The Hope)," our unofficial national anthem. It was really impressive. Suddenly the men stopped what they were doing and stood up straight. Amid the lengthening shadows of the setting sun we all joined in singing the sixty-year-old hymn, the sound of which grew as more and more men joined in. Even a cynic like me could not remain dry eyed as I sang:

> Our hope is not yet lost,
> The hope of two thousand years,
> To be a free people in our own land,
> The Land of Zion and Jerusalem.

I quickly wiped my eyes as Yossi and Danny came over to me.

"Come on, Benny. We've got to go to our lorries now. We'll be leaving soon. So get the rest of your gear and your pack and we'll see you over there."

I did not need to be told twice. Soon we were given the order to switch on our engines, and our convoy of one hundred fifty lorries passed through the gates of Sarafend and headed south toward Gaza and Egypt. After a few miles we entered Rishon LeZion and had to slow down as hundreds of people lined the road and started throwing flowers and cakes at us. I told the soldier next to me to keep the side window open, as I was hungry and the more cakes that were thrown into the cab, the better.

This same joyous scene was repeated a few miles further south when we drove through Rehovot. Apart from receiving some more cakes, it was very encouraging to hear the cries of "*kol hakavod*, well done" and "*b'hatzlachah*, good luck" as we drove slowly down the main street. However, soon this joyful noise turned to silence – silence that is, if you don't count the sound of our heavy lorry engines as we approached the drier, arid areas of the northern Negev desert.

We spent that night at Bir Asluj, where German engineers had built a railroad station for the Turks, but which had been taken over by the British at the end of the Great War. We set up our camp and climbed into our bedrolls, exhausted. Luckily, as Danny, Yossi and I were drivers, we did not have to stand any guard duties that night or any time when we were on duty as drivers.

"You see," I said to my friends just before we fell asleep, "It paid to volunteer to be drivers. No guard duty and no route marching."

Danny yawned in agreement but Yossi was already asleep.

The next day we continued driving, but now in a more westerly direction. In our lorry, we had to make sure to keep our distance from those in front of us as they were throwing up great clouds of fine sandy dust, which made it difficult to see ahead. One lorry, in fact, did drive into the back of another but, apart from smashing his headlamps and denting his wings, no major damage was caused. We had a short break near Shivta by the ruins of an ancient Nabatean city, and then spent the following night at Nitzana, another old desert post built by the Germans for the Turks.

Early the following morning, we crossed into Egypt.

"Do you realize," I said to Danny and Yossi the following morning, "that we've been driving for three days now and our lorries look like they haven't been cleaned for weeks? I looked under the hood this morning and – "

"Don't you mean bonnet?" Danny smiled.

"Hood, bonnet, whatever you call it. My engine is filthy. It's caked in oil and sand. It'll be impossible to keep it clean."

"I'm sorry, *Chabibi*, we've got no choice. You may be happy that we don't have to do guard duty, but you're responsible for Bella and I am for Beverley."

"Bella? Beverley? What are you talking about?"

"I've adopted Yossi's idea of giving my lorry a name. Bella and Beverley, the Bedfords. See, I've painted 'Beverley' on the back."

So now, together with Bella, Beverley and Betty and the rest of the convoy, we drove another two hundred miles to Cairo, where we arrived on December 30. We were given the next day off, and on New Year's Day 1941 we were ordered to drive back east to the Suez Canal.

"Why?" asked Yossi. "We just came from there."

"We've been told to clear the docks at Port Suez. There's tons of equipment there and it's blocking up the place. We have to bring it back west if it's going to be used to fight the Germans."

However, it was while we were in Cairo that one of the most important events of my life took place. I met Tamar. Tamar Mizrachi, to give her full name. She was a Jewish girl of my age who originally came from Alexandria and was now living in Cairo. When I joined the British army in Palestine, she had done the same in Alexandria by joining the Auxiliary Territorial Service (ATS), a unit for women in the British army. She was now working as a secretary in Cairo. She told me that unlike me, who had joined the army for patriotic reasons, she had joined in order to escape from her horrible uncle.

"What do you mean, uncle?" I asked the first time I took her out, as we were sitting in a café. "Don't you live with your parents?"

"No," she said, and her bright black eyes clouded over. "They're both dead."

I immediately felt uncomfortable about opening my big mouth.

"Don't feel bad about it," she said, laying a soft hand on my arm. "It's not your fault. They died two years ago in a car crash outside Alexandria and since then I've been living with my horrible uncle, Obadiah."

"Why is he so horrible?"

"Because he is. He's tightfisted and won't give me any money even though he is well off. He won't let me go dancing or do anything like that and all he wants me to do is to be his servant. To run and fetch and carry for him."

"So how is it that you're in the ATS in Cairo?" This pretty girl with her black curly hair and intelligent face intrigued me.

"It may not be nice to say, but this war has done me a big favor."

I looked surprised.

"Yes, joining the ATS meant that I had a good excuse to leave my uncle. I first heard about it because my friend

Miriam joined up and she told me all about it. She said they were looking for a girl who could type in English and Arabic."

"And how do you know English so well?"

She blushed at my compliment. "My parents were both high school English teachers back in Alexandria and they made me speak English much of the time at home."

"Well, they did a good job," I said, and ordered some more coffee. "And now you live here in Cairo?"

"Yes, just outside the base. I share a little flat with Miriam, and the pair of us work as secretaries and translators. I know some French, too, which is also very useful. You know these English; they're so bad at foreign languages. They think everyone should speak English, and if you don't, they think you're stupid."

"I know, we had that problem back at the base in Tel Aviv. Some of the officers and NCOs thought that if you didn't know English but they shouted it at you, then you'd understand what they wanted that way. But in the end, Captain Aron made Hebrew the language of the base and some of the more intelligent officers actually made an effort to learn a little Hebrew. It was pretty funny to hear their accents, but of course we never said so."

"Well, I'm jealous of you. You speak English and Hebrew fluently. My Hebrew is terrible. It's mainly words to do with prayers and religion."

"Let me hear you," I said, and we continued talking in simple Hebrew until the conversation broke down. She burst out laughing after she had made a mistake mixing up *chavitot* and *chaviot* – fried eggs and barrels. She laid her hand on my arm again. I could feel it, warm and soft.

"You see," she said. "I can say the blessings in Hebrew and the prayers, but I can't really ask you questions about yourself."

She was right, and from then on English became our language.

We stayed in the café for another hour and I walked her back to her flat. I told her we had to go to Suez the next day for some time and I asked her if we could meet again when I came back.

"Yes," she nodded, "I'd like that. You can always ask where I am at the ATS office." She leaned forward, gave me a quick kiss on the cheek and dashed into the courtyard of her building before I could kiss her back.

That night I was in seventh heaven. I had to see her again, but before I could, I had to spend ten days working at the docks at Suez.

We arrived there late the following day and were immediately set to work unloading the heavy Leyland and Fodor lorries, and then driving them to the depot where they were to be stored. We didn't have to drive these monsters for long distances, but we learned a lot about judging their lengths, widths and turning radii, and how to maneuver them into small parking spaces. But even though we were gaining more experience as drivers of heavy vehicles, I noticed that as the days passed, the rigid discipline we had become used to was starting to fall apart.

"You know, Yossi," I said one day as we were resting in the cab of a huge khaki Fodor, "it looks like things are getting slack around here."

"What do you mean?"

"I'll tell you: we're all Jewish Palestinians here, but we've become sloppy and unprofessional. There have been a few driving accidents and the men often leave their tents in a horrible mess, and I heard a private arguing with an NCO about going on guard duty."

"You're right. He'd never have done that at Sarafend or even on the way here. And look over there. See how those men are dressed," and he pointed to a small group who were standing and arguing over what to do with a stack of large crates waiting to be loaded. "Look at how that tall guy has his shirttail sticking out and the one behind him isn't even wearing a belt."

"Er, yes," I said, hastily tucking my own shirt into the top of my trousers.

And we were not the only ones to notice this general sloppiness. Captain Aron did as well. That night he called us all together and slammed into us. We all felt like small schoolboys in front of a particularly strict principal as he pointed out all our failings. Of course, he was right. After listing all the things we had done wrong, he told us that we would have to improve our personal appearance, behavior and punctuality, and that our work would also have to be more serious and efficient.

"You must not forget," he continued, "you have to set an example of what Jewish soldiers can be and do. Always remember that. There are enough people out there who think that we Jews cannot be good soldiers. It is up to us, each and every one of us, to do his job properly and prove them wrong. Every time you turn up on parade in a scruffy uniform or have a dirty rifle or arrive late for whatever occasion, or argue with an officer or NCO," he said, counting off these "crimes" on his fingers, "you are telling the non-Jews that we Jews are not fit to be soldiers. I know there are non-Jews here who also do those things, but they don't have others telling them they're not suitable to serve in the army. You do, and don't forget that, ever. Every time you leave your tent in a mess, break a wing mirror through carelessness or carry a dirty rifle, you are giving ammunition, so to speak, to those who are against having Jews as fighters in the British army. You must do your best to remember this and make sure that we have a good name. All this sloppiness has to stop, and it must stop now. Dismissed."

It did. In the few days that we had left at Suez we made a real effort to improve the situation. We made sure our uniforms were clean, our shirts buttoned and our boots polished. We had very few accidents, and those that we did have were very minor. We all felt proud of what we were doing. The next time Captain Aron called us together, he told us that we were to form a new unit: the Palestine Motor Transport Works Services. Our commander would be Major Belk, and Captain Aron would work with him. His next two pieces of news were better. The first was that we were to finish our work at Suez so that we could drive our lorries and supplies to Tobruk, a town on the North African coast. The second piece of news affected us personally: several privates in our unit were to be promoted – Jewish corporals in the British army. Danny, Yossi and I were not granted this honor, but we really did not mind. If one of us had been promoted, it might have put a strain on our friendship. All that concerned us now was the chance to drive to Tobruk.

That night I got hold of a large map and started looking for the place. "It's here," Danny said, pointing to a black circle four hundred miles west of Cairo. "Here, on the coast of Libya."

"Wow! That's five hundred miles away from here. Are there any Germans between here and Tobruk?"

Danny, as usual, had the answer. "No, but I've heard there are plenty of Italians. It sounds like we're supposed to go there as soon as possible and deliver supplies to our men who are fighting them."

And that is what happened. Ninety of our lorries drove right across the north of Egypt and crossed the border into Libya. The driving was not easy. For much of the time we were accompanied by sandstorms, which blew most of the days and nights. Sometimes our visibility was down to ten yards, and we had to crawl slowly along in our lorries, always looking out for the one in front of us, and being careful not to drive off the road into the soft sand that bordered it. And perhaps even more annoying was that the gritty sand got everywhere: in our eyes, in our clothes and in our lorries. We had to stop frequently to wipe the sand off our radiators so that they would not overheat. These conditions also meant that we had very little hot food to eat. Cooking for the convoy as the sandy winds were blowing everywhere was impossible, so for much of the time we had to make do with fruit and sandwiches, all of which came with their own portions of sand. Fortunately, by the time we reached Tobruk, the town had fallen to the British, but the place was in a shambles.

However pleased we were to see the smashed-up enemy tanks and lorries and the thousands of Italian prisoners of war being herded off into prison camps, we all felt very sorry, as we had suffered our first casualties. In an effort to break through the British forces besieging the town, the Italians had bombed our convoy and killed four of our men. Since we were such a close-knit unit, this affected everyone deeply. We all felt this terrible loss, and instead of working with our usual noisy camaraderie, we were now a very quiet and subdued unit.

This killing also made me think more seriously about the war. Until now I had been more concerned with trying to do a good job, making sure that any lorry I was responsible for was working properly. I enjoyed being with my friends and it was fun to take part in our noisy social life of games and the occasional drinks in the army canteens.

But that night as we sat in a circle around a small campfire listening to what the others said about our first casualties, it came home to me that the war was more than just keeping your lorry in good condition and obeying your superior officers. It was about life and death. Four families back home in Palestine – two in Tel Aviv, one in Haifa and one in Jerusalem – were soon to learn that their sons or their brothers had been killed in action on the northern coast of Libya. They would not be coming home again. Not now, not ever.

However, we could not dwell on this sad aspect of war for long; the following morning, we were ordered to drive to our new quarters in Tobruk. They were in the center of the town, and when we got there, we saw that the area was in a terrible state. Some of the buildings were still burning or smoldering, and the floors of the gutted shops we were to occupy bore witness to the fighting and the Italian ransacking of the place before they surrendered. We found a few bodies, which were taken to a central place where they were recorded, and then given a decent burial.

The morning after I arrived I was clearing away a few boxes of garbage when Danny came over to me, holding a piece of paper.

"Look at this, Benny. It's a page from a *siddur*."

"What's it doing here in Tobruk?"

"I don't know. Come over here. There are more pages like this."

Five minutes later, while we were stacking up half-burnt prayer books, I found some more religious documents.

"This is a *ketubah* and here are some other certificates," I said, putting them into a box.

"I wonder what they're doing here."

"So do I. And look, here are some more, and they've got the Jewish National Fund badge on them.

"The JNF?" Danny asked.

"Yes," I guessed. "This shop or whatever it was must have been used as a synagogue."

I was right, and soon several men in our unit together with some Jewish soldiers in an Australian unit were working to clean up the synagogue and some of the Jewish houses nearby. About an hour after we had started an old man shuffled into the building and approached me. "*Tagid li, chayal, atah yehudi?* Tell me, soldier, are you Jewish?"

"*Ken*, yes."

"Then," he said, continuing in Hebrew, "I'll get some other Jews to come and help you clean up this mess. You see you are in the Jewish quarter of the town and all the buildings around here belong to us."

"And who smashed them all up?" I asked.

"*Atem*, you."

"Me?" I didn't understand what he was saying.

"No, not you personally," he said, smiling, putting his hand on my shoulder. "But you, the British, when you shelled the Italians who were fighting here. At first the Italians ransacked these buildings looking for valuables, and then the British shelled them and they surrendered. But enough of that. I will go now and find some people to help you." He shuffled off, taking care not to tread on the pieces of broken glass and pages of prayer books that were still lying around.

For the next few days, when we had time off from our other duties, we helped the local people to clean up the smashed buildings; we also repaired windows and cleared out the rubble. We all worked very hard so that by the time Friday evening arrived we were able to combine the Shabbat evening prayers with a short consecration service for the newly cleaned-up synagogue.

It was all very moving, and I remember thinking that this was really something very special. "Look," I whispered to Danny as the rabbi of Tobruk led the service. "There are Jews here from everywhere. There are the local ones, us from Palestine, some from England and over there in the front there are some from Australia, New Zealand and South Africa."

He nodded. "That's what we're here for. To help and protect them. Let's hope we'll be able to do the same for the Jews in Germany. But you know, my friend, from what I've heard, I think we're going to be too late. I heard on the BBC that the Nazis there are making life very tough for the Jews – for the Jews in Germany and in the other countries they've conquered as well."

We had heard news like this before, but at the beginning of 1941 we were still ignorant of what was really happening inside Hitler's Germany, and we knew very little about the concentration camps and Hitler's plans to kill all of Europe's Jewish population.

The following week we had hard work of a different sort. Our unit had received orders to hand over the ninety lorries we had driven from Palestine and Egypt to another unit in the British army. We never found out why. All we were told was that we were to go out into the desert around Tobruk and repair and rebuild some of the smashed-up lorries we found there. We set out in scouting parties to look for them and, sure enough, out there among the sand, rocks and desert scrub, we found dozens of wrecked lorries and jeeps – mostly in very poor condition – lying around. We towed the better ones back to our base, but then I saw we had a problem.

"Look," I said to Yossi and Danny as I stood on the exposed engine of an Italian army Fiat. "We've towed in all these vehicles, but we don't really know how to fix them. What do we know about Italian Fiats, Lancias and the rest? Yes, we know how to replace wheels and change filters, but we don't know all the more detailed specifications, like tuning carburetors and things like that. What we need are instruction manuals or the mechanics who used to work on these vehicles."

"You're right," Yossi replied. "I suggest you fly out to the Fiat factory in Turin and come back with a few mechanics."

"Very funny. No, what I was thinking," I told the others, "is to see if we can get hold of a couple of mechanics from the POW camp."

"You think the officers will agree to let them out?"

"Why not? It's for our benefit, isn't it? We're supposed to be a transport company and at the moment we don't have any transport."

"How do you know these prisoners will want to help us?" Danny asked. "After all, they could be accused of helping the enemy."

"Tell me, Danny, if you were a prisoner just hanging around in a desert prison camp getting bored and eating lousy food and you were given the choice of doing a job you like and getting better food, what would you choose?"

"All right, you win. So let's start asking questions and see if we can get ourselves some Italian motor mechanics."

We did, and the simplicity of our idea impressed our officers so much that within two days we had twenty prisoners who were allowed out under guard to help us. We drove out to what looked like a graveyard for army vehicles, and began towing in more mangled mechanical junk for spare parts. As we bumped our way over the rutted desert tracks, the tubby Italian prisoner sitting next to me suddenly burst out laughing.

"What's so funny?" I asked.

"You British are mad," he said in bad English. "Mussolini was right. Do you ever expect to see these lorries working again? We dumped them here on purpose because they were broken."

But he stopped laughing after a few days. The lorries may have been useless to the Italian army, but to us they had to be made into working vehicles again. And so, helped by the POWs, who were paid with extra food rations, we all set to work. Within a week we had managed to rebuild several of the wrecks and turn them into working lorries again. I really enjoyed doing this. I was using my knowledge to make new – well, reconditioned – vehicles, and I also felt I was doing something positive to earn a good name for our unit.

One day after I had just run the engine on one of our "new" lorries to see how it sounded, I felt a light tap on my shoulder. It was Yossi.

"Stop what you're doing, Benny, and come over here. Come and see what Yacov Schmidt has done."

We strolled over to Yacov's lorry and there on the front wings and doors of his Lancia he had painted a Star of David and three letters in Hebrew.

"What do the letters mean?" I asked.

"*Yud, ayin, lamed*?"

"Yes," I said. "I can see that they spell 'Yael.' Is that the name of your girlfriend?"

"No, of course not. You know she's called Debbie. It stands for *Yehidah Ivrit L'tahburah*."

"The Jewish Transport Company," I translated.

"Right. Doesn't it look great?"

It did. "But Yacov," Yossi said, "you might like it, and we think it's great, but will the top brass agree to let you paint your lorry like this?"

Fortunately, after Captain Aron had a brief discussion with some of his superior officers about nurturing pride in the unit and keeping up our morale, the "top brass" agreed. From then on, all the vehicles in our unit had these new badges painted on them. It was also at this point that our transport company received its new name. From now on we were to be known officially as the Fifth Motor Transport (Works Services) Company. The other name changes were less official. We renamed the main street in our base Tel Aviv Street, and we made street name notices both in English and Hebrew for the other streets as well. Although a few old-fashioned British officers objected at first, they kept quiet when some of them were reminded that twenty-five years earlier, the British soldiers fighting on the Western Front in France had given English names to their muddy trenches.

We worked hard for a few weeks and luckily the dry weather allowed us to put in many hours of overtime. At the end of this period we had rebuilt one hundred fifty reconditioned lorries and felt very proud of ourselves. In fact, the *Magen David* badge became so closely associated with reassembling broken equipment that an Australian soldier who had broken his leg painted a *Magen David* on his cast.

When Danny asked him why, he said that if this badge was good for lorries, then it might be good for his leg as well!

But there was a grim price to pay for all this progress. At the end of February 1941 the German air force bombed our base and my friend Moshe Cohen was killed. A dozen men were injured by flying glass and bits of hot metal, and we were soon to learn that this was just the opening stage of the enemy's counterattack, whose aim was to recapture Tobruck.

CHAPTER FOUR
To Derna and Back

On March 24, 1941, two events happened. One was important to me, personally, and the other was important militarily. I was sitting on an upturned crate sorting out some nuts and bolts when Danny handed me a postcard. The picture showed the Tombs of the Caliphs of Cairo and when I turned it over, I saw that it was from Tamar. She had written a short message telling me what she had been doing, though naturally, because of the army censor, she had not written any details about her life in the ATS. She wrote that she was enjoying herself and ended the message, "I received your card from Suez. Please look after yourself and I hope to see you soon in Cairo. *Shalom*, Tamar."

I was ecstatic. This was the first time that she had written to me since we had met. It was hardly a love letter in the conventional sense of the word but I felt very happy that she had told me to look after myself and that she wanted to see me again. Just as I was savoring these happy thoughts, Danny came over to me.

"Benny, do you have any three-eighth Whitworth bolts over there?"

I answered him with a question. "When do we next get leave to go to Cairo?"

He shrugged his shoulders. "Not for ages yet. Why? And *do* you have a three-eighth bolt?"

I gave him the bolt and said we had been in the army long enough to get some time off.

"You might be right there, but go and tell that to the top brass. Didn't you hear on the radio that the Germans have defeated the Brits at El Agheila?"

"That's west of us."

"That's right, and they're moving east very fast."

"And can't we stop them?"

"I'm not sure, Benny. From what I've heard, the Brits weren't expecting this attack and so they sent a lot of men to Greece, Crete and the Middle East. I tell you, my friend, from what I overheard in the communications bunker an hour ago, it doesn't sound good."

"So there'll be no leave for Benny Levi."

"That's right. And no leave for any of us. Not now and not for a while, I'm afraid."

Danny was right. The German Afrika Corps under General Rommel, together with a few Italian units, was rapidly advancing eastward and in three weeks had reached the Libyan-Egyptian border some seventy miles east of us. They had smashed the British Second Armored Division and had bypassed us in Tobruk. This meant that we were now in an isolated pocket completely surrounded by the enemy. All leaves of absence were canceled, and meeting Tamar would have to wait. When I told Danny about this, he tried to cheer me up. "Don't worry – you know the old saying: 'Absence makes the heart grow fonder.'"

"Yes," I replied. "And what about that other old saying: 'Out of sight, out of mind'?"

From then on life under siege was an unnerving experience. It was like living in a box, except that you couldn't see the sides. We knew that the enemy was just a few miles outside the town, but although we could not see them we were always aware of their presence. By day we could hear the sound of the German artillery moving and practicing. At night the sky would light up with their artillery flashes and the ground would shake as they fired various explosive devices. Living in this situation meant that we also had to be careful about using our basic rations and equipment. We learned not to waste food, water or medicines, and we did our best to get used to this situation. We, as a transport company, would drive our reconditioned Italian lorries down to the docks and load them up with crates of ammunition. We would then deliver them to our forces that were out guarding the perimeter defenses. More than once our Fifth Motor Transport Company became actively involved in defending Tobruk from advancing German scouting groups prowling around like wolves looking for weak spots in our defense system.

It was on one of these delivery trips that we came under fire from German shelling. We had just unloaded several crates of QF – quick firing – tank shells when the enemy's shells started landing dangerously close to us. Our only means of defense were some old Lewis machine guns and a Fiat quick-firer. We immediately increased the distances between the lorries in our convoy, so that if one was hit, it would not affect the others. As soon as we had gotten ourselves into the best positions possible, we left the lorries, as we knew that individual soldiers presented a smaller target to the enemy. We also did not want to be blown to pieces if an enemy shell hit one of our lorries. Fortunately nothing dramatic happened and their shelling tapered off. After half an hour of lying in the sand, we climbed back into the lorries, delivered the crates and returned to base.

The next time we went out on a delivery mission, this time at night, we did see a little more action. Yacov Schmidt, one of our men who had arrived in Palestine in 1938 as a German refugee, suddenly put his finger to his lips and signaled us to stop talking.

"What's up?" I whispered.

"I think there are some German soldiers out there trying to sneak through. Let's see if I am right and we can grab them."

Following his instructions, Yossi and I and a dozen others crawled out from behind our lorries and broke up into four small groups. Before moving out, we agreed on a simple flashlight code so that we wouldn't shoot each other in the dark.

Slowly the sound of three Germans talking grew louder.

"*Wo ist das Tor?* Where is the gate?" one asked.

"Over there on the right. Now stop talking. They'll hear us."

But it was too late. At a prearranged signal we jumped up and quickly overpowered and disarmed them. We tied their hands behind their backs and blindfolded them. We did not want them to see our defense network. We then took them back to base and handed them over to our intelligence officers. The next day at dawn before we were told to take them to a POW camp, I took them to the front of our lorry so that they faced it. Then we took off their blindfolds.

"What are you doing that for? Now they'll see everything," Yossi said.

"Not everything. But just enough." And I showed them the blue and white *Magen David* I had painted on the front wing of my lorry. The three of them looked at the badge with amazement.

"Jewish soldiers?" the tallest one asked in English.

"Yes," I said proudly.

"But you are fighters."

"I know, and we'll fight you till we've beaten you."

We replaced the blindfolds, helped them into the back of the lorry and then they were driven off.

When the word got around about what I had done I was congratulated by everyone, although one officer said that perhaps the Germans had seen things that they shouldn't have.

"Don't worry," I said. "They saw only what I wanted them to see. They were in such a state of shock that they didn't look around at all."

A few days later, our commanding officer, Major Belk, was ordered back to Egypt, and Captain Aron took over. This meant he was promoted to major, and we could see he was very pleased to replace his captain's shoulder pips for a major's crown.

And this was not the only good news we heard about Jewish soldiers serving in the British army. Back home in Palestine the 1039 Port Operating Company, a unit of Jewish soldiers and British officers, was earning itself a good reputation for the unloading and distribution of war supplies, and the Commando 51 unit had fought well in Eritrea on the northern Ethiopian border. In addition, a unit of Jewish sappers had also been praised for their good work in Egypt.

However, despite our pride in learning about these new developments, we also heard that 1,500 Jewish sappers and stevedores had been taken prisoner by the Germans in Kalamata in southern Greece, and another 170 Palestinian Jews had fallen into enemy hands in Crete. We hoped that none of those taken prisoner in Crete were ex-German Jews.

If so, they would be in for a very rough time, as they would be considered traitors as well as Jews.

In addition to our driving duties we were ordered to "dig down" and camouflage our tents so they would be less visible to low-flying enemy aircraft. This meant we had to spend days digging huge pits and then covering up all our tents, both the ones we slept in and those used for storage. All of us hated this backbreaking work but we knew we had no choice. It was all part of living under siege.

"Danny," I said one day, trying to ignore the blisters on my hands. "I joined the army to fight and drive, not to dig holes in the North African desert."

"Well, just think how lucky we are that we're near Fort Pilastrino. We can use some of that old fortress's stones instead and save ourselves some digging."

"That's a very good idea; my hands and my back have had enough. I'll be very happy when we can get back to driving again."

That came sooner than we expected. The next day we received orders to stop digging (hooray!), as we were to drive one hundred miles west to Derna, a small Libyan town on the North African coast. This meant sneaking out of our defense perimeter and hoping that the enemy didn't spot us from the air. We were lucky and reached our destination unscathed.

However, as soon as we arrived we were told that if we wanted clean billets, we would have to clean out and disinfect some old bug-ridden buildings. As I was moving a pile of trash outside to be burned, my "walking encyclopedia," Danny, came up to me.

"Did you know this place used to be a slave port?"

"What do you mean 'used to be'? I feel like a slave now. First I'm digging holes in the desert and now I'm cleaning out stinking old buildings. And you know what's not fair? Every time we clean someplace up and make it fit for living in, we're ordered to move on to somewhere else. I'm telling you, Danny, I'm beginning to wonder when we'll see any real action. I'm fed up with digging, cleaning and diving for shelter every time we hear the sound of an aircraft overhead. This isn't what I had in mind when I joined the army."

Danny put his hand on my shoulder. "I know and I agree with you, but forget all this cleaning for a bit. I'm supposed to tell you we have to join Major Aron's convoy in the center of town. Let's go."

Being part of the major's convoy proved a very moving experience. We had just driven into the somewhat dusty main square next to the town hall, when suddenly we had to stop. Hundreds of people appeared out of nowhere and started swarming around our vehicles.

"Look," I heard them say in Arabic. And then they would point to the Star of David badges painted on our front wings and doors.

A young boy wearing a *kippah* stuck his head through my window. "*Shalom*," he said.

"*Shalom lecha*, peace to you," I replied.

"Are you really Jewish?" he asked in Hebrew, his sharp black eyes open in amazement. "Can you speak Hebrew?"

"Yes, all the soldiers with me are from Palestine. We're Jewish soldiers in the British army. We've come to fight the Germans and the Italians."

He turned around, clapped his hands and then told everyone around him what he had just learned. After that, our convoy was mobbed by the happy crowds and it took us some time to finish off the remaining few yards until we reached our parking places by the town hall.

When Danny and I eventually managed to enter we were in time to hear Major Aron talking to some of the leaders of the Derna community.

"How many Jews live here?"

"Five hundred."

"And how is it now that the Italians have left?"

The three elderly Jews shrugged. "*B'seder* – It's all right."

"Why? What's wrong? You don't seem very happy."

"Oh, we're happy you Jewish soldiers are here. It's just that the Arab Senussi Ghaffirs – "

"Who are these Ghaffirs?"

"Guards. They make their rounds at night. They've been robbing us, taking our food and money at gunpoint," said the oldest one.

"So why don't you complain?"

"It doesn't help." He shrugged. "And maybe you will leave like the Italians did and then we'll be at the mercy of the Ghaffirs again."

"Nonsense," said Major Aron. "We're here to stay and protect you."

But little did we know that we would not be staying in Derna for long. Within two weeks we would become part of the British army's retreat in the face of Germany's North African offensive.

However, as they say, ignorance is bliss. In the meantime, as we had done in Tobruk, we helped the Jews in Derna clean up their ruined buildings, and gave food to fifty or so half-starved little children.

On March 28, just two weeks after arriving in Derna, the phone rang in our office and we were asked if we had any lorries in good condition.

"Yes, one hundred and fifty."

"And drivers?"

"Yes."

"Then dispatch them to Advanced Force Headquarters immediately!"

"But it's nighttime now."

"Doesn't matter. Send them now! It's a matter of top urgency."

Two hours later, Danny, Yossi and I were driving in a convoy toward Benghazi. As we headed west we saw long lines of British army vehicles of all shapes and sizes stream past us in the opposite direction.

"What's happening?" I shouted to a driver of a slow-moving ten-tonner.

"We're pulling back to Egypt. We're going to regroup there."

"So why is our convoy heading west?" an Australian Jewish soldier sitting next to me asked.

"Don't know. I guess we'll find out when we get there. You know what army life is like."

"Sure I do. Run, run, run, wait."

I nodded in agreement. "But I still want to know what this is all about."

We found out soon enough. Our company had been sent to the rear of the retreating British army to help them fight a rearguard defense action and to try to slow down the advancing German forces. As soon as we reached our temporary base, we had to transport troops and supplies, and move ammunition and stores. We also had to transport all sorts of explosives so that we could blow up bridges and do everything possible to slow down the German advance.

Apart from the sheer physical demands of driving heavy duty lorries at all times of the day and night, we were also constantly strafed by the enemy dive-bombing aircraft. It was not long before we suffered casualties, and temporary gravesites could be seen topped with Stars of David made out of strips of wood.

In contrast to the sadness we felt when we saw these Jewish graves, we were pleased that we were able to rescue isolated pockets of British and Australian soldiers whose vehicles had broken down in the desert leaving them stranded.

"What's that badge on your front wing?" an exhausted young soldier asked as he clambered aboard my lorry.

"Our unit's badge. The Fifth Motor Transport Company."

"So why the Jewish star?"

"Because we're a Jewish company."

"Blimey! So you Jews *can* fight, after all. Well done! Now let's get the hell out of here. Me and my mates have had enough of this place."

And after setting fire to our abandoned vehicles so that the Germans wouldn't be able to use them, we set off back for Derna, our convoy full of tired but relieved British soldiers.

We stayed in Derna for a few days and then – again at short notice – we were ordered to join the rest of the army and head back east for Tobruk. This we did as the orange-red sun was setting in the clear blue sky. To the south we could make out the flashes of heavy guns while at the same time we could hear the constant roar and thunder of heavy artillery – the enemy's and our own. We knew that an Indian Infantry Brigade was trying to break out from where Rommel's Afrika Corps had surrounded it at Mekili. Owing to the overcrowded roads we were not able to drive faster than fifteen miles per hour, and I found this very frustrating.

CHAPTER FOUR: TO DERNA AND BACK

"Can't we go any faster? We're like sitting ducks for any German plane out there!"

"Don't worry, mate," the Australian next to me said. "Jerry doesn't usually attack at night and besides you lot are driving with no lights on."

And his friend added. "You've got to allow your slower vehicles to keep up with you, haven't you?"

He was right, but I still found it annoying to keep my speed down so low.

However, it was not only the crawling pace that annoyed me; we also had to stop for routine checks every hour. Officers with flashlights would walk down the lines of vehicles looking for any mechanical problems, and checking to see if any vehicles had gotten lost in the dusty darkness.

"How can you get lost?" I asked. "We're not bicycles that you can't see in the dark."

"You'd be surprised," an officer said when he heard me. "More than one lorry has gone missing or driven into a *wadi* in the dark. So stop complaining, laddie, and keep your eyes peeled for the lorry in front of you."

We were to learn later that driving off the dusty tracks into the desert and falling into *wadi*s were not the only dangers. Just as we were approaching the perimeter defenses of Tobruk and beginning to feel good – "home and dry," as my Australian passenger said – several sharp rifle shots suddenly rang out. Beams of light cut through the darkness and started flashing, and within seconds we found ourselves surrounded by some heavily armed British troops.

"What's going on?" I shouted to a lieutenant carrying a machine gun. "Can't you see we're on your side?"

"What do you mean?" he shouted back over the rumbling sounds of our engines.

"We're the Fifth Motor Transport Company, the Jewish unit," I replied, leaning out of the cab.

"Well, why didn't you say so? We're all uptight here about Rommel's lot trying to break through our perimeter fence and suddenly we saw your Italian lorries looming out of the dark."

I grinned. I had forgotten that we were driving captured enemy vehicles.

"And then one of my men heard some of your lot shouting in a foreign language and he thought it was German."

"Well, it wasn't," I laughed. "It was probably Hebrew or Yiddish or Polish."

"Oh," he said, lowering his weapon and telling his men to do the same. "Well, just know you were all very nearly dead. Now drive on toward that gap in the fence to your right and you'll be OK after that."

We had arrived in Tobruk, but our problems were far from over.

CHAPTER FIVE
Tobruk under Siege

The first thing I did when I had the opportunity was to write a short letter to Tamar. As I could not include any details that the censor would remove, my letter was fairly vague.

> Dear Tamar,
>
> Thank you for the postcard, which I received recently – it was probably a bit late as our unit was on the move. But this short note is to let you know I am alive and kicking and even more suntanned than when you saw me last.
>
> We've been driving a lot and I've gotten used to the Italian Lancia and Fiat lorries (see – I've gotten used to using British English, too!), which are heavier than the British Bedfords we had before. They are also slower and we all feel more exhausted driving them than the British ones, but it is true that they can carry more men and supplies, so I guess the extra effort is worth it.
>
> Our unit and our lorries with the *Magen David*s painted on the front wings and doors have earned a good name for hard work and reliability. At first there was a certain amount of anti-Jewish prejudice but this is no longer the case. In fact, one stupid British soldier who called me a "dirty Jew" was bashed up by some of the other men in his unit. These were some of the men we had rescued in the desert after their lorry had

broken down and left them stranded in the middle of nowhere.

When we're not driving or looking after the lorries, we spend our time on guard duty or reading. I just finished *The Black Knight*, a book about a heroic knight in England in the Middle Ages who everyone thinks is a bad guy, but of course they're wrong. In the end of course, his good side is discovered, especially when he rescues Angelina, the fair princess. It's not my usual kind of reading but I found it in the back of my lorry and it makes a good escape from the driving.

We also play cards and football when we have the time. My friend Danny, who is a pretty serious guy but still looks like a kid, is teaching me to play chess. He is a good player and has beaten some of our officers. They seemed pretty impressed that they were beaten by this skinny nineteen-year-old private.

I have to finish now; I have to check the oil, petrol and water in my lorry, Lara the Lancia, before I put her to bed! Don't be jealous!

How is life in Cairo and in the ATS? Are you allowed to tell me what you are doing?

I'll give this letter to one of our officers who's returning to Cairo, so I hope you get it soon. I also hope I'll see you again soon.

          All the best.
          Shalom,
          Benny

I had just finished writing this when all of the drivers were ordered to stand by our vehicles. It seems that we were parked in the wrong place and would have to find somewhere else.

CHAPTER FIVE: TOBRUK UNDER SIEGE

After scouting around for somewhere new, we found a place by the road leading out of Tobruk toward Egypt.

"Danny, we can't park here," I said, looking around. "This place is full of holes and *wadi*s."

"Look again, Benny. Can't you see? There, in the sides of the *wadi*s, there's loads of dugouts. They'll make perfect air raid shelters. The Italians must have dug them when we were attacking them. Now it's our turn to use them against the Germans."

Of course he was right. We parked our lorries in them and used some of the other dugouts as our new sleeping quarters, if you could call them that. We then spread khaki camouflage nets over the area and waited for the Luftwaffe, the German air force, to attack us.

They did. Their Messerschmitts and Heinkels returned on the eve of Passover. We were sitting around planning who would read which parts of the Haggadah – and figuring out who was the youngest soldier, to read the *Mah Nishtanah* – when the air was shattered, as a hundred German planes flew over and started bombing the town of Tobruk to our rear. We rushed out to our deeper dugouts and, like prairie dogs, stuck our heads out and looked up to see the large German crosses on the wings as they flew in low to dive-bomb the town and the military supply depots. Then, as suddenly as they had come, they banked away and headed back into the blue sky, leaving smashed and burning buildings behind them and large clouds of black oily smoke swirling around the dock area.

The raid was short but it was certainly not a good feeling to be stuck underground while the enemy, doing his best to kill you, was dropping highly explosive bombs all around. It is true that we had some anti-aircraft guns, and that some of the men managed to fire off a few rounds, but their actions were born of frustration rather than efficiency. As it was, none of our men was hurt in any serious way and only one lorry was destroyed.

As soon as the "all clear" signal was sounded, three of us were told to drive to the port to pick up some specific supplies – "and let's hope that Jerry hasn't blasted them to smithereens." Imagine our surprise when we found our supplies waiting for us on a ship, the *Atid* (meaning "the future"), which had just arrived that morning from Palestine. Apart from the regular supplies, I was very happy to find a parcel from my parents, which included a letter containing family gossip as well as news about what was happening in Palestine. I was also glad to read that my two sisters, Dina and Rachel, were doing well at school, and that my dad had been promoted at the bank, but I was sorry to learn that my Uncle Sol had died. My mom also wrote that my neighbor had crashed his Harley-Davidson, but that he had been thrown off and had only broken his arm. At the end of the letter my dad added a few words in his own scrawling handwriting. He said that it was ironic but the war was good for the local economy, as many people were now working for the British army. And he added that there was serious talk of introducing compulsory military service for all men between twenty and thirty years of age.

As I was reading these lines, I overheard Major Aron ask the captain of the *Atid* if he had any *matzot* and wine for a seder table for the base.

"How much do you need?"

"Enough for over 250 men."

"I can spare only four big boxes of matzah and a half-dozen bottles of wine. Will that do?"

The major said that if that was all he had then he had no choice, and that each man on the base would have just a small piece of matzah as a symbol of the ancient festival of freedom.

Sent aboard to bring these supplies back to my lorry, I overheard the captain saying to Major Aron that if he had known there were Jewish soldiers in Tobruk he would have brought much more. I found that the matzot were stored in the hold between petrol-filled jerricans, 250-pound bombs and thousands of rounds of ammunition.

Thinking back to what the *Atid* held, she did seem to have a future, as this ship, full of explosive material, had survived the German air raids on the harbor and had not been damaged in any way. Before driving back to base, I wrote a short letter to my parents in Tel Aviv and gave it to the captain, who promised he would mail it to them "if we get back OK."

What we did not know at the time was that the brief air raid was a trial to see how we, the British army, would respond. Luckily for us, the anti-aircraft guns were working in Tobruk, but our unit, parked some ten miles away near the perimeter fence, did not know this.

A few days later the German air force and artillery began their combined assault on Tobruk. The normally clear blue sky was suddenly filled with the sound of rolling thunder and huge clouds of thick black smoke. The attack continued throughout the day and into the night. Now the dark, starlit skies looked as though a lightning storm was taking place as the enemy artillery boomed and flashed, their lights combining with the red and green Verey flares to create one huge but deadly fireworks display over the north Libyan desert to the south of Tobruk.

We fully expected our forward positions to be overrun at any minute, especially at dawn, when we were subjected to another massive air raid. Well over one hundred enemy planes dive-bombed our lines and we were ordered to make sure our defenses were as secure as possible. This order was soon followed by another, to set up roadblocks using our heaviest lorries and anything else we had at hand, and to be prepared for any enemy tank offensives.

"This is where the British army goes communist," Danny muttered as we lay in a slit trench near the perimeter fence.

"What do you mean?" I asked.

"Because these are Molotov cocktails we're going to throw at the Germans," he said. "But just in case they don't work, make sure your rifle's ready."

Luckily we did not need to try out our primitive defense weapons, as some of our more forward-based men stopped the German assault. During this lull in the fighting, we improved our lines with land mines, deeper anti-tank trenches and caches of ammunition; we also made sure we had plenty of food and water readily available. The air raids continued sporadically over the next few days, but fortunately they caused no major damage to our defenses. A few men were injured by flying glass and shrapnel, but no one was seriously hurt. Ironically, we, the lower ranks, were in a better defensive position than our officers. We ate and slept in our cave-like dugouts, while they, in their usually more comfortable tents, had to spend much of their time running for shelter when the air raids started. Major Aron was heard to mutter, "most undignified," as he ran as fast as possible to safety.

And as we were being bombed, the German planes attacked the *Vita*, a hospital ship lying in wait in Tobruk harbor. This could not have been a mistake because, like all hospital ships, it was painted white with huge red crosses on its hull. Obviously this made no impression on the enemy pilot who, on turning around to make a second attack, was caught by our anti-aircraft guns. As his burning plane began falling like a rock into the sea, he managed to parachute out. The wind carried him to the center of Tobruk where he was immediately tied up and taken prisoner.

For the next six weeks we spent our life under siege in Tobruk. It was not like living in a besieged medieval castle of long ago, as the perimeter fence was ten miles outside the town. We also had the harbor and the coast as an open route to the rest of the world. But what it did mean was that we had no overland connections to Benghazi to the west or to Cairo to the east. It also meant that we were constantly aware of the presence of the huge enemy forces that threatened to overrun us. At any time of day or night you could hear the sound of distant artillery practicing, while at night, German thunder flashes would light up the sky.

Living under siege was a weird situation. Sometimes we were very busy, such as during a bombing raid or immediately after, while at other times it seemed like time stood still, and there was nothing to do. We spent most of these quiet periods making sure that our lorries were in good running order, reading or playing indoor or outdoor games. And although we, as a transport company, were officially designated a second echelon unit, we found that owing to the siege situation we were asked to maintain our weapons and to be as efficient as the regular frontline combat units.

Not all our newly acquired weapons were taken from the abandoned enemy vehicles we found lying around. Some of them, including a load of heavy German machine guns, were "donated" to us by the enemy, "airmail" style – that is, we took them from recently crashed enemy aircraft.

One of the things that relieved the boredom was watching the aerial dogfights between the RAF Hurricane fighters and the German Messerschmitts. The RAF's job was to prevent the Germans from flying over the center of the town and the docks. As the weeks passed and more and more British planes were shot down, we looked on the remaining pilots as real heroes. One of them, a Free French pilot serving in the RAF, developed a trick of deliberately nose-diving toward the ground as if he were out of control and then, as the German plane dived after him for the "kill," the Frenchman would suddenly swoop up into the sky leaving the enemy pilot to dive into the desert.

It was also during this period that word began to seep through about what the Nazis were doing to the Jews in Europe. Normally we heard these stories from the occasional Jewish refugee who had managed to escape and find his way by boat from southern France to North Africa. One of them, a thin teenager called Daniel Cohen, told us how the French Vichy police and the Gestapo had started rounding up Jews and Gypsies from off the streets or from their houses. These unfortunate people were either held in camps or put on trains and sent to concentration camps in Germany and Poland.

"How do you know all this is true, and not just stories?" we asked.

"Because before I escaped from one of the camps near Paris, I heard the Nazis talk about what was in store for us. They wanted to frighten us, and they did. They frightened me so much that I was determined to run away. I managed to hide myself in a delivery truck, but I was not able to save anyone else in my family. I am sure they were taken away and…" He could not continue and started crying quietly.

Later we heard that a Jewish French-speaking family in Tobruk had taken him in.

As well as learning about what was happening to European Jewry, we sometimes went to lectures our officers organized for us. Many of these were about Palestinian history and geography, but on one occasion, Danny gave a talk about *Hamlet*. It was very funny for me to hear the men in their different accents recite "To be or not to be," especially as I did not understand most of the languages they used.

But one language we all understood was the language of war. On June 15, 1941, General Wavell launched Operation Battleaxe, the aim of which was to break through the German lines and relieve us in Tobruk. For three days the British tried to hammer Rommel's Afrika Corps, and although they were sometimes victorious in the skies, the enemy's ground forces were too strong and the Brits lost over half of their tanks on the first day, and managed to capture only one of their three main targets. This meant that we continued to be stuck in Tobruk, and General Wavell was relieved of his North African command.

Our life in Tobruk continued for another month under siege – a life of repairing lorries and captured artillery, guard duty, lectures, Erev Shabbat services and endless games of cards. We were also subject to endless rounds of rumors.

"Did you hear that Gideon Cohen has been made corporal?"

"Have you heard that Moshe accidentally drove his lorry into a *wadi*?"

"Did you know that General Auchinleck is replacing Wavell?"

"Did Haim tell you that Rommel has returned to Germany?"

But the best piece of news I heard was in mid-July. While I was busy cleaning out the barrel of a machine gun, Yossi tapped me on the shoulder.

"Benny, have you heard? We're leaving."

"Leaving what?"

"Tobruk."

"Yeah? Why? Has Hitler had enough of us here?"

"No, it's not that. But I was talking to Fat Moshe in communications and he heard we're leaving here tomorrow."

"Yeah? And the Germans will just sit around and let us go?"

"No, of course not. Moshe said we're going to leave tomorrow at midnight on two Australian destroyers."

"But won't the Germans bomb them like they did to the Brits at Dunkirk?"

Yossi shrugged. But what he'd heard – and what I'd dismissed as just another battlefront rumor – did actually happen. At six o'clock on July 22 we were officially told that the Palestinian companies were to be evacuated from Tobruk that night, and that we were to pack only our own personal equipment.

"What about our lorries?" I asked. "Aren't we taking them?"

"No, they're staying behind here and the Australians will be using them instead. Any more questions? No? So listen up."

We were then told to be packed and standing ready by our lorries by ten o'clock that night, when we would take them down to the docks and then hand them over to the Aussies. It was a strange feeling to leave behind all our lorries and equipment, but orders are orders and we drove down to the docks as planned. Just as we arrived, the Germans started shelling the harbor. As we watched some of the buildings and stores blow up we felt helpless and defenseless – just like on the first day out in the desert when we had only had a few suitable dugouts in which to take shelter. The attack lasted for about an hour, and as soon as it was over and we saw that none of our men had been hurt, we scuttled aboard HMAS *Stuart* as quickly as possible; soon we were out at sea heading east toward Egypt. The following day we sailed into the harbor at Alexandria, most of us looking pretty dirty and disheveled, especially after our rushed evacuation from Tobruk.

"I haven't seen such a scruffy bunch of men as you for ages," one of the sailors laughed. "You'll all need a good scrub up before they'll let you lot out on the town."

I grinned back at him and walked down the gangway with Danny and Yossi. We had lived through seven months under siege at Tobruk, had come though it all unscathed and were now wondering what the future held in store. It was a strange feeling to be back in a normal situation – that is, a normal wartime situation. People were bustling about: there were civilians, as well as soldiers, walking around and it was good to see cafés and restaurants open for business. Even though there was talk of Rommel attacking Egypt, no one seemed very concerned, and Alexandria seemed to be thriving very well on the war.

"I know what I'm going to do," I answered Yossi's question. "First I'm going to phone Tamar and then I'm going to have a long hot soak in a tub. We've got ten days' leave and I don't intend to waste one single minute of it."

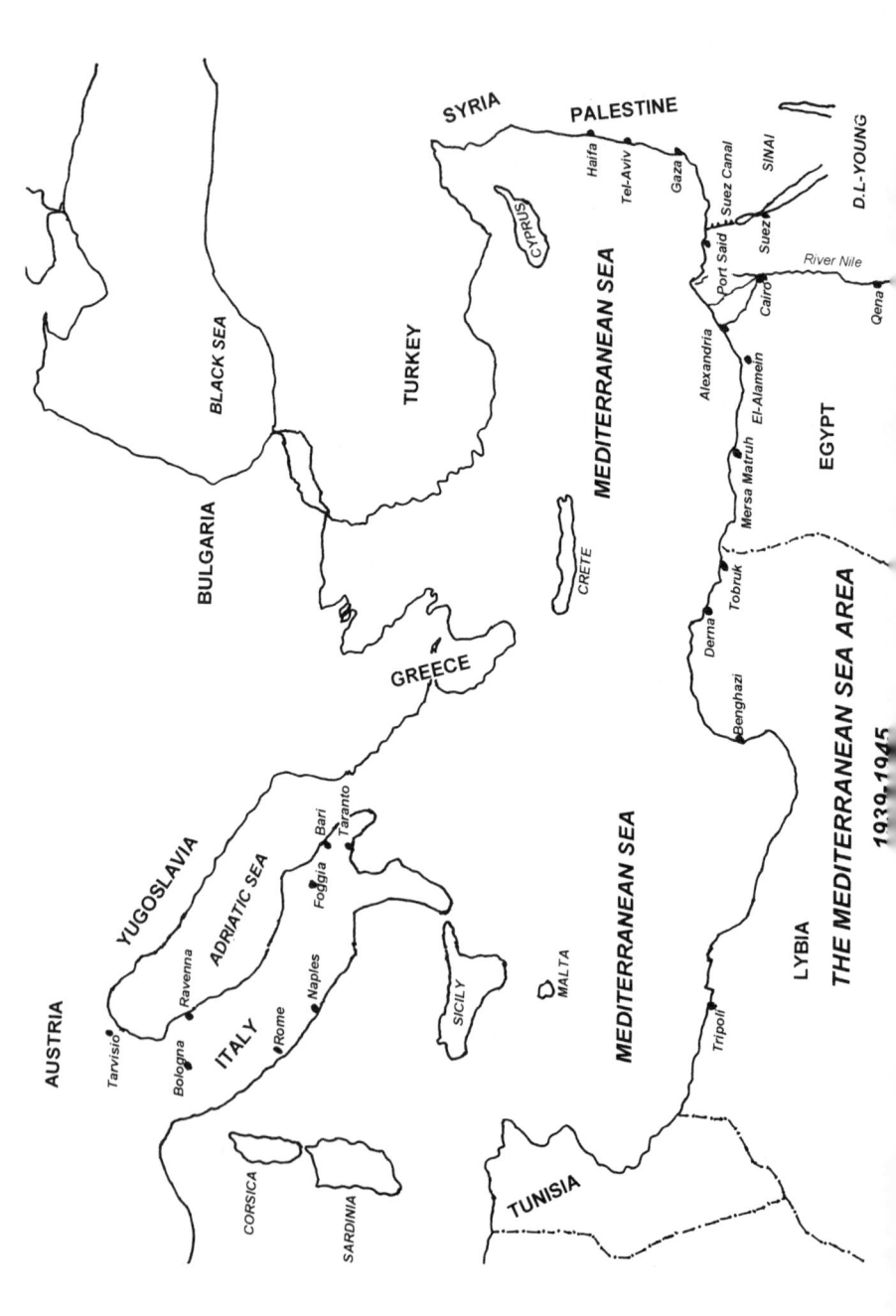

CHAPTER SIX
Cairo and Tel Aviv

The next day I arranged to meet Tamar at the base where we had first met. We were both in uniform and she looked very good. Her black hair was curling out from under her smart ATS hat, while I had tried my best to look sharp in a uniform that had really seen better days.

At first, it was slightly embarrassing to meet up with her. So many months had passed without seeing each other. I had spent them on the front lines in the North African desert in all male company, and she had been working in the more civilized environment of the Cairo ATS offices. As we walked toward each other I hoped we would not be like two strangers at a party, not knowing what to say to each other. At first we kept saying, "No, after you," as we started telling each other what had happened in the meanwhile. However, as time passed, our conversation became less awkward and more natural. To me, she looked much better than the picture of her I had kept in my mind all those months. Her eyes sparkled more, her skin looked smoother and her curly hair was shinier and seemed to ask me to stroke it. I could only hope that I looked equally good to her.

After walking for half an hour along the promenade overlooking the Nile, we stopped at a small café and ordered orange juice, cakes and ice cream. I was longing to eat something cool and fresh after having survived a monotonous army diet for several months.

"You don't know what this is like for me," I said as I offered her a piece of the light, nonmilitary cake. "Just sitting by the river, relaxing and being out in the open without any fear of German bombers and air raids."

"But weren't you scared a bomb would fall on you when you were driving out in the open or when you were on guard duty?"

"Yes and no." I said, enjoying my vanilla ice cream topped with chopped nuts. "It's true, I did think about it from time to time, especially when I saw German aircraft flying over, but after a while you have to learn to live with these things, otherwise you'd go crazy, wouldn't you?"

"Yes, I suppose so," she said. "And we also had a few false alarms here and it was rather worrying having to rush to the shelters. At first I was quite scared but, as you say, after the third or fourth time you become used to them and become rather blasé."

"You see, as I said, you can't think all the time of what could happen. But I must admit, two or three men in Tobruk did start suffering from shellshock, and they were given jobs that kept them sheltered underground most of the time."

After a while we got up, left the café and continued walking toward the Egyptian Museum. This impressive building with its arched windows and solid walls near the river sat handsomely among the well-kept green lawns and flowerbeds. As there was so much to see inside, we decided that Tamar, who had been there many times before, would act as my guide. She would show me the sections containing Tutankhamen's treasures. As we stood there looking at the famous golden bust of the ancient boy-king with its heavy gold striped headdress and collar, she told me about his life. She explained that this magnificent piece of work was more a symbol of his power, rather than a true likeness.

"Do you know, he lived over three thousand years ago in what was known as the New Kingdom, and he was only eighteen when he died?"

"Does his name have a meaning?" I asked.

"Yes, it means the living image of Amen."

"Who was that?"

"He was one of the ancient gods," she said, and then began telling me about them. I found this fascinating and enjoyed my lesson in ancient Egyptian history, especially as my personal "tutor" was so enthusiastic about her subject. "I love the history of this country," she said. "And if you think about it, Egypt's place in the world today is so different from what it was when Tutankhamen was king. Then we were a rich country, the center of the world; today we are a poor country and one that is exploited by the British for its geographical position. I'm sure that if we didn't have the Suez Canal, nobody would think about us at all."

After this we went outside and sat on a bench in the beautiful museum gardens. There we talked about Palestine – well, I did most of the talking. I told Tamar what it was like to live in a country where in many aspects of everyday life, we had our own Jewish country, even though it was not yet an independent one.

"Many of the newspapers are printed in Hebrew, the children speak Hebrew even if many of their parents can't, buses don't run on the festivals and the most fantastic thing is that the whole country comes to a complete stop on Yom Kippur: the only vehicles you see being driven are the British army ones. Everyone else is either at home or in *shul*. It's really something to see. You know, maybe one day when the war is over, the British will see how good we Palestinian soldiers were and then help us establish our own Jewish state."

Then, just as we were leaving the gardens, Tamar tripped on a loose paving stone and held out her hand for support. I took it and she straightened up but did not let go of my hand. After that we continued walking hand in hand and I was in seventh heaven – and I hoped she was feeling the same. Since then, I have often wondered if she tripped on purpose.

We walked and talked for another hour and then stopped at another café where we drank more juice with our pita, hummus and olives. As I was wiping up the remains of the hummus with the last piece of pita, Tamar took my hand and said, "Let me show you the Kasr El Aini gardens. They're even more beautiful than the museum ones and there's a fantastic view of the river from there." I paid the bill and we left immediately. Tamar was right. Looking out over the Nile from the gardens surrounding the medieval school and hospital, the view was as Tamar had described it: fantastic. The wide river flowed along, and our view of it and the boats with their triangular sails and the steamers plying their trade was perfectly framed in the leaves of the overhanging branches.

"Now look up at the dome of the hospital – there, that building to your left with the little tower on the top. Doesn't it look like a huge orange-pink *kippah*? I think this is one of the most beautiful sights in Cairo," she said, and squeezed my hand. I squeezed hers in return and said, "I agree, though I haven't seen many sights yet."

"Then in that case, we'll have to do this again tomorrow afternoon. I'm not on duty then. And would you mind if I bring my friend Esther with me? She's dying to meet you. I've told her so much about you already."

I felt really flattered that even though we had not been dating in the usual sense, she had talked about me with her best friend.

"OK, but on one condition."

"What's that?"

"I bring *my* best friend, Danny, with me. That way we'll make up a foursome. And from what you've told me about Esther – "

"Esty."

"Esty – I think she and Danny will get on very well together. But now I'll take you home, since I have to be back at my base in an hour."

We walked back to her flat and just as I was turning to leave, she squeezed my hand and gave me a quick kiss on the cheek. I was about to do the same to her, but she had run up to the top of the steps and was waving goodbye.

"*Ashufook bukra*, see you tomorrow," she shouted in Arabic.

"*Lehitra'ot machar*," I shouted back in Hebrew and started walking back to my base.

I felt great. Not only had we had a terrific day out, but she wanted to see me again, too. It was certainly a better way of spending my time in a foreign city – that is, walking around with a pretty girl in uniform – than just killing time sightseeing on my own or going to movies and cafés with some of the others in my unit.

I must have been walking without paying attention, because as I was thinking about Tamar and remembering our conversations I found myself suddenly and unexpectedly back at the base.

"And just in time, too," Danny greeted me. "We're on guard duty in five minutes."

During our turn guarding the base I told Danny about the time I'd spent with Tamar; then I saw that after some time he was beginning to look a little depressed.

"What's the matter?" I asked.

"Well," he began. "It's that just that while you've been playing tourist in Cairo, and Yossi has gone off to visit some long-lost aunt, I was left behind to read a boring book about how the pyramids were built."

"But I thought you liked that sort of stuff."

"I do, normally, but not over five hundred pages of it, and in small print too."

"Danny, my friend," I said, slapping him on the back. "Your problems are over. Your fairy godmother has been looking out for you. Tomorrow you shall come with me when I go out with Tamar again."

"What, and hang around like a spare wheel while you two are being all chatty and lovey-dovey?"

"No, Danny, nothing like that. Tamar is bringing a friend along with her who wants to meet you. Tamar says she's very pretty and we'll make up a foursome."

And that is just what happened. The next day Danny and I walked over to the ATS base and met the two girls at the main gate.

To my great delight, Tamar immediately took me by the hand and introduced Esty to Danny. She was a bit shorter than Tamar but had the same slender figure. Instead of Tamar's black curly hair she had shoulder length straight brown hair. I was pleased to see she was also pretty and that Tamar hadn't brought some fat spotty girl with her.

We had another great afternoon and soon it was clear than Danny and Esty had a lot in common. I overheard them talking about ancient Egyptian history and who was responsible for building the Great Pyramid of Giza. Esty said it was built by King Cheops.

"You mean King Khufu," replied Danny.

"That's the same name but in Greek. It took him twenty years."

"I read that it took longer," Danny countered, "but let's not argue about that. All I know is that for nearly four thousand years it was known to be the tallest man-made structure."

We returned to the Kasr El Aini gardens and wandered around the mosque before going to a riverside café for coffee and cakes. The afternoon passed so quickly that I was somewhat surprised when Danny tapped me on the shoulder and said we would have to break up the party, as we were both on guard duty again that evening.

"When will I see you again?" I asked Tamar.

"I don't know. Here's my phone number on the base in case you can't reach me at home," she offered, and we all scribbled our numbers down on the café's paper napkins.

Before parting, I managed to give Tamar a kiss, which lasted somewhat longer than the peck on the cheek that she had given me yesterday. And out of the corner of my eye I noticed that Esty had given Danny a quick kiss just before we left.

To my great disappointment, and I hoped that Tamar felt the same, we were not able to meet again for the next five days. This was because as soon as we got back to the base, Yossi told us that a notice had been put up that we were to return to Tel Aviv early the next day for a big parade.

"What for?" I asked. "I thought we'd finished with that stuff."

"It's a recruiting parade," Yossi explained. "The army has decided it wants to recruit as many Jewish soldiers as possible, especially as more Arabs are joining up as well."

"So we'll have more Jewish transport units," I said.

"I guess so, and more trained Jewish soldiers as well."

When I thought about it from that angle, I did not feel so bad. It was true that I would miss seeing Tamar, but I hoped at least I would be able to fit in a visit home and see my family, whom I had not seen for over a year. And besides, as I said to Danny, the more Jews who join the army, the better. We were going to need a strong, well-trained army in the future.

"That's right," he agreed. "From looking at our past history, one day we're going to have to fight the Arabs in a big way. Not just ambushes and things like that, but open battles with tanks and artillery. I'm telling you, the more we know about these things, the stronger we'll be."

To our relief, our guard duty was canceled that night and instead we were told to use the time to pack our equipment and clean up our uniforms and rifles.

We were up very early the next morning and set off after a brief inspection parade. This time, Yossi, Danny and I were sitting in the back of my lorry, but later we knew we would take over the driving. We didn't mind not driving; we stretched out on some blankets to sleep for another couple of hours. If there was one thing I had learned in the army, it was this: if you get the chance to grab an hour or so of sleep, don't turn it down.

After waking up, I took over the driving from Amos, a tubby soldier from Gedera. As we drove through El Arish we could see the triangular sails of the felucca fishing boats with the fishermen hauling in nets full of silvery fish. The clear blue sea contrasted with the swirling clouds of dust our convoy was churning up as we headed east. After crossing the border into Palestine near Gaza, the expanse of light brown desert landscape began to give way to small green fields. I took a break from driving for an hour and then took over the last section, the sixty-mile stretch from Beersheva to Tel Aviv. We arrived at our base at Sarafend late in the evening, and those who lived in Tel Aviv were allowed to go home – "But make sure you're back here by ten o'clock sharp."

It was a wonderful feeling to go home again, but, oh, how everything seemed so small and neat! For the past year while I'd been away I'd gotten used to living out in the desert or in large army buildings. Now I had to move carefully around a small suburban apartment, making sure I didn't break anything. My parents and sisters were in a state of absolute shock when they opened the front door and saw my dusty self standing there, complete with backpack and .303 rifle. I had tried to call them from Beersheva but hadn't gotten through.

After the first few hugs, kisses, slaps on the back and cries of "How big you've grown," my mother told me to take a shower while she prepared a meal.

"But *Imma*, it's nearly midnight," I protested.

"Doesn't matter," she said, pushing me into the bathroom. "What Jewish mother isn't going to feed her son who's been away for such a long time? Now be quick or your food will be burned. It's lucky I've still got some food left over from Shabbat."

Twenty minutes later I was sitting down to eat roast chicken and vegetables and trying to answer everyone's questions at the same time. Naturally they asked me what I had been doing and where I had been, since, apart from a few letters and postcards, they hadn't heard much from me.

I told them quite a lot but omitted the stories of how a piece of flying glass in an air raid had cut my arm and how I had nearly broken my leg when falling down a *wadi* on guard duty one night near Tobruk.

However, my sharp-eyed mother noticed the scar on my arm and asked how I got it.

"Oh, that – just working on the lorries," I lied.

Dina laughed. "Listen, Rachel, he calls them lorries instead of trucks. And Benny, do you fill up your lorries with gas or petrol?"

"With petrol, of course." And then I changed the subject by comparing my army experiences with my father's in the Jewish Legion, some twenty years earlier.

He commented, "At least we didn't have to fight Hitler and his Nazis in those days. Then it was a case of fighting the Turks and trying to drive them out of Palestine. Now we are hearing all sorts of terrible stories about what the Germans are doing to the Jews in Europe."

"But aren't those stories, the ones about concentration camps, just rumors and propaganda?" I asked. "We also heard stories like that when we were in North Africa and we met some Jewish refugees from France, but is it as widespread as they say?"

"Yes, my son. I'm afraid it is. None of the letters we or our friends here write to our families there ever get a reply. And the Jewish Agency officials we know now say that what we, too, thought was just propaganda is really true. The Jews have to wear yellow stars on their clothes and many have been taken away to work in all sorts of terrible camps. And yes, they've been forced to move into ghettos. And the synagogues and other Jewish buildings have been destroyed as well."

"But, Dad, that sounds just like the Middle Ages," I said, remembering my history lessons.

"I know that, Benny, but that's what everyone is hearing now. All these terrible stories. And we can't do anything about it. Some people are even saying that Hitler and his Nazis – may they be blotted out – are determined to kill all the Jews in Europe."

"It's true what your father is saying, Benny," my mother added. "There have been reports of mass shootings of Jews, and of using them for all sorts of terrible medical experiments. I'm telling you, this Hitler is the worst thing that has ever happened in our history, believe me."

"Yes, and Rommel is trying to fight his way here, to the Suez Canal and Palestine," I said. "And so far it looks like he is succeeding."

"That's what we've heard, son," my father said. "That is why you and the rest of the men with you must stop him. You have no choice. It's not just for the British that you have to win; it's for us Jews as well. I wanted to join the army as well, but they told me I was too old, and my bad leg wouldn't let them take me anyway. So tomorrow, you tell the men with you to put on a good show. It's very important. Do you hear me? We want as many men as possible to join up and stop this Hitler before it becomes too late. But I must tell you, son, that even though your mother wasn't very happy when you joined up –"

At this point *Imma* cleared her throat and *Abba* corrected himself: "That is to say, even though your mother and I weren't very happy when you joined up, we're now very proud of you and hope you know what you're doing, and that you look after yourself when you're out there."

If I had felt proud then, I felt even prouder the next morning when I was on my way to Sarafend. People whom I did not know on the bus and in the street would see the "Palestine" shoulder flash on my smartest uniform and pat me on the shoulder and say, "*Kol hakavod!* Well done!"

I must admit that despite my somewhat cynical attitude when I first heard about this recruiting parade, I was truly impressed when it took place. It consisted of a thousand Jewish soldiers from all different units, and before our turn to march into the stadium, a New Zealand military band marched in, their brass instruments blaring out some really inspiring tunes. Five hundred civilian volunteers, all wearing armbands, marched behind us. They were carrying banners bearing slogans like "Enlist Now" and "Join Us to Defend the Homeland." We marched past the district commander and saluted, and as we did so, fifteen thousand spectators in that packed stadium stood up, clapped and cheered as loudly as they could.

Then Mr. Israel Rokach, who looked more like a successful businessman than the mayor of Tel Aviv, started to read out his dramatic recruitment speech. Suddenly he was cut off as some RAF fighter planes flew low over the stadium, their noise drowning out everything else before they disappeared into the clear blue sky.

Later we were told that only one thousand new recruits had signed up that day, and that the army and the Jewish Agency were disappointed by this poor response.

"But don't worry about it, Major Aron," an Agency official told our commander. "More men are joining up at the other army bases and I'm sure that when more people hear about what the Nazis are doing in Europe, even more will join up." He was proved right. By the end of the war, over thirty thousand Palestinian Jewish civilians had volunteered to serve in His Majesty's army.

After the parade, we had another day in Tel Aviv to see our families and also to help out at the recruiting stations. It was a good feeling to be part of all this and to tell people face-to-face what we had done on the battlefields of North Africa.

"So you are not just pen pushers then?" a young man asked me.

"No, we drive lorries and do guard duty, and we've also taken part in several attacks on the enemy."

"The Afrika Corps?"

"Yes, that's right." And after I told him in the typical, time-honored way some exaggerated stories of what our unit had gone through at Tobruk and Derna, he signed up on the spot.

Early the next day, with my pack stuffed full of cakes, fruit and clean clothes, I left my parents' apartment for the base. As before, I played down any danger I might be in and told my mother that I would be busy with lorries and supplies. I don't think she believed me and I'm sure that my father did not. He had told me that while he was serving in the Zion Mule Corps in 1915, he had officially been in a supply unit, but had also taken part in some of the fighting at Gallipoli.

When I arrived at Sarafend, I saw that all the others also had overstuffed packs like mine, while several were carrying extra bags as well, all full of home-baked cakes and bottles of fruit juice. We had a quick roll call, then climbed up onto the lorries and soon we were on our way, driving back to Cairo. Throngs of people were in the streets to see us leave, and it felt good to see our lorries' large blue and white flags flapping in the wind.

I was sad to say goodbye to my family, but I was also looking forward to seeing Tamar again. I still had one day's leave left and I was planning to make the most of it.

CHAPTER SEVEN
Qena

Apart from my last day of leave, which I spent with Tamar, the next few months were the most boring part of my time in the British army. It all started with Danny waking me up on the first morning after our ten-day leave.

"Get up, lazybones! We're driving to Qena in two hours."

"Where's Qena? Who's driving what?" I asked, still half-asleep.

"We've got new lorries and Qena is south of Cairo. Now get up."

"How far south?"

"Don't know. I'll tell you later. Now I'm off to eat. I'll save you a place in the canteen."

After breakfast, Danny, with his usual thirst for knowledge, filled me in about Qena.

"It's about four hundred miles south of Cairo and is the local capital of the area. It's well known for its pottery and there are famous ruins there."

"Sounds fascinating," was my sarcastic reply.

"And it's only forty miles from the ancient Valley of the Kings at Luxor."

I was not impressed. "Oh, yeah – and four hundred miles from Tamar."

"That's true, and also four hundred miles from Esty," Danny added, his face suddenly looking sad. "Well, I just hope we'll be able to get back here to Cairo on leave from time to time."

"Yes," I said. "If we get leave. Now let's go find Yossi and check our engines before we go. All we need is to break down in the middle of nowhere with a dry radiator."

We arrived at Qena two days later, after making an overnight stop near El Minya. The drive was boring and our convoy headed south, down the valley of the Nile, without any incidents – exciting or otherwise. The only thing that broke the monotony was that one of the lorries' radiators started bubbling over, as the driver had forgotten to check it before leaving. We had to wait for it to cool down before he filled it up and then we got going again.

The worst part of the journey, however, was dealing with the tropical heat and the flies – two "enemies" that were to return and plague us for much of the next few months.

"At least we had fans and fly screens in Cairo," I complained to Danny and Yossi.

"I know," Yossi said, rubbing his neck where he had been bitten. "These flies are much worse than those in Cairo. I think they've got teeth as well. They bite like crazy."

"Here, rub some of this cream on," Danny said. "It might help."

"But why are we going to Qena anyway?" I asked. "Surely all the action, like fighting Rommel, is taking place in the north, near Tobruk and Benghazi?"

Danny shrugged. For once he did not have the answer. "I guess we'll be told when we get there."

We were. Our job was to provide the transportation for the building of a new road from Qena in the west to Port Safaga in the east, on the Red Sea.

"Danny, Yossi, I found out why they need a road and railroad down here," I said the first evening at our new base. I took out a screwdriver and sketched out a simple map in the sand. "It's like this. Here is Cairo and here is Suez, and here is the Red Sea, right?" I explained. "Now, our job is to work on the road and railroad here in Qena, because it's the shortest distance between the Nile and the Red Sea."

"So what if it's the shortest distance between here and the Red Sea?" Yossi asked. "Why do the British want this road and railroad at all?"

"They want them as an alternative road to those in the north. They're scared of Rommel overrunning the roads up there."

"But that's impossible," Moshe, a tubby mechanic, said. "Rommel and his Afrika Corps are hundreds of miles away."

"I agree, but the road we're building here will be part of the Brits' contingency plan, you know, if anything goes wrong in the north. Our job is to help with the building of this new road and railroad."

And help we did. Every day we would transport food, water, road and railroad building equipment and supplies from Qena to the east. As the work progressed and the new road and the railroad began snaking their way over the desert dunes toward the Red Sea, our journeys became longer. I knew our work was strategically important but I had not joined the army to transport gallons of water and sacks of cement through the Egyptian desert.

To break the monotony we watched old cowboy movies and others on a somewhat primitive and noisy projector. We also had talks and lectures every so often, and one evening Danny gave a talk about how the pyramids were built. We also had a Friday night service every week followed by *Kiddush* and a better meal than usual.

The only good thing about Qena as far as I was concerned was that I could write regularly to Tamar without waiting forever to receive her letters in reply. I usually kept these letters fairly short, as, frankly, there was not much to tell. I mean, how many times can you write, "Today we drove east and my lorry was full of concrete blocks"? It was enough that I was bored – I did not want Tamar to become bored as well. However, I did tell her about the minor incidents that happened, such as Gideon's lorry having a flat tire in the middle of nowhere or how Moshe managed to drive into a soft patch of sand and how I had to tow him out. I also told her how Avram had forgotten to close the tailgate of his lorry properly, and so when he arrived at the building site, he found that all of his jerricans of water had fallen out of the back. But to be honest, it was not really exciting stuff, just stuff to read and write to pass the time.

Perhaps the most interesting letter I wrote was after I had come back from visiting the ancient city of Luxor with Danny, Yossi and a couple of other men.

> Dear Tamar,
>
> Thank you for the letter in which you told me about the broken typewriter and the Egyptian clerk who kept stealing stamps and envelopes.
>
> For a change I will not tell you about driving lorries in the desert, but about the trip we made to Luxor. This place is really fascinating. Have you ever been there? If not, I promise to take you there some day. Luxor includes Karnak and the ancient city of Thebes, and both of these places are joined by a paved road that's over one mile long. (Don't I sound like Danny?) There are all sorts of ancient buildings here including a long temple dedicated to King Amenhotep III and a tall

painted obelisk to Ramses II, who is, I think, the same guy mentioned in the Haggadah.

There are also hundreds of stone columns that Danny told me are called "colonnades," but I think the most impressive things to see here are the three huge statues of Ramses II. Danny (who else?) told me that there used to be six of them, and that one of them is now somewhere in Paris. He also told me that this Ramses guy lived about 2,700 years ago and fought several battles and in the end married a Hittite princess.

We spent the whole day wandering around here, and drove the forty miles back to base in the dark. We had to keep on the alert, as the sides of the road are lined with soft sand and we didn't want to get stuck like Moshe did last week. The good thing was that at least it was cooler than driving in the daytime and the flies seemed to have gone to sleep, or decided they had eaten enough of me!

When we got back to base we gave our Luxor guide book to one of the officers, who said, "Now you'll agree with the old saying: 'Join the army and see the world.'" I'm not sure Luxor is the whole world, but at least it made a change from delivering railroad sleepers and gallons of water to thirsty construction workers in the middle of nowhere. However, even though it was very interesting I'd still prefer to drive back to Cairo and see you. In the meantime, I sent you a postcard so please let me know if it has arrived.

                      Please write soon. I miss you,
                      Benny

P.S. Danny has just told me he says "Hi!" to Esty and says he will write soon.

And so, apart from the occasional trip to Luxor or to some other desert sites which all looked the same to me, the days stretched into weeks and the weeks stretched endlessly into even more boring months. Perhaps to keep us motivated, we were reminded time and again of how important our work was and that, like the American Pony Express of the old Wild West, we always managed to deliver our supplies – especially the water – come what may.

"Always bear in mind that there are ten thousand men out there working in that heat. You are their only source of supplies and communication. You are their lifeline. Never forget that," we were constantly reminded. And so we would drive our convoys through the barren tawny desert and cause huge clouds of fine dust to rise in the air, making the drivers behind us keep their distance while they did the same to those behind them. You could hardly see anything green, just a few scrubby saltbush plants and a stunted tree or two trying to survive among the rocks and the sand. I always wondered how the lizards that we saw sunning themselves on the rocks by the roadside or suddenly flitting away on our approach managed to find water, but I guess they did. Danny told me later that they drink the early morning dew before it evaporates in the heat of the day.

"Yes, either that or the water that fell off Avram's lorry," I said.

For me, the worst loads we had to carry were the live cattle, which would later be served up as meat for the workers. At the beginning of the journey the cattle would be "persuaded" by us, armed with sticks, to walk up the gangplanks into the open backs of our lorries. Usually, once we had persuaded the lead cow to climb up, the rest would follow more or less without too much trouble. We had to make sure we packed enough cows in so that they could not move from side to side and tip our lorries over. Then, once we arrived at the building site, we would have to reverse the process and unload them. Of course, once they were up there, they did not want to come down again. The good thing was that the unloading was usually quicker than the loading. Our last view of the cows was seeing them standing patiently in the pens outside the slaughterhouse, flicking away the ever-present flies with their tails.

"So it's not just a case of 'Join the army and see the world,'" I said to Yossi after we had delivered yet another load of cattle. "It's 'Join the army and learn to be a cowboy as well.'"

Occasionally our routine would be interrupted, as important military officers or politicians came to inspect us and check the progress of our construction project. Then we would have to tidy everything up and go through the "spit-and-polish" ritual so beloved by the British army. We would polish our boots, tidy our rooms and tents and make sure that our lorries were as dust-free as possible. Of course we hated these interruptions, not because they broke the monotony, but because of all the cleaning up we had to do. However, sometimes it was worth it, like when Danny and I managed to get ourselves a few days' leave and a lift back to Cairo with some of the visiting party's drivers. This meant we could see the girls for a day or two and we could also make use of our ATS connections to call our parents in Tel Aviv.

It was during my last call home that my father told me about the Japanese attack on Pearl Harbor.

"It was a complete surprise, Benny," my father said. "The Japanese planes had the upper edge and although some warnings had been posted, it seemed that no one took them very seriously. The reports on the news say they attacked in two waves and sank four battleships including the *Arizona* and the *California*, as well as at least half a dozen destroyers and cruisers. And they also blew up well over a hundred planes. I guess that these were on the decks of the aircraft carriers or possibly in nearby airfields. And not only did they drop bombs, Benny, but they also used torpedoes. Of course it's too early to know all the details but the radio said that over three thousand men had been killed or wounded. It's terrible, son. I don't know what's going to happen now. I don't know what Roosevelt will do."

"I guess he'll declare war on Japan."

"He's already done that, Benny, and Germany and Italy have declared war on the United States."

"So that means the Americans will support the Brits, which I suppose in the long run will be good for us."

"I guess so, but what a price to pay. All those poor men, to say nothing of those ships and planes. But I have to hang up now. So look after yourself and keep writing. We love reading your letters, even though you can't include any interesting details."

I told the others what I'd heard and from then on, we made sure we listened to the news regularly.

On the evening of our third day in Cairo, Tamar and Esty accompanied us to the station, and we returned to Qena on the overnight train. Although we had to pay for the journey, it was much more comfortable than traveling back by road.

Of all the official inspections, the one I remember most clearly was the one when Moshe Shertock, the head of the Jewish Agency, arrived at Qena during Chanukah 1941. This time we did not resent tidying up the base and forming a guard of honor for him. It also became quite obvious that he was very pleased with what he heard and saw.

Before he left, we were assembled on the parade ground, and this government-style official with his thick mustache and slight Russian accent addressed us. He gave a short speech in English and then in Hebrew, and even added a few phrases in Arabic as well. Although we could not have known this at the time, this would not be our last meeting with him; we would meet him later in the war in Italy under completely different circumstances. Later he would become Israel's first foreign minister and its second prime minister, but looking at this short, stocky official in his dark gray suit as he faced us from his raised platform, none of us could have guessed this.

Three months later, we had to go through the whole "spit-and-polish" routine again as Yitzhak Ben-Zvi, the Chairman of the Jewish National Council, made an official visit to our base. He seemed to know more about the military than had Moshe Shertock; in fact, he told us that he had served in the British army during the Great War. He added that his son was also serving in the army, in the Royal Army Service Corps.

Like Moshe Shertock, Ben-Zvi, with his slight Russian accent, told us that our work, however boring it seemed to us, was very important for the British war effort. We should do our best, as it was important for us as Jewish soldiers to keep our good name for hard work and reliability. Again, none of us could have guessed that one day this bespectacled and unassuming official would rise in the ranks of the future State of Israel to become the country's second president.

The next nonmilitary activity that succeeded in breaking up our routine was celebrating Passover in 1942. Since there was no lack of space in the desert, we roped off a large square with our lorries, which we decorated with palm leaves. We then set up long tables to seat six hundred men and covered them with white tablecloths. These were decorated with flowers, and stood opposite a large archway that bore a huge banner welcoming the various civilian visitors who had arrived from Palestine and Cairo. Before the seder, we had arranged who would read each passage, and when I began, "*Veyered Mitzraimah*, and he went down to Egypt," I noticed quite a few of the men smiling as they noted the relevance of this sentence.

After the prayers, the meal and the songs were over, Danny said to me, "I can't help comparing this seder with the one we had last year at Tobruk. Do you remember?"

"You mean when the Germans were shelling us and carrying out air raids? Well, this one is much better. But, as we've just sung, let's hope next year we'll be in Jerusalem."

He nodded. "Or at least in Tel Aviv."

We felt good about our Passover celebrations, but two months later we received some bad news. At the battle of Gazala near Tobruk, Rommel, in a successful flanking attack, smashed our forces in North Africa and destroyed over five hundred British tanks.

"What does that mean?" I asked Danny that evening as we were listening to the radio. "The BBC thinks we've really been hammered up there."

"I think they're right. It means that the Germans are free to move east toward the Egyptian border and the Suez Canal."

"Toward us?"

"That's right."

That night, Baruch Schmidt, a soldier in our unit who had fled Nazi Germany in 1938, confirmed Danny's opinion. He had managed to tune in to a German army broadcast and had heard more details about the battle.

"It's true what Danny said. The British Eighth Army had to withdraw from Gazala, and Tobruk has fallen to the Germans. They said that thousands of British soldiers have been taken prisoner and that Rommel has been promoted to field marshal. It seems that the Brits have retreated to El Alamein and – "

"El Alamein!" I interrupted. "But that's well inside Egypt. It's only about seventy miles west of Alexandria."

"I know," Baruch said with his German accent. "The radio said the Brits have abandoned their position at Mersa Matruh and have fallen back to El Alamein."

"Well, all I can say is, I hope they make a strong stand there. If not, we'll all be sunk." And thinking of Tamar, I said, "I bet they're all panicking now in Cairo and Alexandria."

That night I wrote to her to ask what the situation was like in the north. A few days later I received a reply. She had given it to a soldier in our unit who had been sent to Cairo for medical reasons, and so did not have to submit her letter to the censor.

> Dear Benny,
>
> This will be a short letter, as Jacob has to return soon and is waiting for me to write this. The news in Cairo is not good. As soon as people heard about the German successes, a few anti-British riots broke out. As you know, the British aren't popular here. There are also rumors that once the Germans arrive, the laborers' wages would go up. I'm sure this is just pro-German

propaganda but it has added to the general tense atmosphere that you can feel everywhere.

I am well and so is Esty. I miss you a lot and hope you'll be able to find an excuse to come up here for a few days. However, seeing how things are at the moment, I doubt if you'll be able to. A friend of mine in the Intelligence Corps told me that the army is not giving much leave now.

Please look after yourself (and Danny).

Write soon. *Shalom* and kisses,

Tamar

Wow! Kisses! This was even better than her last letter. Things were looking up.

The other hopeful incident during this period was that we were quietly told to load a few crates of rifles and ammunition onto a captured German vehicle and to make sure it was in "tip-top condition, ready for a long trip though the desert."

"What's going on?" Danny asked me. "Why have we spent the morning cleaning that thing up?" he said, pointing to the now spotless Opel lorry standing behind some camouflage screens.

For once I was able to answer his question.

"Danny, have you heard of the German unit?"

"The German-speaking unit in the British army? The men who are going to sneak behind the enemy lines?"

"Yes, well, officially we're preparing this lorry for them."

"And unofficially?"

"They're for our people at home, the Palmach."

"Are you sure?"

"Yes. It seems that their commander, Yitzchak Sadeh, has asked us to send this stuff over to him."

"To send this stuff? You mean to smuggle it."

"Possibly," I muttered, keeping a straight face. "But we can't admit that to the Brits, can we?"

And so, shortly afterwards, the Opel and three lorry loads of captured machine guns, rifles, grenades and ammunition were sent back home. There they were to be used for training purposes and for defending outlying settlements.

Apart from sending weapons home, we also heard a positive piece of news – that Winston Churchill, the British prime minister, had paid a visit to Cairo to see firsthand how Rommel's Afrika Corps could be stopped in their drive east. One of the results of his meetings was that we were given permission – and this time it was official – to wear shoulder flashes bearing the word "Palestine."

"Why not 'Jewish' as well?" I asked Yossi.

"Don't know, Benny. It's probably something to do with politics. It seems the Brits are not prepared to go that far. So for the time being, we'll just have to resign ourselves to being a Palestinian regiment in the Buffs."

"Yes, sir," I mock-saluted Danny. "Hooray for the Buffs, the Royal East Kent Regiment."

Another change of name was that from now on, our new official name was to be the 178th General Transport (GT) Company.

It was also at this time that I heard the best news so far about the war. I was in my room preparing my kit for an inspection, only half listening to the radio. But then, as the military correspondent was explaining the situation, I put my rifle down and started listening very carefully. It seemed that Lieutenant General Montgomery, later called "Monty" by everyone, had smashed the combined German and Italian armies at El Alamein on the North Egyptian coast. The correspondent described how Monty had drawn the enemy forces into an area between the coast and the Quattara Depression. In this way, Rommel was not able to bypass the British Eighth Army and continue his drive to the east. As a result, a weeklong enormous infantry and tank battle had taken place, and Rommel had lost over thirty thousand men and seven hundred tanks and heavy guns.

Leaving my kit on my bunk bed, I rushed out to tell everyone that the British had "hit Rommel for six." Later that evening we learned that despite Hitler's orders to "stand and die," Rommel had retreated, and so Cairo and the Suez Canal were saved – at least for the time being.

"But don't forget," Danny reminded us, "Rommel is still around. He's not out completely."

"That's true," I said. "But he and his Afrika Corps have retreated west into Libya and they lost more men than we did. And that's not saying anything about their smashed-up tanks and guns."

"I wonder if we'll see them again," Yossi thought aloud. "The Germans have a bad habit of reappearing, but there must be a limit to what they're prepared to sacrifice in North Africa. And besides, I think the Italians have been more of a liability to them than a real help."

"Well, I doubt whether *we* will see them again," I said. "At least not as long as we're stuck in this sandy hole in the middle of nowhere."

"But that's just it, Benny," said Yossi. "I just heard we're moving out of here."

"From Qena? When?"

"Tomorrow or the day after."

"Where to?"

"Somewhere in the north, though I don't know exactly where."

And indeed, the next day, after nine months in Qena, we were ordered to get our lorries ready for a four-hundred-mile journey to Cairo and the northern Egyptian coast. There, our convoy would meet up with the rest of the British army, pushing Rommel and the battered remains of his Afrika Corps westward in the direction of Tripoli.

"And guess what?" Yossi added. "We've been allowed to paint our unit's badges on our lorries, on the front wings and on the doors."

It was with great pride that we painted or touched up the light blue circles with white *Magen David*s on our vehicles. Then, amid the noise of heavy clutches being released and gears being engaged, the 178th GT Company of the Palestine Regiment started heading north. We were off to fight the enemy once again.

CHAPTER EIGHT
Pushing the Germans West

It took us two days to return to Cairo, and when we got there we were told we would be stopping overnight.

"Just make sure that you're ready to leave at six o'clock tomorrow morning," we were told. Of course Danny and I rushed off as soon as we could to Tamar's apartment, where we hoped to meet the girls. Imagine our disappointment when their neighbor told us that they had left the day before – "in their nice ATS uniforms" – but he did not know where they had gone. We returned to the base, and after carrying out the usual checks on gas, oil, water, tires and radiators we set off the next morning and headed west for Alexandria and El Alamein.

Our progress was fairly slow, as we had to stop several times at various ammunition dumps and depots to pick up extra supplies. This meant that most of the lorries in our convoy were overloaded, but our slow speed allowed us to witness the aftermath of the destruction of much of Rommel's forces. We saw hundreds of burned-out tanks and lorries, lying in the desert, black, heavy and useless, contrasting sharply with the bright scenery of the desert sands and rocks.

"Look over there," I said to Yacov Cohen sitting next to me. "Just look at that smashed-up tank, that Panzer over there. The one with the turret upside down on the top. Once it looked so massive and so strong, as though nothing could possibly destroy it – but now look at it. A useless lump of burned-out scrap iron."

Yacov nodded. "And I suppose you can say the same about the heavy lorries over there. When they're new, they also look indestructible, but now look at them, just like the tanks, burned out with all their *kishkes* spread out all over the place."

Apart from the extra weight, another reason for making such slow progress was that we no longer had the road to ourselves. It seemed as though every British military vehicle in North Africa was joining our convoy, and they were all sending up huge clouds of engine smoke and sandy desert dust. Since we were being urged to move as fast as possible, and because there was little traffic coming from the opposite direction, we sometimes drove four and even six vehicles abreast.

Occasionally a lorry would drive off the road and then have to be winched back from where it had sunk into the soft sand. But these were the only incidents as we chased Rommel's Afrika Corps west toward Tunisia.

Two nights out of Cairo we stopped at Mersa Matruh, a small coastal town halfway to Tobruk, and there a huge surprise awaited me.

I was sitting down on a couple of jerricans with Danny and Yossi in the late afternoon, discussing our situation when suddenly, from behind, I felt a pair of hands clap over my eyes.

"Guess who?" a deep, strong voice asked.

"General Montgomery."

"Try again."

"Winston Churchill," I replied and yanked the hands down. I looked up and saw the happy smiling face of Tamar.

"What are you doing here?" I asked, standing up and giving her a kiss.

"I'm here with the ATS," she said in her normal voice.

"And so am I," Esty added, suddenly appearing from behind one of the lorries. She ran over to Danny, who was as surprised as I was.

"But what's the ATS doing out here in the desert?"

"We've been sent here as cooks and clerks and drivers," Esty said.

"And what are you?" I asked looking at the two girls who were clearly enjoying the surprise.

"Drivers," they answered in unison.

"Tamar, I didn't know you could drive," I said.

"I couldn't, but I took a course with the army in Cairo and passed it last week. And so did Esty."

"What are you going to drive?" Danny asked. "Lorries like ours?"

"Yes, but the lighter ones. Those and staff cars for the officers."

"And jeeps," Esty added.

We were so happy that the girls had found us, and the four of us left the main camp and walked over to the perimeter fence where we split up into pairs.

For the next two hours I sat there with Tamar on two old ammunition boxes as we held hands, talked and watched the evening sky darken over the camp. We talked about everything: her time with the ATS in Cairo, my time in Qena, our families and the war. And most of all how we had missed each other. I was just running my fingers through her curly black hair when I felt an urgent tapping on my shoulder. It was Yossi.

"Benny, sorry for breaking up the party, but we've been called over to the lorries – now."

We hurriedly broke apart and I quickly followed Yossi back to the central parking lot. Shouting, "*Shalom*, see you later," over my shoulder I made my way over to my Bedford.

"What's up?" I asked, when I saw how busy everyone was.

"We've got to get everything packed up now and ready to move out at a moment's notice," Micky Feingold told me. "The Brits want to keep the pressure on Rommel, so we'll be off again soon. And check your headlights as well as your oil and water. It looks as though we'll be doing a lot of driving through the night. By the way, do you have a spare headlight bulb? One of mine burned out." I gave him one, and within an hour our 178th GT Company set off west along the North African coast. Once again we were part of the huge mechanical fat snake of cars, lorries, tanks and artillery that was following hard on the heels of the retreating enemy.

I must admit it was a great and powerful feeling to know we were chasing the Germans toward Tripoli. It meant that we were pushing them further and further west – that is, further away from the Suez Canal and further away from our homes in Palestine. Of course there was also the sweet feeling of revenge, that the tables had been turned. It had certainly been an unnerving experience sitting in our underground dugouts in Tobruk during the German air raids.

I told Baruch, sitting next to me as reserve driver, of my feelings.

"You're right, Benny. Up to now the Nazis have had it all their own way. Now they're getting a taste of their own medicine. And not only here," he added, "but I heard on the radio that things aren't going well for them in Russia, either."

"You mean at Stalingrad?"

"Yes. The BBC reported that the freezing weather there is doing to the Germans what it did to Napoleon's army over a hundred years ago."

"Very good. So let's hope that history repeats itself," I said as I remembered learning how "General" Winter and the Russian army had decimated the invaders.

We continued on our frantic drive westward, all the time pushing the enemy further along the northern desert road. We drove all night with very few stops, and when we did stop it was only for a quarter of an hour or so, to change a punctured tire or carry out some other simple repair.

Our next major stop was near Sidi Barrani, where I looked for Tamar. It gave me a warm feeling to know that while I was driving she was also somewhere in this huge convoy, but I had no luck. Perhaps she was there somewhere among the dust-covered staff cars milling about, but neither Danny nor I succeeded in finding the girls.

Just as we were checking our radiators and cursing our bad luck, we were suddenly blown to the ground as a massive roar and thunderclap shattered the air. One of our lorries had driven off the road into the soft sand and set off a land mine. This lorry, a petrol tanker, had exploded and burst into a huge bright ball of vivid orange flame. The lorries closest to the explosion hurriedly backed away, and all we could do was hope that the driver had somehow managed to survive. Fortunately he had. The blast that had felled Danny and me had blown him out of the cab. The last we saw of him, he was being carried away on a stretcher, shocked and burned, to a waiting ambulance.

Before we set off again we were all gathered together for a short lecture on safety. Among other things, we were warned to watch out for British army vehicles standing innocently by the roadside.

"Some of them have been captured by the Germans and placed next to land mines, and others are booby-trapped," the lieutenant told us. "So no one is to have anything to do with them until the sappers have checked them out first. You saw what happened when one of our vehicles hit a mine, so take that as a warning. Now let's get moving."

We drove on for the rest of the day. Fortunately, as this was November, it was not too hot and made for a far more pleasant driving experience than driving supplies from Qena to Port Safaga.

That night we slept in the cabs and in the backs of our lorries. It was bitterly cold, and I ended up wrapping myself up in a piece of German camouflage material for extra warmth. My last thought before I fell asleep was that it was ironic that a piece of German army equipment was now being used to keep an enemy soldier warm – and a Jewish soldier, to boot.

I was woken up by a heavy hammering sound on the roof of my cab. Stretching myself, I muttered, "What the heck?" when I realized that it was raining. And very heavily, too. Shivering, and still not fully awake, I pulled on my khaki greatcoat and looked outside. The normally dry and dusty desert was now a dark brown and muddy expanse. Streams of water were flowing in all directions. The current in one was powerful enough to carry away a dead sheep, which it then deposited by the side of the road. Luckily I had parked on a rocky area, so my lorry did not get stuck in the mud.

As I was taking all this in, I saw Yossi making his way over to me, jumping from rock to rock. He signaled for me to open my window.

"Drive over to where Baruch is stuck," he said, pointing to where one of our lorries, its rear wheels stuck in the mud, was standing at a crazy angle.

The next half hour I spent attaching chains to the front axle of Baruch's lorry and hauling it out of the sticky squelching mud. By the time I had finished and Baruch's lorry, with patches of mud all over it, was standing firmly on the road, the sun had come out. Immediately everything started steaming, including us and our slab-sided vehicles.

"Baruch, you were lucky you weren't loaded with even more stuff," I commented as we both downed a mug of coffee. "Otherwise we'd still be trying to pull you out."

Fortunately, the rest of the day passed without any mishap, apart from the usual flat tires and overheated radiators. One lorry had to be abandoned, as its engine had seized up, but other than that, we reached our next stop for the night in good condition. The only other incident took place when we stopped for a short break for sandwiches. We saw a notice saying "*Prima comp. Ebreo lavore.*"

"What does that mean, Danny?" I asked. "I know that *Ebreo* is Italian for 'Hebrew' but what does the rest of it say?"

"If I remember my Latin, it means something like 'First Company, Hebrew Labor.' I guess it means that some Hebrew or Jewish unit in the Italian army had repaired the road at this point."

He was right. Later we learned that the Italians had conscripted a Jewish labor company from Tripoli to repair the road.

The next day we continued west to Capuzzo; both sides of the road were littered with the burned-out remains of enemy tanks and other military vehicles. It was sobering to think that Rommel had brought over all this equipment originally to the east in order to overcome Egypt and to capture and conquer the Suez Canal and Palestine. Now it lay here, burned, black, mangled and useless.

We spent the night at Capuzzo, a small town that had changed hands several times in the past three years. There was nothing special to do that night apart from checking over our vehicles for the next day, chatting and playing cards. I went for a walk with Danny to look for the girls but we had no luck. Two other ATS girls told us that they had probably gone ahead and maybe we would catch up with them at our next major stopping place.

We had now settled into a routine. We would get up early, make any last-minute checks and then start driving. As before, apart from a few planned stops and some unforeseen ones for flat tires and other repairs, we made good progress chasing the enemy west.

That night, unexpectedly, Baruch and I were woken up at three for guard duty.

"We drivers don't have to do guard duty," I protested, still half-asleep.

"Maybe that's what the rule book says," replied the unsympathetic and burly sergeant. "But not this time. Get your boots and rifles and get out there, now."

We had no choice. We got up, grabbed our equipment and, muttering things about injustice, set off for the camp's perimeter fence.

It was a clear and cold night and the unfeeling stars twinkled in the dark sky above, not caring about two soldiers, cold and fed-up, who were now on guard duty in the North African desert below. All I wanted to do was sleep; "This downy sleep, death's counterfeit," I remembered learning from Shakespeare's *Macbeth*. All I wanted to do was to lie down and wake up fresh, ready to do my part in pushing the Germans ever westward. But instead, here I was, wrapped up against the chill, holding my rifle and looking out over the desert. I was just about to say something to Baruch when suddenly I noticed three figures moving like dark ghosts in the desert. They were some distance away from our camp.

"Quick, Baruch," I whispered, pointing out into the desert. "Lie down so they won't see us."

We lay down and watched them approach the fence. They did not seem to be in a hurry or to have any special purpose in mind. It occurred to me that they were walking as if they were on a leisurely Sunday afternoon stroll. I could not make out whether they were armed or not, and neither could Baruch. When they were about one hundred yards away, I gave the prearranged signal and we both jumped up, rifles at the ready, to face them. They were in complete shock. Suddenly the silence of the nighttime desert had been shattered by these two forms that had sprung up out of nowhere.

"Hands up!" I shouted. "Throw down your rifles!"

"No rifles," a guttural voice shouted back. "*Wir sind verloren*! We're lost!"

"*Ja, ganz verloren*, absolutely lost."

"Listen, Baruch," I said. "This may be a trick. You know, something like the Germans using our lorries as a decoy. I'll go and see what's up and you cover me. When I whistle, come up and join me. Only don't shoot me by mistake."

Making sure my rifle was loaded and ready, I slowly advanced to where the three shadowy shapes were standing in the dark. It was true, they were not carrying rifles, but they could have had their pistols with them. Two of them had their hands in the air. The third one was using an old piece of wood as a crutch and as soon as I got close to them he sat down. Covering them with my rifle I made them take off their coats. None of them was carrying a pistol. I whistled for Baruch to join me.

"Who are you?" I asked, using the very little German I knew.

"Hans Bach."

"Yosef Schmidt."

"And I'm Wilhelm Weiner," the wounded one said.

"Which unit?" Baruch asked.

"Fifteenth Panzer Division," Hans said, and Yosef nodded in agreement.

"I'm from Twenty-First Panzer," Wilhelm added, rubbing his badly sprained ankle.

"What are you doing here?" I asked.

They shrugged. They really did not seem to know what they were doing in the middle of the desert in the dark. Hans, the tallest one, who spoke the best English, tried to explain. "We were *mit unser* tanks and suddenly a big boom, how you call it? *Eine* big explosion, and I was thrown into *eine* hole in the ground. When I woke up I saw *mein* head was bleeding. I must have hit it on a rock."

"*Ja, ja,*" Yosef added. "Me also knocked out."

"But why aren't you with your men?" I asked.

They shrugged again. They seemed to have no idea of what was going on. Their reactions were like those of groggy drunks, like boxers who had been punched in the head too often. I signaled Baruch to come over to me and we had a quick discussion. We could not abandon our guard duty so we tied them up to take them back to camp when the relief guards turned up. This happened an hour later. We blindfolded our three prisoners and escorted them back to camp. As we were setting off, I could not help telling them that they had been captured by Jewish soldiers. Their reactions were interesting to see and hear. Hans looked shocked. Yosef shook his blond head in disbelief and Wilhelm tried to protest.

"But Jews don't fight. Hitler said you Jews are all soft and *untermenschen*, not people."

"Well, the next time you see Hitler, tell him that we Jews are not soft and we fight really well," I said proudly. "Just take one look at us and remember that you were captured by Jews."

We handed our prisoners over to the intelligence unit. They would know what questions to ask and what to do with them afterwards. For us, their capture was one more wartime incident; for them it was the beginning of a long period of captivity.

CHAPTER NINE
Tripoli and Malta

Tripoli. We reached the end of our westward "pushing" of the enemy along the North African coast on the eve of Passover 1943. We had driven our heavy lorries well over fifteen hundred miles since leaving Cairo. We had driven in howling dust storms when you could hardly see the vehicle in front of you, we had driven in wintry torrential rain, we had crossed flooded *wadi*s and had become stuck in axle-deep sticky mud and had driven by day and by night. In short, apart from large towns, we had driven through every situation possible.

As our convoy entered Tripoli, I could not help but think about the times when we had had to haul each other out of soft sandy dunes or thick brown gluey sludge, and how we had had to clean our engines of all the dust and mud afterwards. As I mentioned this to David Goldsmith, the mechanic sitting next to me, he grinned.

"You know," he said, "I've cleaned so many filters and other blocked-up engine parts in the last few weeks that I think I could do it all in my sleep. Who would have thought you'd get so much rain out here? And I thought we were on the edge of the Libyan desert. Since when has this place been known for its rainy climate?"

I had to agree with him. Fortunately, we passed through the area reasonably well and with few losses. Apart from having to abandon several lorries that broke down or had burned-out engines, we also lost a few men. They had driven over some of the thousands of land mines the Germans had sown in a desperate attempt to slow our progress.

One of the men was a driver called Izzy, whose proper name was Itzhak Levine. He was a stocky, suntanned soldier, whose natural strength allowed him to tighten and loosen nuts and bolts with his fingers, when the rest of us would have had to use a wrench. He had joined the army on the same day as I had, and in fact had stood behind me for our health inspection. He had lived in Rishon LeZion, a small town south of Tel Aviv, and was very proud of coming from there. "You know," he would say, "Rishon was one of the first towns to be built in Palestine. It was built by the *Bilu*, the first pioneer immigrants from Kharkov." Izzy had been an only child and had helped his parents with the family dairy. And now he was no more. He had been blown to bits by a land mine while trying to haul another lorry stuck in a sandy hole.

Naturally we were shocked by his death, and it reminded us that we, too, could easily be blown up driving in this God-forsaken, barren, tawny landscape.

"And it's not as if he were doing anything heroic," David said to me when I mentioned Izzy's name. "He just happened to be in the wrong place at the wrong time. It wasn't as if he were attacking the Germans or defending a position or anything like that. It was just pure bad luck."

So it was with a mixture of feelings – the joy of reaching our journey's end and having beaten the Germans, mixed with sobering thoughts of those who hadn't made it – that we drove into the main square in Tripoli. This ancient city, situated between the desert and the sea, had been founded over twenty-five hundred years earlier by the Phoenicians. Danny told me that it had a population of over one hundred thousand, and we wondered if the Jewish community had survived the fighting and the German administration. It did not take us long to find out. As our transport company, the 178th, with its *Magen David* badges on the doors and wings of our lorries, made its way through the crowded streets where most of the Jews lived, we found ourselves greeted by lines of happy, smiling people, all waving wildly and cheering loudly. Our convoy was led by Major Aron in his staff car, a large, impressive vehicle which had been cleaned up and washed for the occasion. A large *Magen David* and a badge of the 178th were painted on the car's front wings.

It seemed that everyone, all of the fifteen to twenty thousand men, women and children of Tripoli's Jewish community, had come out into the warm sunshine to greet us. There were ancient-looking bearded rabbis and young men together with young women in flowered frocks, holding their small children. Most of the cheering crowds were wearing modern clothes but some people were dressed in the traditional North African long, flowing *galabiya*s.

"Look how they're all pointing at the *Magen David*s on our lorries," I said to David. "I feel as though I'm the Messiah who has arrived."

"Sure," David grinned. "Didn't you know the Messiah will be a dusty Palestinian driving a British-army Bedford?"

Suddenly a young girl broke free of the crowds and, clambering up on to the running board, kissed me on the cheek and thrust a few flowers at me. It was a great feeling.

"Don't worry, Benny. I promise I won't tell Tamar," David laughed.

I laughed as well and told him I would tell her myself, if I ever found her here. When I did find her later in the day she said, "What, only one girl tried to kiss you? I thought I had got myself a real catch!"

"Well, I was a bit scruffy and unshaven," I said.

"Huh! It was because of the *Magen David* that was painted on your lorry. Anyway, let's go to the seder service they've prepared for us. I've asked Esty to save us places there next to her and Danny."

Now washed and shaved, and wearing my cleanest uniform, I took her hand and we made our way over to a large courtyard on the edge of the town. The sight was impossible to believe. Yesterday we had been driving through the endless and empty-looking desert. Now we were about to sit down at a huge, traditional seder and celebrate the festival of freedom. Yes, we had brought freedom to the Jews of Tripoli. Apart from the cleanliness and the order of the tables with their bright white tablecloths, shining silverware and copies of the Haggadah, we ourselves were now looking fresh and clean. And if we of the 178th looked good, then Tamar, Esty and all the other ATS girls looked even better. It was clear they had cleaned themselves up and washed their hair, and a few were even wearing lipstick. This was a seder I would remember for a long time. It looked even more impressive than the one I'd attended the year before at Qena. After saying *Kaddish* and washing his hands, the chief rabbi of Tripoli stood up and made a short speech.

"*Bruchim haba'im l'Tripoli*, welcome to Tripoli," he began. "Jewish soldiers and our liberators. We, the Jewish community of Tripoli, welcome you here as our brothers," and seeing the ATS girls he added, "and sisters, to this traditional celebration of Passover, the festival of freedom. What does it celebrate, you may ask. It celebrates freedom – the freedom of Moses and the Children of Israel when they left Egypt to start a new life as a real nation. They were no longer a nation of slaves. They would become a nation who believed in the Holy One, blessed be He, and in His Torah. Like you, my khaki-uniformed brethren, they too crossed the desert and passed through many trials in order to reach the Promised Land.

"I will admit that Tripoli is not the Promised Land, but one day, God willing, we will all rise up and settle there and live a Jewish life in the land our God promised to our forefathers, Abraham, Isaac and Jacob.

"Now all that remains for me to do is to thank you all for liberating us from the Nazi yoke and for having defeated them on the field of battle. Let us hope and pray that the Holy One, blessed be He, sees fit to grant us and our persecuted brethren in Europe peace and salvation from Hitler, *y'mach shemo*, may his name be blotted out, and from his wicked Nazi forces. May the troubles of our poor fellow Jews across the sea come speedily to an end. So let me wish you all, to my community and to all the brave Jewish fighters who are here with us tonight, *chag Pesach same'ach*, a happy Passover. Amen."

There was hardly a dry eye among the people sitting around those tables that night as everyone said "Amen" in reply to the rabbi's final wish and blessing. From under the table I felt Tamar reach out for my hand and give it a loving squeeze. I turned and gave her a quick kiss on the cheek.

The youngest soldier – also called Benny – then stood up and read the *Mah Nishtanah*, and after that, the seder proceeded as it has always done over the centuries wherever Jews have settled, a combination of prayers and the retelling of the ancient story of the Exodus from Egypt.

Sometime later as we were eating the traditional meal, I suddenly felt a light tap on the shoulder. I looked around. It was Tamar.

"Where were you, Benny? You looked miles away."

"I was thinking," I said, coming back to the here and now. "I was thinking about my family's seder, back home in Tel Aviv, and I was wondering if they were thinking about me."

"After all that you've told me about them," she smiled. "I'm sure they are."

"Yes, and I was also thinking about last year's seder at Qena and where we'll be next year. Will we still be here in North Africa or will we be back at home?"

"That's funny," she said, squeezing my hand again. "I was also thinking where we'll be having our seder next year. Let's hope the war will be over by then."

"You know, it's strange," I said, giving voice to what I'd been thinking as I had looked around the table. "Here we are in Tripoli, all sorts of Jews from all over the world. Me from Tel Aviv, you from Alexandria, Danny and Yossi from German and Bulgarian families – and yet when it comes to certain prayers and celebrations, it's as if these differences in language and background don't exist; we all know what to do, and there's a unity among us."

"You're right," she agreed. "Even though the food and the tunes and our local traditions may be different, when it comes to prayers like the *Mah Nishtanah* and the blessings for wine and for food, they are all the same."

By the time we finished "Chad Gadya" and "Echad Mi Yode'ah?" it was very late, but looking at the clear, starry sky, Tamar and I felt it was just the right time to go for a walk before retiring to our separate base camps.

The next day some of the local youngsters took us for a tour around the old city of Tripoli – the part where most of the Jewish community lived. The streets were narrow and winding, and it made me think of what I had heard about the old medieval ghettos of Italy. When I asked Avraham, my fifteen-year-old guide, where the houses were, he explained that they surrounded the courtyards that lined the shady streets. However, despite the peeling and cracked walls and the torn posters, the people did not seem poor or unhappy at all. In fact, the opposite was true. The men in the Jewish quarter were all wearing their best hats and suits, while the women were wearing their prettiest dresses. I told Tamar that in my khaki uniform I was feeling positively drab in comparison.

"Don't say that," she said fiercely. "You should be very proud of wearing it, especially with your 'Palestine' shoulder flash. Just look how the people are looking at you."

"No," I replied. "It's you they're looking at – with your pretty face and your ATS uniform. The way you wear your hat, it looks very chic."

"Oh, thank you, kind sir," she said, bobbing a curtsey. "I'll remember that." And she kissed me on the cheek.

We wandered through the twisted alleys for the next two hours, looking at the old buildings and stopping every so often to speak to the little children who, together with the older members of the community, seemed to be everywhere. Everyone wanted to be outside in the warm sunshine, and a holiday atmosphere filled the air.

Just as we were leaving the Jewish quarter, we saw a group of soldiers in completely different uniforms speaking English.

"They're American," I told Tamar. "I wonder what they're doing here. Let's go over and ask them."

"We came over on Operation Torch, you know, our invasion of North Africa, to get the Nazis out of Morocco and Algeria," a soldier in a light tan uniform explained.

"Yes, and out of Tunisia, as well," his friend added. "We arrived a few months ago and here we are," he summed up.

But every holiday has to come to an end. The next ten days were spent in the army garages and workshops where we did much-needed maintenance on our overworked lorries. Tires were changed, radiators drained, cleaned and refilled, worn and torn fan belts were replaced and broken lamp bulbs and other faulty electrical parts were checked and replaced. It felt good to be working on the lorries – and this time we were not under pressure that an air raid might suddenly wreak death and havoc. While I was cleaning a particularly dirty carburetor, Jonathan Wasserman came running into the workshop.

"Benny, Danny, you know we're supposed to be sailing to Malta in a few days?" he began.

"Yes."

"Well, I've just heard that the ship taking the 462nd Company has been torpedoed and – "

"What! When?"

"I don't know many details. I've just heard the news. It seems that the men in our other company, the 462, had set off before us for Malta when their ship was hit by an aerial torpedo."

"Where?"

"Off the coast near Benghazi."

"When?"

"A few hours ago."

"What happened to the men?"

"Most of them, if not all of them, drowned. Over a hundred of them."

Soon afterwards we learned that what Jonathan had told us was true, and it was a very gloomy unit that set sail on the *City of Florence* for Malta a few days later in May 1943. I had said goodbye to Tamar the night before, and knowing what we had heard about the men of the 462, it was a very subdued farewell. This was also due to the fact that we did not know when and where we would meet again. Her last words to me were, "Look after yourself, Benny, and write to me as soon as you get there. I won't sleep till I get that letter."

I promised I would, and as we boarded the painted gray ship, there were no jokes about being seasick or "How do you make a Maltese Cross?" We were all wrapped up in our thoughts – mourning the tragedy of a few days earlier. We had all had friends in the 462 and had shared a friendly rivalry with them. We had played football against them; we had taken part in shooting competitions and had beaten them and been beaten by them in various athletic events. Now it was all over. They were all lying dead on the bottom of the sea, off the North African coast, never to run or shoot again. However, despite any dark predictions, we pulled into Valetta harbor, Malta, after a peaceful crossing.

At various times in the past, this strategic harbor had been filled with the sounds of Phoenician traders and Roman, Norman and Saracen soldiers, as well as those of the Knights of Saint John over four hundred years ago. Now the ancient brown defense walls echoed the sound of Hebrew as our lorries and tons of military supplies were winched overboard or carried from the hold to be transported to the quayside stores.

Soon after we had unloaded all our vehicles and equipment we were told to line up for a parade. There we were told that we, the 178th GT Company, were the first unit of General Montgomery's Eighth Army to be sent to Malta and that we would have to smarten ourselves up. "Any sloppy uniforms, general appearance or behavior unbecoming His Majesty's Army will not be tolerated," the major said. "And the same goes for your vehicles and your driving. Enough of you have died or been wounded. We don't want any more."

We were also told that our barracks would be in the Luqa Poorhouse, a long building next to the old leper hospital. We noticed quite a few shell holes that had not been filled in, and the walls of our new quarters showed signs of recent bomb damage.

Danny, of course, was one of the first to find out what had happened here. "I heard that the Germans bombed this area pretty heavily because it's near the airport."

"Well, they're not here now," I said. "And I hope after what happened to them in North Africa, they won't be coming back here soon."

"That's why we're here now," Danny said. "Malta is a stop for us on the way to Italy. I've heard that we and the Americans are going to attack the Germans from the south. As someone in the canteen put it, 'from the soft underbelly.'"

"And who is going to attack them from the north?"

"The Brits and the Americans, I guess."

"And the Russians will move in from the east," I added.

"Probably. That makes sense. They can't be all that fond of Hitler, especially after what he did to them at Stalingrad and Leningrad. He killed millions of them there."

"To say nothing about what he did to the Jews in Russia and Eastern Europe."

A few days later we heard that the German and Italian armies in North Africa had surrendered to the British general, Alexander. This meant that the whole area we had driven through was now in the hands of the Allies, and that a quarter of a million enemy soldiers had been taken prisoner. It really seemed that the course of the war was changing, and that we were no longer hearing any news of German successes on the battlefield.

We remained in Malta for seven months, until December 1943. Most of the time was spent on routine army duties and waiting for more exciting events to happen. To relieve the boredom we played football and took part in sporting events with other units that arrived, but in general, we spent much of our time hanging around feeling that we were missing out, and the war was passing us by.

Of course, as soon as I arrived I wrote to Tamar to say we had crossed safely, and, without too many details, she replied, describing what they were doing in Tripoli.

Later I wrote her a letter in a similar style, telling her how we were passing the time like we had back in Qena, "but without delivering sacks of cement and gallons of water to workers in the desert." I also added some words about the international situation.

> I'm sure you've heard that all sorts of partisan groups are rising up against the Nazis, especially in France, Russia and Eastern Europe, and that the Allied air forces are now bombing German cities and industrial areas. This is a good thing and I hope it shortens the war.
>
> We've also heard news about the Americans' success in their war in the Pacific, and how they beat the Japanese in New Guinea. The papers and the radio

have also reported American victories at Bougainville and the Solomon Islands, and these are important as they affect the fuel supply situation for the Japanese.

I added that I hoped that these successes would bring us together soon and that somehow we would meet up again in the not-too-distant future.

But however happy we were to hear of the various Allied victories and other positive pieces of news, it was terrible to hear reports of what the Nazis were doing to our fellow Jews in Europe. We had heard about the fall of the Warsaw Ghetto and how tens of thousands of Jews from all different places in Europe had been marched off or forced onto trains and taken to death camps. Apart from the tragedy of the news itself, we also had the feeling that we were wasting our time sitting on the sidelines, not being able to do anything. It was all terribly frustrating and we could not lift a finger to help. Here we were, all able-bodied Jewish soldiers, and all we could do was passively read reports or listen to the radio about all these horrors.

"You wait," warned Heinrich Grunwald, a mechanic in our unit who had fled Germany at the last minute. "When I get back there, I'm going to kill every German I can see with my bare hands. Especially if anything has happened to my family."

No one told him it was wrong to think like that. Many of us agreed with him. And when the time came, many of the men with me did indeed take the law into their own hands. As more and more news of the Holocaust began to filter into our base, the feeling expressed in the biblical passage "an eye for an eye" grew stronger and stronger. But for now, stuck on the island of Malta in the middle of the Mediterranean

Sea, there was nothing we could do but wait – wait for the day when we would be sent to Europe.

At last this longed-for day arrived. It was Christmas Day 1943 when we set sail from Malta. We were bound for Taranto, our first stop in the south of Italy.

CHAPTER TEN
Italy

The first inkling that we were approaching the port of Taranto occurred when, as though drawn by an enormous magnet, all the men began to gather on the forward deck. Quietly, and without anyone giving a specific signal, a muted song grew in volume as we all found ourselves singing songs in Hebrew: songs of war, songs of Eretz Israel and the most important song of all, the song of hope – "Hatikvah." At last we had come to fight the Germans in Europe and rescue our fellow Jews from the Nazi concentration and extermination camps. With luck we would bring them back to a life of freedom and happiness and all that they had been praying for.

As the sounds of our national anthem died away from our blacked-out ship and we glided into the port, we began to make out its buildings and installations, which loomed up from the still waters.

Taranto is one of the most ancient ports in southern Italy. Founded by the Spartans 2,500 years earlier, it had brought great wealth to the surrounding town. Later the economy collapsed and the town was destroyed by the Saracens before rising again. A few months before we arrived, the German army had retreated and now, completely unopposed, we were to land there.

"Look at those beautiful old buildings," I said to Danny as we sailed into the harbor. "Just look at that castle. Doesn't it look a bit like the one at Tel Afek? I'm telling you, they certainly knew how to build in those days."

Danny nodded in agreement. "And look at those holes in the walls. That's what the Brits did three years ago when they bombed the Italian navy."

"And you know who was here before them?" I asked.

"The Romans? The Phoenicians?"

"No, my father."

"What was he doing here? Was he on holiday?"

"No," I answered him proudly. "He came here over twenty years ago, during the Great War. You know, when he was in the Jewish Legion and on his way to Palestine from England."

"With General Allenby?"

"That's right. Taranto was the port from where they sailed to Egypt and then carried on to Palestine."

"So they came here from the north and we've arrived from the south. Their enemy was back home in Palestine and ours is here, in Europe."

The following day as we were beginning to find our way around the town, we received orders to pack up all our gear, check out the lorries and start driving to Bari, a small town forty miles to the north on the Adriatic coast.

"Danny, what's in Bari?"

"Nothing special," he replied. "Except that it has an old cathedral named after San Sabino, and the town's been in our hands since September."

"How do you know all this stuff?" I asked. "Next you'll be telling me that the priest there is called Tomas Verdi or something like that and that he likes eating spaghetti bolognaise with red peppers."

Danny shrugged. "I don't know. I guess I just pick up stuff like this the same way you know more about engines and carburetors than I do."

As with Taranto, we did not stay in Bari for long. But while we were there we learned how important it was to the Jewish communities we encountered that there were Jewish soldiers fighting in a regular army. It quickly became clear that we meant a great deal to both the local Jewish population and the Jewish refugees who had joined them.

Two days after our arrival I was walking in the center of town with Yossi. I had just posted a letter to Tamar and was wondering when I would see her again. Suddenly my thoughts were interrupted when two old women walked up to us and one of them asked me in Yiddish, "*Du bist a Yid?* Are you Jewish?"

"*Ja, Ken*, Yes," I replied in Yiddish, Hebrew and English.

"Are you sure?" she continued in English.

"Sure, I'm with the Palestine soldiers in the British army," and I pointed to my shoulder flash.

Her eyes filled with tears and she pulled me over and gave me a big, soft kiss on my cheek.

"*Broruch Hashem*, Thank God," she said. "Sarah," she said to her friend. "Now we're safe. These boys, they're *unsere*, they're ours."

Sarah's eyes were wet with joy and she threw her arms first around me and then around Yossi. Then she stepped back and looked at us and then touched our Palestine badges, testing them, as it were, to see if they were real.

"*Broruch Hashem*, Thank God," she said like her friend. "Now you must save those of us who are left." She took out a large handkerchief and dried her eyes. "Oy, we're so happy you've come," she continued in heavily accented English. "We had heard about you Jewish soldiers but we didn't know if you were real or it was just another wartime story. But now we can see you're real," and she threw her arms around us again.

They then told us there were a few hundred Jewish refugees in the area and they were in desperate need of food, money and warm clothes.

"But I don't know what we can do to help," I said. "We're soldiers in the British army, just ordinary soldiers. We're not officers or anything like that. We're just drivers, that's all. I'm sorry."

"Benny, don't say that," Yossi said. "We're Jewish and so are these two ladies. We must help them. Remember, we didn't join the army only to fight the Nazis; we joined to help our own people as well."

I felt ashamed of myself. Yossi was right. I had not been thinking clearly. Suddenly I had an idea. "Come with us," and I led them to where our lorries were parked on the far side of the square.

"Here," I said, leaning over the tailboard and grabbing some bags of vegetables and a couple of khaki sweaters. "Take these, and I'm sorry I said something about not being able to help you. I wasn't thinking."

For a reply, Sarah pulled me over to her, hugged me again and said, "Bless you, my son. No, bless all of you," and after Rachel had also hugged and thanked us, they walked off telling us they would tell the other Jews we had come to save them.

"What have we done?" I asked Yossi, not knowing that this simple action and similar ones carried out by our fellow soldiers would grow into a huge international organization that would bring thousands of Jews to Eretz Israel.

We did not stay long in Bari before we were ordered to drive seventy miles west to Foggia. Knowing nothing about the place, I asked Danny what he knew about this city.

"I didn't find out much about it. All I know is that it has an impressive cathedral, and that the emperor Frederick II liked to live there. And after the Americans had smashed it up completely, the Allies then took the place over from the Germans. The Americans are now using Foggia as one of their forward bases."

It did not take long to see what Danny had meant about the scale of the American bombing. Many buildings were left half-standing, piles of rubble lay everywhere and the streets glinted with shards of broken glass. However, despite these scenes of destruction, the army had commandeered some buildings that had survived the bombing, and they were to be our base for the next few months.

Life in Foggia was never quiet, and we were always aware of the war that surrounded us. Apart from the sounds of fully laden lorries arriving and leaving the base at all times of the day and night, we could hear the nonstop sounds of the large American air force bombers. They were always setting out or returning from their bombing raids on the Nazi and industrial centers in Vienna and central Europe.

A more pleasing sound was that of the Jewish refugees, later to be known as DPs – displaced persons – who began to make their way to our base. A week after our arrival, lorries began returning carrying sad-looking and often shabbily dressed individuals and groups of people.

"Who are they?" I asked.

"You remember Sarah and Rachel in Bari?" Yossi said. "Well, the word has gotten around that we Jewish soldiers are helping these people and that's what they're here for. To get help."

"But there's dozens of them," I said as three more lorries drove into the courtyard.

"You're wrong, Benny. There are hundreds, if not thousands, of these people. Didn't you get a form about them this morning?"

"No, what form?"

"The captain gave out forms to all the drivers and told us to record where we see or hear about any Jewish refugees when we're driving around."

"I missed out on that. I had to leave very early this morning to take a supply of shells and ammo to Cerignola. The journey took longer than I thought. The road was full of potholes from the bombing. But tell me what's going to happen to all these people? They won't be able to stay here. I can't see Montgomery allowing our base to become a refugee camp."

Yossi nodded in agreement. "You're right. Once we've fed them and given them clothes and medical help, we're to take them to Bari."

"Why there?"

"That's where the Jewish Agency is collecting them. They'll be looking after them there."

"But where are all the supplies coming from – the food and clothes and medicine? I mean, there's a war going on and we haven't beaten the Germans yet. They're still controlling the northern half of Italy, not to mention much of the rest of Europe."

"I know that, Benny, but we're getting some help from King George."

"King George?"

"Well, maybe not from him personally, but we're quietly getting extra supplies and rations from the army."

I nodded. Now I understood why I had been asked to store a few boxes of food and clothes in the back of my lorry. When I had asked Sergeant Berkovitch at the time he had just put his finger to his lips and said, "Shhhh!" I had thought at the time that he had been involved in some shady black market deal but now I knew better.

"And now," Yossi said, "we need some volunteer drivers to take these people to Bari. Are you willing?"

"Yossi, my friend, that's one of the dumbest questions you've ever asked me. Of course I'm willing. When do we start?"

"We'll be leaving tonight. Go and tell Sergeant Berkovitch you'll be ready when he gives the go-ahead."

I found the pot-bellied sergeant in the supply depot and told him to count me in as a driver. He shook my hand warmly and told me to be ready to move out after Shabbat.

I always enjoyed these evenings. Apart from those unfortunate souls who were on guard duty, everyone was there, clean and in their most respectable-looking – well, in their least grubby – uniforms. Even though I did not consider myself an observant Jew, I enjoyed the relaxed and friendly atmosphere of military camaraderie. The chaplain would say a few prayers and we would all sing the well-known traditional Shabbat *zemirot*. Sometimes the lesser-known tunes sounded a little strange to me, but as time passed I got to learn those Sephardic ones as well as my own Ashkenazi melodies. But however they sounded, there was always a warm feeling as hundreds of us soldiers, together with the refugees, sang them. For many of the refugees it was the first time they had sung these Shabbat songs in a long time. They would sing and smile and their eyes would shine wetly as they remembered their past and felt safe in the knowledge that for them, at least, the horrors of the Holocaust were over.

The next night, when it was good and dark, we escorted our passengers to our lorries, helped them climb aboard and then added some boxes of supplies and extra rations. We also threw in some extra blankets to protect them from the cold night's drive to Bari. Yossi asked me why we were stacking the boxes near the tailgates. "Shouldn't we put them further inside?"

"No, we want to put them there in case we get stopped by the military police. We can easily show them these boxes and hopefully they won't see our passengers at the far end at the back in the dark. And that's another reason for the blankets. To cover them up in case we get stopped."

Now that I was involved in all this I was really enjoying the "cloak-and-dagger" aspect of it. Even if we weren't directly involved in fighting the Germans at this point, we were still doing some very valuable work. Besides, this breaking of the rules appealed to the mischievous side of my nature.

We set off just before midnight. It was a dark and cloudy night and heavy rain clouds threatened to soak our little convoy of three lorries.

"I hope it does rain," I said to Danny as I climbed into the first lorry. "It'll probably mean there won't be many cops around asking questions and looking for smugglers."

"Smugglers?"

"Yes, there's a lot of smuggling going on right now. You know, people stealing rations and supplies from the British and American bases and selling the stuff on the black market. But let's get moving and let's hope that all of His Majesty's redcaps are safe at home, tucked up in their beds."

They weren't. As we were halfway along our route, just near the entrance to Canos di Púglia, a large flashlight was suddenly turned on signaling us to stop. Praying that the police would not be too thorough, we drew to a halt in front of their makeshift barrier.

There were two policemen: a redcap and an Italian civilian. The tall military policeman walked over to Danny's lorry and asked to see his license and transport documents. I wondered what would happen next. Would Danny accidentally give the game away? Would my bookish friend be able to bluff his way out of this situation? Then I saw Danny lean out of his cab and hand a piece of paper over to the redcap. He looked at it and returned it almost immediately.

"You!" he shouted to me. "Turn off your engine!" As I did so, I muttered to Baruch sitting next to me that our next stop would probably be the military prison in Bari.

"Don't worry, Benny. Danny isn't as green as you think. He knows what he's doing."

"I hope so. Look, he's going around to the back of his lorry with the cop." It was true. While one of the policemen was standing in front of Danny's lorry, the other had gone around to the back. He climbed halfway up the tailgate and lifted up the heavy khaki flap. All he could see were boxes bearing official British army insignia. I could see he was about to investigate further when there was a flash of lightening, a clap of thunder and suddenly it started to rain heavily. Dropping the soggy flap in a hurry, the redcap jumped down and ran over to his own vehicle in which the other policeman was already sitting. Before anything else could happen, we switched on our engines and drove off.

"Bless the Lord for the rain," Baruch said. "He couldn't have made it come at a better time."

"How right you are!" I said, remembering a line from *The Merchant of Venice*. "'The gentle rain from heaven.'"

"Yes, I also learned that line, Benny, except it's not so gentle now. By the way, I hope it's not leaking into the back or our passengers are going to have a pretty miserable time from now on. Anyway, just drive carefully and look out for potholes."

We had no more problems with the military police that night, and after delivering our passengers and supplies we headed back to Foggia. As soon as we had parked our lorries I rushed over to Danny.

"Danny, you have to tell me what was written on that paper you handed over to the redcap at the barrier. I didn't know you had a pass. I thought I had the only one. Was it a real one?"

"Of course. Sergeant Berkovitch has a whole stock of them. He always fills them out and stamps them for these special deliveries. Don't worry, Benny, it's all kosher. Even Major Aron is in the know." He grinned. "Now let's get some sleep. We've been up all night and if you haven't forgotten, we're on duty this afternoon."

That journey was the first of many. Later, the small-scale organization of this journey would grow into a larger one called *Reshet*, the Net. It would spread north from Italy to Germany and Austria, and its aim would be to save as many Jews as possible.

But as the sun rose on me lying on my bunk that morning, I was not thinking of any large international organization; I was just thinking that I had taken a part, however small, in helping my fellow Jews get further and further away from the Nazis and all they stood for.

The only thing missing from that night was that I did not have Tamar nearby to tell her what had happened. The only way I could do this was to write her a letter at her last known address and hope that she would get it in the near future.

The next day when I came off duty I wrote her a detailed letter about our trip to Bari. Then just as I was about to sign off with "*Shalom* and love, Benny," I ripped it up. The journey to Bari meant that we had broken some serious army regulations and I could not risk the army censor reading about that. However, still hoping that we would meet again soon, I wrote a much shorter letter saying that we had helped some poor Italian Jews who had escaped from the Nazis. On reading this self-censored version, I could not help thinking how weak it sounded in comparison with the strong emotions (and tears!) that had flowed freely two nights earlier.

CHAPTER ELEVEN
Foggia

We stayed in Foggia for the whole of the winter of 1944. We soon heard from the local population that this winter was exceptionally cold, even for southern Italy. We also learned to keep warm with extra clothing and to use charcoal burners in our quarters, offices and hospitals.

One day as I was sitting on my bed reading a magazine and grumbling about the cold, Danny came in.

"Stop sitting there and shivering, my friend. We've been given a job that'll warm your heart."

"Oh, yeah? A drive to the equator?"

"No, we've been told to drive to the American heavy bomber base near Foggia and pick up some bales of warm clothing."

"Who for? For us?"

"No, you've got your greatcoat. This stuff is for the DPs we've been helping – the ones we've been sending on to Bari. It seems that they don't have enough winter clothes."

"And where do these clothes come from?"

"Ah, Benny, that's a story. I heard that Major Aron was visiting the American base and one of the men there, someone from Philadelphia, heard that we were short of clothes to give our Jewish DPs. So he wrote to his wife who is an active member in Hadassah and they began collecting the stuff to send here."

"And now it's our job to go and pick it up?"

"Right. So let's get moving."

I stopped shivering and soon Danny and I were on our way to get the clothes. While we were there we heard another story of how the Americans were helping the liberated Jewish communities in Italy and elsewhere. As we were standing around waiting, our hands wrapped around hot mugs of coffee, one of the men, a sergeant on the base, gave us the latest information.

"You guys think that this stuff is all you're going to get, huh? Well, you're wrong. Your Major Aron was here recently and he told us what you guys have been doing to help your Jewish refugees. He must have sold himself well, because when he finished, all the men here, the pilots and the ground crews, started dipping into their pockets. Soon your major had a whole sack full of dollars to help you buy more supplies for these poor folk. So all I can say is, well done. That's the spirit."

That night, after returning to the base, we heard that the Americans had started to bomb the German defense lines stretching across Italy, from east to west.

"They call it the Gustav Line," the ever-knowledgeable Danny told me. "The Germans have built quite a few of these lines and if we're going to beat them, we'll have to break through all of them. It's not going to be easy and the Germans are going to try to hang in there to the bitter end."

"Well, I hope we'll get a chance to join the fighting. I don't object to picking up clothes for the DPs, but the reason I joined the army was to fight the Germans."

"I know that, Benny, but listen a minute. While we're forcing the Germans to retreat to the north, the Russians have broken the German blockade at Leningrad and are now forcing them to retreat to the south and the west. The latest report I heard on the radio said that they've been pushed back fifty miles and that the trains are running again in Moscow."

"Good," I said. "So they're caught in the middle – the meat in the sandwich, so to speak. Very good. But my question is this: how long will it take to finish them off, and – "

"And when will you see Tamar again?" laughed Yossi, who had just joined us.

But the next day one of our drivers told us a story that was certainly no laughing matter.

"You know I was sent to Manfredonia yesterday to pick up some supplies…"

"That small port east of here?"

"That's right. Well, while I was there I saw a small boat sail into the harbor and it looked terrible."

"Why? What had happened to it?"

"All the decks were covered with blood and I heard that it was full of refugees who had escaped from Yugoslavia. It seems that while they were crossing the Adriatic, a German plane spotted them and machine-gunned the boat. There were dead and wounded everywhere. I'm telling you, it was terrible. All that blood everywhere and the wounded crying out for help."

"Where were the refugees from? Were any of them Jewish?" I asked, half guessing the answer.

The driver nodded. "Yes, quite a few of them were. And later I heard that in addition to that attack, some of the non-Jews on board started beating up the Jews, saying it was their fault. They claimed that the Germans had attacked them just because there were Jews on board."

"And what's happening now?" I asked.

"That's what I was going to tell you. You, Danny and Yossi, and also Captain Gobernick and a few others, have to drive over to Manfredonia – it's about twenty-five miles away – and take a field kitchen and some stretchers as well as food and medical supplies with you. You'll receive further instructions when you get there."

Once we arrived it did not take us long to find the people we were looking for. They had been herded into a large, empty department store and now the military police were standing guard over the building.

"How are we going to get our people out of there?" I asked.

"You leave it to me," Sergeant Major Bankover replied. "I'll get them out."

We never discovered what he said to the redcaps but soon we were inside. "Now to find the Jewish DPs," I said. "Look, that man over there looks Jewish. I'll go and ask him."

We were lucky. The bent old man in the stained black coat was Jewish and he told us where the other Jews were as well. As we were in British army uniforms, no one asked any questions when we separated the Jews from the others and took them outside to where our lorries were parked. Most of the people were completely exhausted and hungry and obviously suffering from their short but traumatic voyage of escape.

"Tell me, son," an old man asked me in Yiddish, a question I was to hear many times over the next few months, "are you really Jewish?"

"Yes, of course," I smiled, and showed him my Palestine shoulder flash. As I helped him climb up into the back of my lorry, he asked, "So how come you're wearing a British army uniform?"

"We," I began, pointing to Danny, Yossi and the others, "are in a Jewish unit in the British army. Most of us are from Palestine. Me, I'm from Tel Aviv and so is he," I added, pointing to Danny, who was also helping some of the people climb into the back of his lorry.

"*Boruch Hashem*, bless the Lord," he said in Yiddish. "Now I know I'm safe at last. What a world! I escape from Yugoslavia to Italy and find a Jewish soldier from Tel Aviv in the British army. Oy! What a world," he repeated, shaking his head, not really believing what he had just said.

As we were driving back to Bari, I asked Baruch, sitting next to me, what he thought Sergeant Major Bankover had said to the redcaps to allow us to take out "our" Jewish DPs.

Baruch grinned. "Benny, first of all, look at the size of Bankover. Would you argue with him, especially when he flashes his rank at you?"

Now it was my turn to smile.

"And then – and don't say one word about this – I think I saw a certain amount of silver cross a certain redcap's itching palms." I smiled again and then concentrated on the drive back to base.

When we got there, we took our human cargo to an old house we had requisitioned. There, with the help of British army and Jewish Agency supplies, the people began the slow and painful process of trying to rebuild their shattered lives.

It was a good feeling when, that night at Foggia, Captain Gobernick told us we had done a good job. "Always remember this, lads. We're here for two reasons: to fight the Nazis and to help our own people. Well done."

"But when are we going to fight?" I couldn't help calling out.

"Soon, I hope," he replied. "But don't feel that you're wasting your time here in Foggia. You're not."

But I have to admit, it *was* hard for me to feel that I wasn't wasting my time sitting on the sidelines. True, we were kept busy ferrying men and supplies to the troops, and our unit had a good name for speed and reliability, but I still felt as though we were on the edge of things. When I heard dramatic news items, like that the Americans had been carrying out some massive air raids over Berlin or that the Russians were pushing the Nazis back toward Germany, I could not feel a part of these major actions. All I was doing was driving my lorry over the Italian hills.

However, the time did come when we received orders to leave Foggia. Our last action there was to organize a seder service, my fourth as a soldier in the British army. This time we were luckier than in the past, as Rabbi Honig, the American army chaplain, managed to obtain some extra supplies. We had planned to hold as large a seder as possible and to include all of the DPs we were looking after. We would be using a big hall in Foggia and were expecting over a thousand people to attend.

"A *thousand*?" exclaimed Yossi. "Even if we include all the DPs, it still only comes to about seven hundred."

"I know, but some of the Americans are going to join us, and so are some more DPs who are at other camps outside Foggia."

And so, with gallons of British army paint, officially used for making road signs, we decorated the huge hall in preparation for the festive meal. Yossi, more artistic than me, painted large pictures of kibbutzim with tractors plowing fields, and Baruch created dramatic pictures of Moses leading the Children of Israel out of Egypt. To my eyes, the picture of Moses looked somewhat similar to Major Aron, and I don't think Baruch's picture was historically correct, as he showed Moses walking past a sign bearing the badge of the 178th GT Company.

"Baruch?" I asked. "Apart from the army badge there, are you sure there were pyramids at the time of the Exodus?"

He shrugged. "I don't know, but at least you can see that the Children of Israel are leaving Egypt and not – "

"Foggia," I quipped.

Danny, as usual, came up with the answer. "Sure, there were pyramids then. I know the Egyptians built some of them long before the Exodus."

Seder night arrived, as did many visitors to our base. An American rabbi conducted the service, and what with reading the Haggadah, eating the meal and singing the traditional songs, it was well past midnight before it was all over. I felt so good that I had taken a part in organizing it that I had to go back to my room and write to Tamar.

> Dear Tamar,
>
> I don't know if, when and where you'll receive this letter, but I must tell you about the seder I have just attended at our base here.
>
> First of all, it was held in a big hall where the Italian Fascists used to hold their party rallies. Danny, Yossi and I and a few others helped decorate it with large pictures, army badges and *Magen David*s. Some of the DPs brought in bunches of flowers which we put on the tables and on the walls. We also had special Haggadot mimeographed for us.
>
> An American rabbi led the seder and several soldiers and DPs read out the different parts of the Haggadah. The most moving part took place when a ten-year-old DP kid, a pretty girl called Karen, who had spent most of the past three years hidden away in a cellar, sang the Mah Nishtanah in a beautiful voice. There was hardly a dry eye in the hall as the rabbi told

us how some of the American soldiers had found her and brought her to our base.

Just as we were on the point of reading about the Four Sons, we were disturbed by a sudden noise in the doorway, and a group of American pilots, still wearing their flying jackets, entered. They had just returned from flying a bombing mission somewhere over Germany, and so even though we all had to squeeze up on our benches to make room for them, no one minded.

I must say that our cooks really outdid themselves and provided us with a great meal, even though they had to manage everything in a somewhat limited army kitchen.

After the meal and Grace after Meals, we started on the songs. This is the part I like best and I couldn't help remembering how my father used to have (friendly) arguments every year with my Uncle Max over which was the "correct" tune for "Echad Mi Yode'ah?" and "Chad Gadya." What was also touching was that a group of the DP kids organized a little choir and sang "Adir Hu."

But in addition to the soldiers, we had quite a few DPs with us. Some of them were in couples, some with their families and a few were on their own. For them, the seder was probably a sad occasion as they must have been thinking of their own families. Some of them knew that their relatives had been murdered by the Nazis, and some didn't know if their families were still alive or not. And if they are alive, where are they now?

However, the most exciting part of the evening was when a couple that had spent the war hiding in the forests in Bavaria suddenly realized that the eighteen-year-old sitting almost opposite them was their own son! The last time they had seen him was on Kristallnacht in November 1938 when the Nazis had gone on a rampage and smashed up synagogues and arrested thousands of Jews.

The son was in the middle of reading *Dayenu*, when suddenly his mother stood up and shouted in German, "Heinz, is that you?" and she and her husband rushed over to him. Naturally everything broke up for a while as they all hugged and kissed each other and then Heinz moved over to sit between his parents. The mother spent the rest of the service with her arm around him saying, "Broruch Hashem, Thank God" the whole time and hugging and stroking her son. Again, there weren't many dry eyes in the hall for quite a while after this.

But this wasn't the only family reunion I can tell you about. A few days before Pesach, a couple of DPs from Berlin who were waiting for someone near the parade ground suddenly recognized my friend David Goldsmith. "David, is that you?" the older man asked.

"Ja."

"Little David Goldsmith from Berlin? Hershel and Trudy's kid?"

"Ja."

And suddenly they were all kissing and hugging each other, which isn't really surprising since "little" David (now over six feet tall) had really been a little boy when he left Germany soon after Hitler came to power. He had tried to find out what had happened to his aunt and uncle who had looked after him after his parents had been killed in a car crash. But every time he sent a letter to them, it came back stamped with the words, "Address Unknown." Naturally he came to the sad conclusion that his aunt and uncle had been killed or imprisoned somewhere, so you can imagine the joy when they all met up again.

In addition to the DPs, there were also some Jewish Yugoslav partisans with us. They looked rather unusual as they were wearing British army uniforms in addition to their Red Army style hats and boots. There were also a few men from the Free French Forces, and Danny was very pleased to practice his French on them.

So all in all, tonight's seder was not only traditional, it was also a kind of Jewish League of Nations. I guess it's lucky we had a common language – Hebrew – or at least for the service itself.

I hope I haven't bored you with this long letter, but I had to tell you somehow. I have to finish now but I hope we can meet again very soon, although I don't know where or when. I also hope you manage to reply to me from wherever you are. I miss you very much and I know that Danny misses Esty.

After some thought, I decided to sign "Love, Benny," and put the letter into a special army envelope. After addressing it to the last known address I had – a British Forces post box number – I sealed the envelope and went to sleep.

As I drifted off to sleep I found myself wondering where I would be for Pesach 1945. Would I still be a soldier in Europe or would I be back home in Tel Aviv?

CHAPTER TWELVE
Finally – The Jewish Brigade!

A few days after the seder service we were ordered to leave Foggia and start driving to Vasto, a small town on the Adriatic coast, some sixty miles to the north. For once Danny knew nothing about the place, and all that we could discover was that it was an ancient town with a magnificent cathedral.

I was not sure whether I was pleased or not to leave Foggia. On the one hand I had gotten used to our life at the base and our regular journeys to Bari, Manfredonia and other small towns in the east, but on the other hand, moving north meant that – with a bit of luck – we would become more involved in the action of pushing the Nazis back to their homeland.

Although in theory the journey north should not have taken us very long, the fact was that it took three days, as we had to stop every few miles. The Germans, as part of their retreat, had blown up all the bridges as well as large sections of the main road in an effort to slow down the advance of Montgomery's Eighth Army, of which we were now part.

I was driving one of the leading lorries when we had to stop by the blown-up remains of the bridge over the River Triolo. The river was in full flood, its white frothy waters rushing down from the Apennine Mountains.

"How are we going to cross that?" Baruch asked me. "If we try, we'll all get washed away."

"You're right, but the army has a new trick up its sleeve. Bailey bridges."

"What? Those bridges made of steel girders we saw near the San Severo?"

"That's right. I guess the engineering boys will lay one of these Bailey things down here and then we'll cross over it."

I was right, but it was sooner said than done. We reversed our lorries back to the sides of the road to let the engineers move in with their long lengths of steel girders and lattices. It took them several hours to make their bridge, and in the meantime, we spent an uncomfortable night trying to get some sleep in the cabs of our lorries. On the following day, as the sun was climbing up over the horizon of the Adriatic Sea, we were able to continue our journey northward. Fortunately, the next two rivers whose bridges had been blown up were not very deep, so we were able to ford them in our Bedfords; we did our best to make up for lost time.

Just as we were passing Campomarina, a huge blast shattered the air. We saw one of our Engineering Corps lorries blow up; thousands of hot jagged pieces of metal flew out in all directions and bright orange flames started burning up what was left of the lorry.

Certain that this was enemy shelling, we immediately took up defensive positions. Then a shout went up that the stricken lorry had driven over a land mine. It must have happened when the lorry drove off the road to try to pass the slower one in front of it. From then on we were ordered to drive only in the middle of the road. The driver and his co-driver were hauled out of the burning wreckage, moaning in agony, their skin black and peeling. Later we heard that the driver had been taken back to Foggia in an army ambulance but that the co-driver had died.

"What a way to die," I said to Yossi at our next stop. "Driving a lorry in pursuit of the Germans on a road in Italy.

CHAPTER TWELVE: FINALLY – THE JEWISH BRIGADE! 153

And Avi didn't have a chance to defend himself. Boom! And that's it. Now someone will have to let his parents know. I'm just glad it's not me."

In the eyes of the army's planning department we arrived late in Vasto but nothing could be done about that. We were one of the last units to arrive at our new base, and there we found that most of the best facilities had been taken over by the Royal Army Ordnance Corps and other units belonging to the Eighth Army.

It was while we were at Vasto that army gossip trickled down to us that Major Aron and several other officers in the 178th GT Company had been questioned by their superior officers about using British army food, blankets and other supplies to ease the lives of the DPs we had rescued.

"Does this mean we'll have to stop helping them?" Danny asked.

"I hope not," I said. "It probably means we'll have to be more careful about it, but let's see."

A few days later we heard the results of the high-level meeting that had discussed the "DP problem." Those who did not want to be involved would not be pressed to do so, but those who wanted to continue helping our fellow Jews – the majority of us – would be able to do so without anyone interfering with their activities.

And so for the next month our life continued at Vasto as it had in Foggia. We drove men and supplies to where they were needed and helped out any Jewish DPs we found or who found us.

Then one day, after I had returned from delivering boxes of ammo and tank shells to a forward unit near Montesilvano, and was sitting on a toolbox reading the *Stars and Stripes* newspaper, Yossi came up to me.

"Forget the reading, Benny. We're off to Rome tomorrow. We've been asked to take some supplies, especially warm clothes, to the Jewish community there. Now that the Germans have fled the city we can go and take them some much-needed clothes and food."

"Are we being ordered to go or is this a volunteer mission?"

"A volunteer mission, Benny. You've been looking so bored with our daily routine for the last couple of weeks that I thought a break might do you some good, so I signed you up."

Yossi was right. I had been getting bored with our daily routine even though I knew it was for a good cause. But I did not have to be asked twice when it came to driving to Rome – a trip of nearly three hundred miles. This meant crossing the Apennine and Sabine mountain ranges and would make a change from driving around the flat coastal plain. Besides, it might mean that I'd get a chance to see the sights.

Our convoy of six lorries left early the next morning, and by the time we reached the Eternal City my back and legs were sore from almost nonstop driving.

"Danny," I said that evening after we had unloaded our bales of clothing, "the driving today reminded me of the times we were chasing Rommel's forces along the North African coast. Just drive, drive, drive and don't stop."

"I know. I also thought that, but don't get yourself too settled in here. We've got forty-eight hours and then it's back to Vasto."

"That's right, and then we're heading further up the coast north to Ancona."

"How do you know?"

"I heard two of the officers talking about it as we left."

Danny looked rather puzzled as we were distributing the bales of clothing and he explained that he had expected a much larger number of refugees. After all, he explained, before the war Rome had had a fairly large number of Jews. Later, much later, we found out why: Mussolini's thugs had captured almost seven thousand Jews in the north of the country and sent them to Auschwitz. But, as I said, we did not know this at the time and, in fact, had a very enjoyable stay in Rome. In addition to seeing some of the more famous sights – and, in my case, sending two postcards to Tamar – we met some members of the Jewish community who had survived the Nazi occupation.

While we were checking the lorries for our return journey, we heard what was probably the best news of the war so far. The D-Day landings had taken place in Normandy, and the Allies were now pushing their way through northern France, aiming for Paris.

"Baruch, do you realize what this means?" I asked as our convoy started making its way east out of Rome. "The war may be over in a few months, and then it'll be home sweet home. But let's admit it, I hope we'll get the chance to pay back the Nazis before it's all over. I like the idea of Jewish soldiers paying them back for what they've done to us."

Baruch gave me a thumbs-up. "I'm with you there, my friend, but I think we'll be driving these lorries until the cease-fire sounds, whenever that will be."

We got back to Vasto without any problems, although once or twice, Allied aircraft – American, I think – swooped low over us to see if we were friend or foe. Fortunately we had tied a Union Jack onto the roof so nothing happened. The only excitement was when Danny's lorry got a puncture as we were approaching Fossacésia, a small town on the Adriatic coast.

"Just my luck," Danny commented, rolling up his sleeves as he and his co-driver started taking out their tools to change the wheel. "I've driven all over Egypt; I've driven right along the coast of North Africa; I've driven all over south and east Italy and now this happens, just a few miles outside Vasto."

That night we reported to Major Aron what we had seen and learned about the state of Rome's Jewish community and then went to sleep. Two days later we were back behind the wheel on the way to Ancona. It did not take long to drive the hundred miles north up the coast, a welcome sign that we were forcing the Germans to retreat even faster than they had been doing until now.

We stayed in Ancona for only a few months, during which time we cleaned all the rubble out of the local synagogue and prepared it for the High Holidays. Heavy rains started soon after this and it was during this rainy period that our company, the 178th GT, was ordered to drive west to the ancient city of Florence, or Firenze, as the Italians called it.

It was hard work driving our Bedfords over the soggy mountain passes of the northern Apennine range. More than one of our vehicles slid off the road into roadside ditches as their worn tires skidded on the slippery surfaces. The worst case happened soon after leaving a small village called Pratovécchio. While we were hauling a lorry out of a ditch, someone shouted that we should turn on the radios in our lorries, as the BBC was about to broadcast an important announcement.

I wondered if they'd say that Germany had surrendered, or if there would be an announcement about the Allied attack on Arnhem in the Netherlands. Then suddenly, as I was daydreaming, I saw my lorry gently slip off the road into a ditch. I had forgotten to put on the brakes and now it was resting quietly at a strange angle – two wheels in the ditch and two on the road! I made a quick inspection and saw that apart from a crumpled mudguard, nothing serious had happened. As soon as my Bedford was back on the road, we would be mobile again.

Luckily it had stopped raining, and just as the crew of a heavy-duty 6x6 American lorry was attaching their chains to my Bedford, we heard the deep baritone voice of the BBC announcer:

> His Majesty's government have decided that a Jewish Brigade should be formed to take part in active operations. The infantry brigade will be based on the Jewish battalions of the Palestine Regiment. The necessary concentration for training is now taking place before dispatch to a theater of war. Supporting and ancillary units to complete the Brigade, based on existing Palestine units, are being prepared and will join the infantry brigade as soon as practicable. The Jewish Agency are cooperating in its realization.

We all stood around speechless for a moment. The impossible had happened! Moshe Shertock and the Jewish Agency had succeeded in persuading Churchill to override the War Office and establish a Jewish brigade! Then, suddenly we all started jumping around, shouting and clapping each other on the back. We had been recognized at last! Our work over the past few years had paid off! We were no longer the Palestine Battalions and companies, units within the "Buffs," the

Royal East Kent Regiment. We were to be an independent brigade – a Jewish brigade! – a unit with our own organization and officers. Churchill had realized how much our fellow Jews had suffered, and now he was going to reward and recognize us for all of our hard work in the past.

"Danny, Yossi, Baruch, isn't this great! Now we're going to be a Jewish brigade fighting both for our own people and the Allies."

"And about time, too!"

"Right. Shertock's been nagging the British about this for ages and now it's happened."

"I wonder who our commander will be? Will he be Jewish? Will he be a Brit?"

"Don't know," Danny shrugged. "But I guess we'll know when we get to Florence."

Fortunately, with no further mishaps, we arrived in Florence later that day. We spent only one night there, as the next morning we were given instructions to move on to the nearby town of Lastra de Signa. Our base there was in a shattered building that had once been the factory for the Nobel Explosives Company.

"Very appropriate," was all that Danny could say as we surveyed our new home, standing there among the shards of broken glass and lumps of concrete. "An explosives factory for a unit – "

"A Jewish brigade unit," I reminded him.

"Yes, a Jewish brigade unit that spends most of its time driving explosives around the country."

Despite the rain, we managed to repair much of the factory building. We covered up the holes in the roof with large sheets of corrugated metal and boarded up some of the broken windows. One of our men, formerly a plumber from Haifa, succeeded in fixing the water system, and then we unloaded all our stores. Fortunately our cooks were used to working in strange conditions, and that night we were able to sit down to a hot meal.

We spent the next few months working together with the American Fifth Army picking up supplies from the Mediterranean port of Livorno and ferrying them to their frontline positions. All this was in preparation for a major push – a push to force the German army to retreat further north even faster.

During our off-duty hours we would drive the few miles into Florence to pick up any Jews who had survived the Nazi occupation, and help them with money and food. We learned that both the Nazis and their Italian Fascist collaborators had shot or sent many of the city's Jewish population to Auschwitz, an extermination camp whose terrible name was beginning to be mentioned more and more often as we came into contact with more and more survivors.

One evening after a group of us had returned to our "explosive base," as Baruch called it, Danny told us about our new commander.

"His name is Benjamin – Brigadier Ernest Frank Benjamin. He's Canadian and comes from Toronto. He served in the Royal Engineers and he's served in Egypt, India and Malaya."

I asked if he was a desk officer.

"I don't know, Benny. All I've heard is that when he was in Madagascar, he did an excellent job fighting the pro-Nazi Vichy forces there. And I also heard that he's started to learn Hebrew."

Soon after this, as part of the newly organized Jewish Brigade, our whole transport company was told to drive to Rome. Here we learned even more how much the local Jews had suffered at the hands of the Nazis, and again we helped out as much as we could. I had a feeling that simply by walking around among them and wearing our new Jewish Brigade badges with their yellow stars on a blue and white striped background, as well as driving our lorries complete with their *Magen David* badges, we did much to help boost the morale of the Jewish community. In addition, we were also proud to replace our "Palestine" shoulder flashes with new ones bearing the words "Jewish Infantry Brigade Group" in Hebrew.

We also learned that an important meeting had taken place among the Jewish chaplains and officers on how to help the Jewish survivors we had found and were still finding. It was felt that a coordinated action would be needed for our help to be really effective.

During the six weeks we spent in Rome, we also repaired all our vehicles. We then received the order we had been anticipating for so long: we were to drive to Fiuggi, link up with the other units of the Jewish Brigade and prepare for the final assault on the German forces still in Italy.

The weather was wet and miserable as our convoy drove out of Rome. However, despite the rain, hundreds of the city's Jews cheered us on as we headed east. Some waved handkerchiefs; some waved small Italian, American and British flags. But everyone knew that we were on our way to battle the Nazi invasion of Europe and to help our fellow Jews at the same time.

CHAPTER THIRTEEN
Into Battle at Last!

It was cold and snowy when we drove into Fiuggi, a small resort town in the Apennine mountain range. But the heavy gray skies did nothing to dampen our enthusiasm, especially when we noticed signposts written in English and Hebrew.

"Look, Baruch, over there, just behind Danny's lorry. Can you see those signs with *Magen David*s on them? It looks like the brigade has taken over the whole place."

"I know. The 178th is the last unit to arrive, so don't be surprised if you hear everyone talking Hebrew. Some of the others have been here for some time now."

"And look over there. Some of the men have painted Hebrew names on their lorries. Look, there's *Sarah* and there's *Yael* and look at those two parked by the tree over there: *Tel Aviv* and *Jerusalem*."

It did not take us long to settle down in our new base. In addition to our regular driving duties, we now had to undergo training using the latest infantry weapons and techniques. These included conducting attacks in platoon strength, laying mines, house-to-house fighting and learning how to send and receive coded messages. Most of this was new to us. However, as part of the newly formed Jewish Brigade, we understood its importance and hoped to get a crack at the Nazis before the war came to an end. We learned how to fire Bren guns and light machine guns as well as artillery shells, and how to launch mortar shells.

One evening while we were cleaning our newly acquired Bren guns, Baruch came over to us.

"Benny, Danny, Yossi, be ready to drive to Naples in half an hour. We've got tons of stores to pick up from there."

"Why can't they bring them here?" I asked. I was beginning to enjoy firing our new guns and taking part in the artillery training exercises. It made a change from driving lorries over mountain passes.

"Because Major Birt from the Welfare Office told me that a whole load of supplies has just arrived from America for the Jewish DPs here. If we don't go and pick the stuff up now, who knows what will happen to it?"

He was right and really we had no choice. Half an hour later we set off for the hundred-mile journey south. Apart from a short break near Cervaro, we made good time. Each lorry had two drivers and two loaders, who could also take over the driving if necessary. And so with many willing hands, it did not take us long to drive down, pick up the supplies and get ready for the journey back.

"OK, now back to Fiuggi," I said, climbing up into the cab.

"Wrong," Baruch said. "We're not going back to base, at least not directly. We've got to take this lot over to Bolsena. That's where the DP camp is."

"But that's fifty miles north of Rome," I protested, wanting to get back to base in time for the artillery course.

"I know, and that's why we brought the extra drivers with us, in case you fall asleep at the wheel."

"*Me*? Fall asleep at the wheel?"

"And what happened way back when we were near Tobruk?" Danny smiled.

"OK. Point taken. But now, let's get moving."

We got to Bolsena without any problems, unloaded our supplies and then returned to base. The only one who had a problem was Major Aron. We heard later that he had received a mild reprimand for allowing War Office transport to be used for "unauthorized purposes." However, as this "unauthorized" journey was of a humanitarian nature, the whole journey was quickly and quietly forgotten.

Our military training continued unabated and it became more intensive as the weeks passed. We learned to fire live ammunition from the latest weapons, and our bodies became hardened as we were sent out on long runs and route marches over the nearby mountains. I had to admit that I had never felt so tough and fit in my entire life. Our only worry was that the war would be over before we'd be sent into action.

It was during this period, while I was sitting on a large rock catching my breath after a particularly hard run, that Moshe Berliner, a corporal whose family had arrived in Palestine from Hamburg in 1936, tapped me on the shoulder.

"Benny, you know what I heard on the German army radio last night? They said that the British army now had a Jewish Brigade and that we were going to attack and pillage all the poor Christians in Europe!"

"That's ridiculous!"

"Of course it is, but do you know what the worst part of the announcement was? They called us the *Plattfuss* Brigade, the Flatfooted Brigade!"

"What chutzpa! Just wait till we get into battle. Then we'll show them how *plattfuss* we are!"

The order to move to the battle zone came a few weeks later, in fact during the festival of Purim in 1945. We had spent the previous few days dismantling much of the base and loading up our lorries for the journey north. Our personal equipment and lorries were inspected, and after many farewells and much backslapping and wishes of "*buona fortuna*, good luck" by the local Italians, we left Fiuggi at dawn. At first we drove to Rome, then headed northeast to Ravenna, an important town on the northeastern coast of Italy.

It took our slow-moving and very long convoy well over two days to reach the ancient Roman city. In all the towns we passed through en route – Florence, Bologna and Imola – we were greeted by loudly cheering crowds of Jews. They pointed at the *Magen David* badges on the fronts of our lorries and shouted "*mazal tov*," and threw flowers and candies at us. It was a fantastic feeling to know that we in the Jewish Brigade represented all their hopes of taking revenge on the Nazis, as well as bringing about a better life for their own future. Apart from anything else, the fact that they could see Jewish soldiers driving off to war in their own brigade did much to restore their pride in themselves as well.

The morning after we arrived at Ravenna, our commander, Brigadier Benjamin, called for a full inspection and complimented us, the 178th GT Company, on our past record for efficiency and reliability. His last announcement to the assembled parade was that we could expect to be moved up to the front lines at any minute. He was only waiting for the final orders from General Clark of the American Fifth Army Group. Those orders came the next day. At another parade, but a short one this time, we heard that we were to be sent immediately to the front lines in a sector north of Faenza.

Later that morning we were assembled in a large field outside Ravenna and Brigadier Benjamin read out the following notice: "From today, the Jewish Brigade will serve under the overall command of the American Fifth Army Group. The infantry units will take control of the front line at Alfonsine, which is north of Ravenna and south of Highway

16. This is a tricky area to fight in, as it is full of ditches and dykes, and the water has a tendency to seep into any dugout you may find necessary to dig. In addition, our field intelligence units have learned that the enemy have sown lots of mines in this area. You will be situated opposite the Austrian Forty-Second Jaeger Division and the 362nd Infantry Division, both known for their strong Nazi sympathies. This is especially so as both of these divisions contain many SS and Nazi party members."

Danny and I looked at each other. Although we were happy to be at the front at last, we were both very much aware that we would have a tough time ahead of us.

Brigadier Benjamin continued. "Your immediate task will be to carry out aggressive patrols, to improve our forward position and to clear the enemy out of the south bank near the River Lamone. You will also try to capture as many enemy soldiers as possible for the purposes of interrogation and identification."

He stopped and looked around at the expectant faces that greeted this last sentence. Many of us had been waiting to hear orders like this for a long time. Then, leaning forward and pushing his glasses back, the brigadier, looking more like a schoolmaster talking to a group of noisy pupils than the commander of a brigade numbering some 5,500 men, added the following strict warning:

"Needless to say, when it comes to personal contact with the enemy, no acts of revenge will be carried out or tolerated by the military authorities. I know that many of you have members of your families who have been hurt or even killed by the enemy. However, as soldiers in this newly formed Jewish Brigade, we must fight as honorable soldiers, as *menschen*, at all times. This is not a fight for personal revenge against a hated and bestial enemy. This is a fight both to rid Europe of this Nazi terror and also to bring peace and security back to our lives. You must remember this at all times. Good luck and *b'hatzlachah* to you all."

* * *

Danny, Yossi and I were assigned to B Company of the Third Battalion. We were to set out on our first offensive action a few hours after Brigadier Benjamin had spoken to us. There were ninety-six men in our company and a platoon from D Company was to join us. We were all to be under the command of Captain Yochanan Peltz.

"Benny, what do you know about the captain?" Yossi asked me as I was trying to squeeze a few extra bullets into my pouches.

"He's a tough guy and won't take no for an answer. As far as I know, he's a good man to be serving under."

"Good, that's what I wanted to hear."

Just then we heard a few shouts, and B and D Companies were called to fall into three lines. Captain Peltz and three sergeants ran a quick, efficient check over our rifles and uniforms and made sure that we were all properly equipped. As the captain approached me I could see he looked ready to set off, and his sharp nose and pointed chin added to his aggressive air.

After the inspection he had us stand at ease and, standing a few yards in front of us, he gave us our final instructions.

"I'm not going to give you men a *shpiel* about Jews fighting Nazis and how you should behave. The brigadier has said all that had to be said about this point. However, I will say that I know many of you have been waiting a long time for this day, and now you must do a good job. We've been given this particular job by the British army and we must – we must! – do it well. Many of the top brass in this army do not believe that Jews can make good fighters. We must prove them wrong. Now listen up. Our aim is to capture the command post at La Giorgetta, a strategic site on the banks of the Fosso Vetro canal. This is our first mission and we must succeed. Not only that, we must accomplish it with the minimum number of casualties on our side. That is all. Good luck."

We broke ranks and took up our prearranged positions as we began moving in the direction of the German command post. From where we were, we could see the Nazi flag with its swastika flapping in the wind on the roof, and I could just about make out a few soldiers moving around on the roof of the building next to it. Taking out my field glasses I saw that they were armed with M-G42 machine guns, which the Allies had nicknamed "Spandaus." I passed the glasses to Danny and quietly told him what I had seen.

"So we'd better watch out, my friend. Those things fire faster than ours."

Now crouching low in the long grass and bushes, our two companies were stretched out in a long line facing the enemy command post, waiting, tense and expectant. Looking around warily, like a fox scenting the breeze, Captain Peltz raised himself from his crouching position and placed a finger on his lips. We were to maintain complete silence.

Suddenly I felt all alone. Even though I knew that within a hundred yards of me Danny, Yossi and the others were also crouching down, all tensed up, like grayhounds ready for the "off," to my great surprise I felt as if I, Benny Levi, was all by myself. On my own, with just my rifle and my will to do a good job and survive what was to come. On my own, with just my thoughts for company.

I suppose this is a feeling that every soldier has just before he goes into battle – a feeling shared by every soldier in every army throughout history. From the ancient fighters of biblical times to the Greeks and Romans, and now our company of the Jewish Brigade, all tensed up ready to take on the Nazi troops facing us.

By now of course, I knew my fellow soldiers – "my mates," as the British would call them – very well. After all, we had been through everything together: Egypt, North Africa, Malta and now Italy. I knew who I could rely on and who I couldn't; I knew who was likely to panic and who would stay calm. I knew who cracked the stupid jokes, who knew how to rustle up some food out of nowhere and who could fix a rifle or carburetor without any problems. I knew whose friendship was worth having, who was an optimist, who was a pessimist and who was a cynic.

And now, despite all of this knowledge and our collective experiences over the past five years, I suddenly felt alone. Alone facing the unknown. How would I react? Would I keep cool under fire or would I panic and lose it? Up until now, any time I had been in a combat situation it had been on a small scale. This time it was different.

Any moment now, I thought, as I held my machine gun at the ready, they'll start firing at us. But they did not. It seemed the Germans were not aware that we were near them, quietly advancing all the time. I gave a thumbs-up to Danny and, keeping our heads low, we continued advancing.

By now we had crossed the open field and reached the tree line at the far end. So far, so good. Suddenly the tense silence was shattered as the Germans opened up and started firing their Spandaus. We could hear the characteristic "tearing cloth" sound they made, and we could see fragments of wood and bark fly out in all directions as their deadly bullets ripped into the trees all around us. I looked to the right and saw Captain Peltz signal us to stay where we were and lie low in the damp undergrowth. Brushing some grass and twigs off my face, I heard a heavy clanking noise followed by the throbbing sound of a large engine. I looked behind me and saw three Churchill tanks standing there, each one bearing the badge of the Royal Irish Horse Regiment on its turret. Stepping out from behind the thick tree trunk, the captain signaled the three tanks to spread out and continue moving forward. As they carried out his command, we resumed our lines behind them and began to advance uphill toward the old farmhouse the Germans were using for their command post.

The sound of the enemy mortars grew louder, and branches and even trees started crashing down around us. Suddenly a mortar shell split a tree to my left and I became aware of the sweet smell of the freshly splintered pinewood. For a split second I was back in my Uncle Aaron's carpentry workshop in Haifa, but then the sound of more shells and bullets brought me back to the present. I looked around for Danny and Yossi. They were still there in line with me, Yossi flashing me a quick smile. Like me, he had become very impatient about going into action.

For some reason unknown to us, the Germans had stopped firing. Captain Peltz signaled the tanks to stop where they were while he sent Haim Brot and a few others ahead to check for mines. We had been told that the mines had been cleared by our engineers, but we couldn't be sure. There were always a few that remained buried in the ground until an unfortunate soldier or tank set it off. We crouched down again and waited as we watched Haim and his men prod the ground in front of us. We were as tense as coiled springs as they stuck their long rods into the soft ground and slowly advanced. They checked the ground for any signs of disturbance and then carefully poked around the suspicious area. I held my breath as I watched and saw that to my right, Danny was wiping the sweat off his face with the back of his hand. To my left, Motty was moving his lips in a silent prayer.

Haim's team advanced slowly. Our rifles and the cannon on the tanks were ready to open fire at any moment. We still had three hundred yards to the command post, and now I began to wonder if we would make it. Then I noticed Haim straighten his back. "I think we've found the last one now – " he shouted to the captain, but his shout was suddenly cut short. There was a tremendous flash of bright red and orange light, and his body, rifle and steel prod were thrown aside in a wide arc.

"Stretchers! Medics!" Peltz shouted. Two men rushed forward keeping as low as possible as German bullets started whizzing around once again. The medics managed to roll Haim's limp, bloody body onto a stretcher and bring him back into the cover of the trees.

As the captain went over to where they laid the stretcher down I could see him wipe away a tear. Haim Brot had been his special friend; they had been through a lot together. Now seeing he could do nothing for him, Peltz covered his dead friend's body with a blanket and then ran toward a forward ditch. He looked back at the rest of us. Most of us were crouching low in the undergrowth or standing behind the mutilated trees. Then out of the corner of my eye I saw three men lying down at the end of the line. They were not moving. I did not know who they were and just hoped they were just keeping low and were not dead or wounded. I did not have much time to think about this as suddenly Captain Peltz's sharp voice cut the air. "Fix bayonets! Fix bayonets!"

All along the line you could hear the sounds of dozens of steel bayonets clicking into place in their rifle sockets.

"Wait for it!" Peltz shouted as if he were the captain of a sports team. "Wait for it! Ready! Charge!"

We did not need to be told twice. Aware of the machine gun in my hands and my fit body, I ran forward as fast as I could, yelling my head off. I don't know what I yelled, but it was a pure release of pent-up energy and tension. At the same time I could hear the enemy bullets whizzing past my head. But I didn't care. All I wanted to do was find some sort of cover and shoot those men who were shooting at me.

Suddenly I saw a German soldier appear from behind the farmhouse and aim toward the charging man on my right. Without a second's hesitation, I threw a hand grenade at him and followed this by spraying the area with machine-gun bullets. After what felt like ages, I saw the corner of the farmhouse explode in a bright flash of light accompanied by thunderous noise and smoke, and pieces of wood and brick flew out in all directions. Keeping my finger on the trigger I approached carefully to see if I had killed the enemy soldier. I had. He was lying on the ground, the hated SS insignia lying on his torn, bloody uniform.

I did not stop to give him much thought even though he was the first person I had ever killed. I gave the mangled body a quick look and raced on to follow a few others. We smashed in a decayed door, its old rotting wood offering little resistance to our boots and rifle butts. Captain Peltz was in front and there was anger in his eyes. It was clear that despite what he had said earlier about Jewish soldiers behaving on the battlefield, he was out for revenge. His friend Haim had been blown up and someone would have to pay for it. As he ran the first German soldier through with his bayonet, he shouted, "That was for Haim! And so is this," he added as he shot the German officer who had just entered the room in the face.

Suddenly the noise and movement ceased. Had we killed all the enemies or were there other soldiers hiding somewhere else in the command post? I bent down to pick up the dead officer's Luger. In a building it was easier to use a pistol than a machine gun. Then, as I straightened up, I noticed a figure appear in the shadows. I was about to shoot when Danny shouted, "Benny! It's me! Danny!" I had almost shot my best friend! Luckily the officer had not flipped the safety catch on his pistol. The split second it had taken me to do so had saved Danny's life.

Danny told me that there were no more live Germans at this end of the command post, and that we should move over to the other end. We ran up to the roof to get a better view and saw several enemy soldiers retreating toward the river. We saw one of them turn around to fire at us, silhouetted on the roof, but that was the last thing he ever did. The soldier next to me shot him. We saw the gray uniformed body crumple up like a bundle of dirty rags and roll over in the mud, his rifle flying through the air to land a few yards away.

In the meantime, we on the roof and our men below kept up a barrage, firing at the fleeing men so that only one or two survived. When it was clear that these men were well out of range, we stopped firing to take stock of the situation.

The command post was ours, and only a few individual enemy soldiers had escaped. That was good. They could now spread the news that the Jews had beaten them. We had captured a dozen men and these would be handed over to our intelligence unit for questioning. In the meantime, we would let them know they had been defeated by the Jewish Brigade. Whatever Brigadier Benjamin may have said, there was no doubt about it: revenge was sweet.

Making my way down the rickety staircase, I could feel the energy draining away from me. My shoulders slumped under the weight of the machine gun and my legs felt like rubber. Apart from a few scratches on my hands and face, nothing had happened to me. I was alive and unscathed. I had lived through my first attack and although I felt drained, physically and emotionally, I was smiling.

"What are you smiling about?" asked Danny, his face streaked with mud.

"I'm alive," I said, clapping him on the back. "And not only that, my friend, but I think I did OK. I've always wondered how I'd react in a battle and now I know."

"That's strange," Danny said, rubbing some blood off the back of his scratched hand, "but I also wondered about that. I guess all soldiers feel the same way before and after their first battle. You know, how will I measure up? Will I panic or will I do what I'm supposed to do?"

We found Yossi downstairs. He was trying to look fierce as he was standing guard over two captured SS officers. When he saw us approach he grinned and beckoned us over to join him.

"Danny," he said in Hebrew. "You know a bit of German, don't you?"

"Not much."

"Doesn't matter. Just tell these two that they've been taken prisoner by the soldiers of the Jewish Brigade and that this soldier," he said, pointing at himself, "doesn't have any bullets in his gun. That should really annoy them."

"What do you mean, no bullets in your gun?" I asked.

"My pouches got ripped off somewhere as we approached the building and I lost all my ammo. And yes, tell them that this soldier is Jewish. That should really make them feel good. They don't understand why I'm wearing a yellow star on my uniform."

Danny told them and the looks of disgust on the faces of the enemy soldiers told us everything. We also gave Yossi some bullets, and he ordered his prisoners to stand up. Taking some pieces of string and wire we then bound their hands behind their backs and told them to start walking to where the rest of our prisoners were sitting together, huddled in a corner of an outbuilding that smelled unmistakably of pigs.

"Very suitable," was Yossi's comment as he began to push his prisoners inside.

The stockier one began to protest. "*Ich bin ein Offizier*, I'm an officer," he said, puffing out his chest.

"*Sie sind mein* prisoner," Yossi replied in a mix of English and what he hoped was German, and then he tore the SS badge off the man's uniform. "A souvenir for the future," he grinned. "And don't tell me that what I've done is against the Geneva Convention. I'm sure it's nothing in comparison to what this guy has done over the past few years. Now get in there." And he gave his prisoner a push inside and slid the heavy iron bolt into place.

Just as we were getting ready to move out we heard the sound of a few of our soldiers in the courtyard laughing.

"What's so funny?" I called out. "Is the war over?"

"No, but we just heard a funny story about Captain Peltz."

I thought this was strange. The intense captain did not seem to be a "funny" person at all.

"What's the story?" I asked, joining the group.

"You see that building over there? Well, he thought he heard some strange noises coming out of the cellar below. So he went down to check and he saw all this red liquid on the floor."

"Blood?" I asked.

"No, it wasn't. But the captain didn't know that. He thought there were some Germans hiding out down there, maybe a wounded man or two. So he fired a couple warning shots. He didn't hear any noises after that but noticed that the red stuff was now flowing all over the place, and all over his boots as well."

"What was it? Paint?"

"No. It was red wine. The captain had just shot several large barrels of it and he came out of the cellar smelling like the town drunk."

"And what were the strange noises?"

"Don't know. Maybe it was just the wind."

"OK, that's enough wind from you," one of the sergeants said. "Now get yourselves over to the gate. The captain wants to take a roll call to see if anyone's wounded or missing."

Then, just as we were crossing the yard, we heard shouts from the roof. We all looked up and had our guns at the ready.

"What's Zekovitz doing up there?" someone asked. "Look, he's undoing his shirt."

A few moments later we saw what he was doing. He was busy pulling a large blue and white flag out of his shirt.

He gave it one more tug and then tied it to a radio antenna the Germans had been using. Within a minute our flag was flapping proudly high over the command post and, without thinking, we all stopped what we were doing for a minute and saluted it. Then we let out a huge cheer and two prisoners who had not yet been pushed into the outbuilding were forced to look up and witness how the men of the Jewish Brigade were celebrating their first success in battle.

But the battle had not been won without paying a heavy price. In addition to Haim Brot, eighteen men had been killed and a dozen wounded. The dead men were buried the next day and temporary wooden markers, topped with *Magen David*s, were placed on their graves. It was an eerie feeling to see these six-pointed stars now used to top the graves of our fallen comrades. The day before, we had felt euphoric watching the *Magen David* flying over the captured enemy command post. Army Chaplain Reverend Caspar said *Kaddish* over the freshly dug graves. "*Yitgadal v'yitkadash, shmay rabbah*, Magnified and sanctified be His great name," he began, and all of us continued the prayer silently as we wondered how much more work and how many more deaths the brigade was to suffer before we could complete our task.

CHAPTER FOURTEEN
Offensives on the Front Line

A few days later, Sergeant Israel Carmi, a long-serving soldier who had also served in North Africa, was ordered to take a few men with him and go on an inspection tour. This "recce," as he called it, was to patrol the front lines and, hoping it would prove to be more interesting than the patrols I was doing, I volunteered to join him.

The sun was shining when we drove to the Senio, a small but strategically important river that flowed through a deep valley west of Faenza. Our brigade was to take over the area from the Ghurkas, the famous Nepalese combat unit. On learning this, I felt that the British army had recognized that our brigade had proved its worth on the battlefield.

We inspected all the trenches and other important points, and then Carmi made one suggestion: since our soldiers were taller than their Nepalese counterparts, we should deepen the trenches as soon as we moved in.

We then learned that the German forces facing us included the Fourth Paratroop Division, a tough unit made up of zealous Nazis. When Captain Peltz and Carmi discussed this last point later, the captain turned to me and rubbed his hands with glee.

"That's good news," he said, grinning. "Now we'll be able to hit those Nazis again. I'm longing to bring in some more of those swine for questioning."

"You mean 'tongue snatching,'" I grinned back. "At least, that's what the colonel called it."

"Call it what you like, but I'd really like to call it revenge. It's about time those thugs paid for the misery they've caused. I'm telling you, the more we catch, the better."

And Captain Peltz tried to live up to his word. Whenever he had the opportunity, he and a few others would sneak out at night and try to capture a few German soldiers. But to his great disappointment, he always returned empty-handed. These private forays became known as "Peltz's manhunts."

Just as we were beginning to accept that the captain's wish would remain unfulfilled, we received news that one of the German platoons facing us was being withdrawn.

"That's good news," Major Storrs said. "That'll be the best time to catch some of them. They'll be too busy with their changeover and will be unprepared. They'll be so busy with all their briefings and details they won't be expecting anything from us."

Later that day Captain Peltz, Lieutenant van Gelder and eight men including me quietly slipped into enemy territory. I would have preferred to do this at night but the captain explained that we needed to check out the area as well as possible – and he hoped the risk would be worth it.

Taking cover behind shrubs and trees, we advanced to where our air reconnaissance map showed us their central bunker should be. We saw nobody on guard duty, nor could we hear a sound.

"Maybe it's empty," I whispered to Baruch. "Maybe they've left already."

Baruch shrugged. "Maybe. Maybe the new guys haven't gotten here yet. And if that's so, that's really dumb. That means they've left this sector open for us to walk into."

"Or they've set us a trap," I said.

Like us, Peltz and van Gelder were also considering this strange situation.

"Peltz, take my glasses. Can you see anything?"

"No, I can't. I can't see anything. I think they must have moved out already."

"Let's make sure," van Gelder suggested. He got up slowly from where he was hiding and signaled for us to move in quietly and surround the squat concrete pillbox.

Keeping as low as possible, and fully expecting to hear a burst of enemy rifle fire, I advanced with the others. Keeping my eyes concentrated on the bunker's doorways and slit windows, I expected to see a rifle barrel suddenly appear at any moment. My heart was pounding away and I was tensed up for action. By now Captain Peltz had reached the main doorway and was standing to the side of it. There was still no sign of the enemy as he carefully pushed the unlocked door open. Like an inquisitive cat, he stealthily entered into the darkness but, unlike a cat, he was holding a cocked revolver in front of him. There was no reaction from within. Our rifles ready, we closed in behind him and surrounded the bunker. By now my heart was thumping even louder, if that was possible. Then the captain turned around, put his finger to his lips, smiled cynically and motioned for us to join him.

Standing next to him, we saw why he was smiling. Lying on their bunks were fourteen German soldiers. They were all asleep. A few empty bottles of beer were lying on the floor. We were speechless. I had been creeping around the woods for this!

Suddenly Corporal Grossman broke the tension and shouted, "*Heraus, ihr Schweine! Die Juden sind hier!* Get up, you pigs! The Jews are here!"

As one, the soldiers jumped up. Some tried to grab their rifles but we kicked them away. Then suddenly someone shouted, "Benny, behind you!" And I whirled around and knocked the bayonet out of the German's hand. It clattered to the floor and he began rubbing his wounded hand.

Van Gelder pointed to the gray-uniformed men and ordered them to stand in line. One of them, a blond, baby-faced private, started crying. "I'm not a Nazi. I'm just a soldier," he blubbered. He was probably speaking the truth but we were not impressed. And neither were his fellow soldiers. Two of them looked at him with disgust. That did not stop another from pleading, "I'm not a Nazi. I'm a Social Democrat."

We were not interested in his politics and van Gelder ordered them to raise their hands. One of them was a bit slow, but a tap in the stomach with a rifle butt speeded up his reaction.

Now that our "attack" was over I was beginning to relax. My heart was beating at its normal rate and I found myself looking around the inside of the pillbox. Rifles, bayonets and boxes of ammunition were lying around everywhere and Corporal Grossman was stamping on a large Nazi flag. His heel had ripped up the swastika in its center and he was looking very pleased with himself. The baby-faced soldier looked shocked at this act of "sacrilege."

"Let's kill them," Grossman said as he finished shredding up the flag. "It's time they had a taste of their own medicine!" And before anyone could do anything, he pointed his rifle at the face of the tallest prisoner.

"Corporal Grossman! I order you to put that rifle down!" van Gelder shouted at him.

Grossman did not move and sweat began to run down the German's face.

"Corporal Grossman! That's an order! Now drop it!"

We waited. Van Gelder waited. The German soldier waited – and started shaking.

Slowly Corporal Grossman lowered his rifle and just as he did so and the soldier began to look relieved, Grossman butted him full in the face with his helmet. The soldier cried out and spat out some broken teeth. Grossman stepped back. He was smiling. Van Gelder ordered him to wait outside. Sergeant Brauner was told to wait outside with him. Just as Grossman was about to leave the bunker he whirled around to face the soldier nearest the door. The corporal's anger was not over yet.

"Huh! You call yourselves the 'master race'? You murdered my family!" he said in German and ripped the swastika off the man's shirt, throwing it on the ground.

"Now spit on it!"

The soldier looked at his comrades but they said nothing. They averted their eyes.

"Come on, you Nazi scum! Spit on it! Let's see what you really think of your *Führer*, your Hitler!"

The soldier looked around again for help but all he could see was the hatred in Corporal Grossman's eyes.

"That's enough," van Gelder said quietly. "Corporal Grossman, wait outside. We've got a job to do here. I know how you feel, but just wait outside and cool down. Sergeant, take him outside."

This time the angry soldier walked outside, but not before he had spat into the face of the German he had just humiliated.

The tension and pent-up fury of the last few minutes slowly seeped away as we tied up our prisoners' hands and checked that they were not carrying any concealed weapons.

Captain Peltz called for a couple of lorries and soon we, together with our German captives, were back at our base. There we handed them over to the intelligence unit. We never saw them again.

It seems that word of the corporal's behavior got out and it soon became the major talking point in the base. Had he acted correctly or not as a soldier in the Jewish Brigade?

"Correct or not, you must remember what happened to his family," Grossman's friend defended him.

"I know, but we've still got to remember the Geneva Convention."

"You're right, in theory, but did the Nazis think of that when they killed his family?"

"True, but two wrongs still don't make a right."

But whatever we thought, two days later Brigadier Benjamin posted a notice in the mess hall.

> Subject: Prisoners
>
> 1) I want to impress upon all ranks the supreme importance of capturing live German prisoners, and of their being sent back quickly for interrogation through the proper channels.
>
> 2) I fully realize that there are many men in the Jewish Brigade Group who have every personal justification for desiring to revenge themselves upon the Germans, and I am afraid that this may, in some cases, lead them to decide to kill every German they can, rather than take prisoners. This is a very shortsighted policy. Our object is to do everything in our power to hasten the defeat of the enemy and it has been proved time and time again that far more is gained by taking

prisoners from whom information can be extracted under interrogation than by killing the enemy out of hand.

3) I want to stress one further point. However great the crimes which the Germans have committed against international and moral law, I am determined that the Jewish Brigade shall act correctly in accordance with recognized conventions.

E. F. Benjamin
Brig. Comd.

If the brigadier had hoped that by posting this notice he would bring to an end all the talk about how we should deal with our prisoners, he was wrong. That night Danny, Yossi and I had a heated discussion that lasted until midnight. It ended only because we had to go out on patrol.

I tended to agree with Corporal Grossman's behavior. "Don't you see, Danny? He's spent three or four years remembering what the Nazis did to his parents. You can't expect him to put that aside just because he's now wearing a British army uniform."

"I'm not expecting anything like that, Benny. But he – and the rest of us, for that matter – must remember that we are now in the Jewish Brigade and that we can't allow ourselves to sink to the same level as the Nazis."

"Danny, you are exaggerating," Yossi said. "Making a Nazi soldier spit on his badge is not the same thing as herding hundreds if not thousands of Jews onto trains that are going to take them to the death camps."

"I know that, Yossi, but it's the principle of the thing. We mustn't act like Nazis in any way. We captured those guys and that was that. There was no need for Grossman to rub their faces in it."

And so we continued throughout the night until a sergeant arrived and reminded us to grab our helmets, rifles and other equipment to patrol our section of the line.

Our patrol started off quietly. It was a cold, crisp night and the Senio was flowing smoothly toward Faenza and the coast. We – that is, Danny, Yossi, Baruch and I – were wrapped up warmly, and it looked as though we were in for a quiet, uneventful patrol duty. Apart from a few enemy rifle shots coming from their lines, nothing disturbed the peaceful nature of the Italian countryside in our sector. I was just looking at a few small branches drifting along the moonlit river when suddenly we heard some loud splashing noises. Something heavy had moved or fallen into the river. We froze on the spot and then quickly moved behind some large trees on the riverbank.

"Those noises are not ducks," I whispered to the others.

"Sounds like people or maybe a stray cow," Danny suggested. "It's not very deep there. If it is the Germans, they may be trying to cross over into our lines."

"I'll slip back with Baruch and tell Carmi," Danny said. "Just watch out for enemy pillboxes. "We can't count on them being asleep this time." And saying that, he and Baruch silently disappeared along the riverbank toward our base.

Then as I turned back to Yossi I saw a group of silhouettes moving toward us. Their shapes were indistinct. All I could make out was that they were soldiers. They were spread out and their rifle barrels glinted occasionally in the moonlight. I pointed this out to Yossi and we ducked behind some bushes and held our rifles at the ready.

Suddenly a low call in Hebrew cut the tense night air. "Benny! Yossi! Hold your fire!" It was Sergeant Carmi. He was there behind another clump of bushes; his platoon was now crouching down behind some other bushes.

"You two," Carmi ordered us quietly. "Start moving along the river bank and we'll do the same. When you hear me start firing, you do the same," and he pointed to a spot on the opposite bank.

We set off, walking as quietly as we could through the damp, dewy grass and low bushes when suddenly the night was shattered by a long burst from Carmi's tommy gun. That was the signal for us to join in and we fired long bursts at the opposite bank, where we could see the German muzzle flashes lighting up. From the brightness of their flashes and from the area they covered, we saw we were outnumbered.

Then, just as I was realizing this, I heard something whiz past my ear and explode in a thick clump of bushes behind me. It was a hand grenade. Suddenly I felt a sharp stinging pain in my left arm and almost dropped my rifle. Now trying to ignore the red-hot needles in my arm, I rejoined the others in firing over to the far bank while trying to throw a couple of my own grenades as far as possible. After throwing two of them, I had to give up as the pain in my arm prevented me from pulling out the pins.

By now it was clear that the Germans had the upper hand, and I was wondering what we could do. As I was looking around to see if any of the enemy had begun to cut us off I heard Sergeant Carmi shout into his field radio for artillery support.

"Too dangerous," the reply crackled back. "We'll shoot you by mistake in the dark."

"No, you won't," Carmi called back. "You start firing now and my men will raise their helmets high up on their rifles. If you hit them, you'll know you'll have to adjust your range."

I heard the artillery officer. "It's too dangerous. We'll kill you all. I don't know how accurate we can be in the dark."

"Do it," shouted Carmi. "We've got nothing to lose. If you don't kill us, then the Germans will. I'll give you one minute and then fire!"

In that minute, Carmi passed the word that every other man was to raise his helmet on his rifle while the remainder were to continue shooting at the enemy. One minute later – one minute that seemed like eternity – the tables were turned. The artillery unit behind us rained down a deadly torrent on the opposite bank, and the bright muzzle flashes and explosive sounds stopped. They were replaced by calls for medics as well as the groans of wounded men. Now we could hear the sounds of the enemy retreating to their earlier positions.

"Benny, can you hear any more noises from over there?" Carmi asked me.

"No, not really – that is, apart from the wounded men left behind. I did see quite a few retreating a few minutes ago when I used my field glasses."

"Well, let's make sure," and turning to his radio he told Haim to start firing again at the same area and to give it some long, sweeping bursts with the heavy machine guns.

Again Haim's bullets flew over our heads onto the opposite bank. We heard a few screams as some of the wounded men, abandoned by their comrades, were hit for the second time. We watched and listened for any return fire, but everything was quiet. Carmi told Haim to cease firing and an eerie silence took over. The only sounds were the breeze in the trees and the Senio lapping quietly below. A few of the remaining Germans on the other side were still moaning as they tried to deal with their wounds.

We remained crouching down for a few more minutes, alert and waiting for some sort of reaction from the enemy, but nothing happened. The backs of my legs were in excruciating pain from crouching down and carrying a heavy gun, but I didn't dare stand up to relieve my calf muscles. All I needed was to be shot by a lone sniper out for revenge.

At last Carmi gave us the order to stand up, but as slowly and as quietly as possible. He then signaled to us to retreat and make our way to a thick group of trees.

When we got there he began to read out our names.

"Avi Cohen?"

"Yes."

"Izzy Cohen?"

"Yes."

"Wasserman?"

"Yes."

"Yitzhak Levi?"

"Here."

"Benny Levi?"

"Yes."

"Goldsmith?"

No answer.

"Goldsmith? Jonathan Goldsmith?"

We all looked around to see where he was. Suddenly we saw him making his way toward us.

"Goldsmith," said Carmi, breathing an audible sigh of relief. "Where were you?"

"Over there, behind those trees, having a pee."

We all laughed and the tension was broken. And then we felt even better when Carmi finished reading off his list and we saw that no one was missing or killed. The only wounds were those that two others and I had suffered when the enemy's hand grenade had exploded behind us. Luckily, the wounds were superficial – the thick bushes had absorbed most of the flying shrapnel.

"Sergeant," Danny asked. "What about our helmets? Mine's full of holes. It's useless now."

Carmi shrugged. "Thank the Lord that the holes are in your helmet and not in your head," he said drily. "When you get back, go over to the stores and get another one. You and anyone else who needs one. I'll tell the quartermaster what happened. No more questions? Good. Then this is what we're going to do. We'll stay here for the rest of the night and check out the area at first light. Everyone is to go back to where you were and keep your eyes peeled. We don't want any more surprises. You all did well tonight and you can be proud of being Jewish soldiers in our own brigade. *Chazak v'ematz*," he said, adding the traditional blessing, "Be strong and of good courage."

It was a long night, and by the time dawn crept over the hills I was cold and starving. I had not brought any food with me, as I had not expected to be out all night. Luckily Yossi gave me an apple and someone else gave me a few biscuits. This, together with the water in my canteen, kept the worst pangs of hunger away. Nevertheless, by the time it was daylight I felt as though I could have eaten a horse, hooves and all.

As soon as I could, when the first rays of light began to dispel the darkness, I used my field glasses to scan the opposite bank. I then reported what I had seen to Sergeant Carmi. "I made out ten bodies. One or two seemed to be moving and maybe there are a few others hidden in the long grass. But

I couldn't make out any details. I couldn't see anyone over there holding anything that looked like a weapon."

Several of the others agreed with me in their reports; none of us noted any enemy soldiers moving around or being positioned for another attack.

Following a warning from the sergeant, we carefully made our way over to the opposite bank, trying not to splash as we waded through the River Senio. My nerves – and I suppose everyone else's – were tightly strung as, standing there exposed, we expected to hear a sudden outburst of fire from a German soldier left behind hiding in the undergrowth. For a moment I felt like a duck in a shooting gallery. It was not a good feeling.

We reached the other side without any shots being fired and began to climb up the slippery grassy surface feeling just as exposed as before, if not more so. Again nothing happened and we reached the area where the Germans had been. There we counted off a dozen bodies, their field-gray uniforms torn and bloody. Most of their faces showed signs of surprise and agony. Two of the enemy soldiers were resting against the foot of a tree, groaning in pain. One was clearly suffering from stomach wounds and his comrade's legs were all bloody and distorted. The grass was stained red in many places and we could see flattened areas where the wounded had tried to protect themselves from our fire.

"Let's finish them off," Goldsmith said, pointing his rifle at the two men.

"You can't," Danny replied, trying to lower Goldsmith's rifle.

"Why not? It'll put them out of their agony."

"You're wrong, Goldy," I said. "Besides, the intelligence boys might want to question them."

"Benny's right," someone behind me said. "And besides, let them suffer after all they've done."

Goldsmith lowered his rifle, very slowly, very reluctantly. He then walked over to the two Germans and stood over them. "Look, you swine," he said in Hebrew and German. "Just know you've been hit by Jewish soldiers. Here, Jews wear yellow stars, but not your Nazi ones. Yellow stars we are wearing with pride. So if you swine survive, just remember that it was the Jewish Brigade that got you." And he spat and walked away. None of us argued with him; I think we all agreed with him. Brigadier Benjamin was going to have a tough time preventing some of his men from carrying out any private acts of revenge, and I noticed that Sergeant Carmi did not interfere in any way.

It was good to know that we had beaten the enemy, although in the big picture this was merely a minor frontline skirmish. But this action, small as it was, was good for our morale, both as individuals and as soldiers in the Jewish Brigade. It also showed that we, as "green" frontline combat troops, could look after ourselves pretty well.

That night I wrote a long letter to Tamar and told her what I had been doing recently. Of course I told her about the actions I had taken part in but, as usual, left out any incriminating details. I also omitted the fact that my left arm had been injured and was now wrapped up in a large bandage. Danny called this my "white badge of courage." I called it my "white badge of luck" – lucky that I had not suffered more than a deep cut.

I told her about the arguments we had had about how to deal with captured German POWs, but the main point was that we had held our own very well, and that I was proud to be a soldier in the brigade. Needless to say, I ended the letter saying I hoped I would see her soon. I posted the letter in a special box and hoped that the British army's postal service was as good as it was supposed to be. So far, Tamar and I had received all the letters we had written to each other, although some had been somewhat late in arriving.

The next major event that happened while we were based near the River Senio was Passover. Bernard Caspar, the brigade's senior chaplain, managed to obtain some boxes of matzah, Haggadot and wine, and as many men as possible – that is, those who were not out on patrol or otherwise engaged – crowded into the large hall and sat around the tables covered with white cloths.

"Where's Corporal Grossman?" I asked Danny. "He wouldn't miss out on this if he didn't have to."

Danny shrugged and then pulled me aside. "Don't tell anybody, but I understand that he and a few others have gone off to track down some of the Nazi officers still in this area."

"To shoot them?"

Danny shrugged again. "Don't know, but don't say a word. It's just a rumor and you know what the army is like for rumors."

"Yes," I nodded. "Especially a Jewish army."

Putting aside any thoughts of Corporal Grossman, Danny and I made our way over to the seder service and happily joined in with the prayers and the songs. Qena, Tobruk and Tripoli. I thought of those past seder nights and felt rather sad that I was not at home this year as I had expected. I had been away from my family long enough and I was missing them a lot. I also thought of the last seder night, which I had shared with Tamar.

It was halfway through the service when Brigadier Benjamin began a special speech, which would later appear in the Jewish press around the world. After comparing the brigade's hopes for freedom as the Children of Israel had hoped during the Exodus from Egypt, he said that he wanted the world to know that we had been doing a good job. He also said that we had already brought honor to the Jewish people and would continue to do so. He finished his speech by saying, "No soldiers have a better reason to be here on the front line facing the Nazi enemy than the men of this brigade. Their spirit could not be higher, and should be an inspiration to all who make sure our ranks are kept completely filled until the enemy is finally routed. Then, in poetic justice, and as a matter of national honor, we must play our part in any task which may be entrusted to us."

He then wished us a happy Pesach, and that this festival should "usher in the dawn of real freedom for Israel and all mankind."

We then tucked into the festive meal, and just as we were singing the last verses of "Chad Gadya" I felt a light tap on my shoulder. I turned round to see Yossi, who whispered for me to follow him outside.

"What's up?" I asked a few moments later. "Are we going out again on another night patrol?"

"Yes, but this one's a special one. It seems they want us to check out this old house above the river. They think – "

"Who thinks?"

"The intelligence guys in the brigade. But listen. They think the Germans have taken it over as an observation post. We have to check this out to see if the information is true or just a rumor."

"But why us? There are over five thousand men in the brigade."

"I know, but you and I have been in the army for a long time and we were also involved in the La Giorgetta fight and the other one by the river. They don't want to send any 'greeners' this time."

I did not really object. But I had been enjoying the singing and the festive atmosphere around the seder table. Naturally, I was feeling a bit resentful at being taken away from it so unexpectedly.

We went back to our rooms and picked up our helmets, rifles, ammo pouches and other equipment. This time I remembered to take a couple of apples and a chunk of cheese as well. War or no war, Benny Levi was not going to be hungry again on the battlefield!

I met up with Yossi and the others near the vehicle spare parts building. Our group included several of the men who had been with me at the River Senio action. There were also two new faces: Joseph Schneur and Arieh Schechter. They reminded me of Danny and myself. Like me, Schneur was tall and outgoing, while his best friend was shorter, wore thick glasses and was never without a book in his hand. This time it was a book about philosophy.

"You can put that away," Captain Peltz remarked, somewhat sharply. "You won't be needing *that* where we're going tonight."

Then the captain gave us a briefing, and using a map and a flashlight he showed us where we would be going and what the main features of the area were.

"Any questions?"

There were none.

"So let's get moving and remember, no noise. We believe this place is empty but we're not sure. We don't want any surprises that we can't deal with."

The night was inky black as we approached our target. The building was an old Italian house on the top of a hill overlooking the Senio River valley. Although it was dark I could see that it had been built in several layers, and it blended in well with the surrounding scenery. To my non-professional eyes, the house, or rather the mansion, looked as if it were over a hundred years old and must have belonged to someone very rich.

The twelve of us spread out and began a slow, careful and silent approach. Suddenly our boots started making a crunching sound as we found ourselves walking on a rough stony path. We all stopped where we were and crouched down, our rifles at the ready. We waited, and after what seemed like half an hour we stood up. No lights had been switched on in the house and no shuttered windows opened and no German voices shouted, "*Wer ist dort?* Who is there?"

Now standing, we continued approaching the house, but this time we walked on the grass shoulder by the pathway. In a whisper I asked Captain Peltz if we had a floor plan of the house's interior. He shook his head. "We'll just have to be careful," he muttered and hurried to the front of our column.

We reached the house without anyone seeing us or opening fire on us. As we stood on the veranda, I could now see that from close up the building looked less impressive. The shutters were peeling, the walls were cracked and the main doors were falling off their rusting hinges.

I wondered if this was possibly a trap and I hoped that Captain Peltz was thinking the same. Could there be a group of enemy soldiers just waiting in the dark hallway ready to gun us down as we entered? Or was the building really as abandoned as it looked?

We waited again and listened, intently. But all we could hear was a breeze blowing through some nearby trees in the garden, their leaves making a rustling sound. Captain Peltz put his finger to his lips and threw a small rock into the hallway. There was no reaction from inside the darkened house. Putting his finger to his lips again, the captain then indicated that before he went in, he would push the door a little and see what would happen. He pushed the door and nothing happened. He pointed to us to indicate who would go upstairs and who would go below, and we entered the building one at a time. We immediately broke up into three groups and fanned out to cover all the landings. I was in the group with Captain Peltz and we made our way up to the top floor. Schechter took the right corridor and Schneur took the left one.

There was still no sound as we moved as silently as we could. Like stalking cats, we all walked with our shoulders hunched low, our eyes darting in all directions, alert for any noise. Suddenly I saw a shape ahead of me at the end of the corridor. It was silhouetted against the window. It was moving and looked as though it were holding something long, like a rifle. I was about to shoot when at the last second I realized it was myself. I was looking at a reflection of myself in a long mirror! Despite the cool night air I began to sweat, and I could feel it running down my face, stinging as it ran into my eyes.

I wiped my forehead with the back of my hand and we quietly returned the way we had come. We checked out all the cupboards and under the beds, and saw that there were no Germans on the top floor. As we were making our way down the curved staircase we saw Schechter's men move into a dark corridor. Suddenly over the muffled sounds of army boots on a wooden floor a cry rang out followed by a short burst of bullets flying in that echoing building. Where was the enemy? Where had they been hiding? There was no enemy fire. Schneur's men had mistaken Schechter's group for the enemy and had opened fire on them. There were immediate shouts of *"Chadal esh!* Cease fire!" and the shooting stopped immediately. Three men turned on their flashlights. There was blood on the parquet floors. Schneur's blood and Schechter's blood. In that short firefight, the two friends had shot each other. We stood there shaking.

We had been trained to kill Nazis, not Jews. Schneur's friend, Ronni, burst out into tears. "After all we've gone through," he said between sobs, his shoulders heaving. "Getting out of Nazi Germany, crossing Europe…and now to die like this. It's not fair. What a waste! What a tragedy!"

None of us said anything; words would have been out of place. Yossi put his arm around Ronni's shoulder but it made no difference.

Captain Peltz made us snap out of our shock. "There's no Germans here," he said coldly. "Schneur's group, get a blanket and a stretcher and put him on it, and you," he said, pointing to the soldiers who had been in Schechter's group, "you do the same for him. I'll call for transport and the rest of you come with me."

Carrying out his orders like robots, we followed him outside. Together with Danny and Wasserman, I was ordered to comb the building again and look for any documents or maps that might have been left behind. We found a few papers in a broken desk and stuffed them into our packs.

Half an hour later we were sitting in the back of a Dodge lorry driving back to base. No one said a word. There was nothing to say. It was a cliché, and I knew it was a cliché, but both Schechter and Schneur had paid the price of being combat soldiers at war.

CHAPTER FIFTEEN
Tragedy at Mount Ghebbio

That same week five of our men were killed in action and fifty-two were wounded. While this growing list of casualties saddened us, it also made us more determined to beat the Germans as quickly as possible. It was with these mixed feelings that we heard that Moshe Sharett, whom we had known as Shertock at Qena, the head of the Jewish Agency's Political Department, was coming to our base to present the brigade's official flag to Brigadier Benjamin.

"Does this mean we're going to have to attend another boring ceremony?" Yossi grumbled when I told him. "I wanted some time off to sleep and write a few letters home."

"You can forget that," I said, even though I sympathized with him. "We have to be ready in one hour in the large field behind the base. The whole thing: clean uniforms, polished boots, the lot."

"What? I won't be able to wear the shirt that I tore on the Nazi barbed wire fence?"

"Sorry, 'Mr. Hero' Yossi," I grinned as I left. "See you later."

One hour later, all the available men were assembled in a wide semicircle facing the central platform. Brigadier Benjamin stood there with a few of his senior officers, all in their best dress uniforms. Mr. Sharett, who had come all the way from Palestine, stood next to them just as he had done at Qena, looking somewhat out of place in his gray suit. Apparently he had been one of the most influential people who had pushed for the formation of an independent Jewish brigade within the British army. Now he wanted to see the result of his labors.

"He looks like a bank clerk," Yossi muttered to me.

"Shh!" I muttered back. "I want to hear what he's saying."

Speaking clearly in Hebrew, the "bank clerk" began. I was not expecting much of a speech apart from the usual clichés about Jewish soldiers defeating the Nazis, but when he began talking he seemed to be a different person. Gone was the picture of the bureaucrat. His voice rang out across the field so that each of the hundreds of men felt that he was talking to him personally.

"This is a great moment in the life of every single one of us," he began. "We have attained the privilege of hoisting the flag of the Jewish people in the front line of the battle for the liberation of Europe, in this world war against the oppressor of the Jewish people." He then spoke for a few more minutes about how essential it was to defeat the Nazis and to bring pride and honor to our nation. He finished his words with a rousing "Long live the standard of Israel's war on the battlefield!"

Yossi and I looked at each other. We were both impressed by this man. We were glad that we had cleaned ourselves up for this parade.

We were then ordered to stand at attention as he presented the brigade's flag to Brigadier Benjamin. Our commander then handed it over to Sergeant Major Spiegel to be unfurled. Spiegel hauled the flag to the top of the flagpole and then, as if on cue, a light breeze caught it and the blue and white flag flew bravely over the parade below. Despite my external cynicism, I felt very proud at that moment and was thinking about what this flag meant for me. My thoughts were interrupted when I felt a light tap on my shoulder.

"Why Spiegel?" someone whispered behind me.

"Because he's the oldest enlisted man here and because his whole family was wiped out by the Nazis," I whispered.

"How do you know?"

"I heard it yesterday. There's lots of news coming in like that. Now keep quiet and let me listen to what the chaplain is saying."

Chaplain Caspar then said a short prayer, and we all sang "Hatikvah." It was certainly an unforgettable moment to hear hundreds of men singing our national anthem with such fervor. And in the middle of a field in Italy! As I looked around I could feel a tear rolling down my cheek. Immediately I brushed it away but I could see other men doing the same.

As the dying strains of "Hatikvah" mingled with the noise of the distant German artillery in the hills to the north, we were dismissed. Some of us were also told to be ready to go out on patrol in an hour's time. Then, walking back to my room, I noticed a woman with a familiar mass of black curly hair among the hundreds of soldiers.

"Tamar!" I shouted. "Behind you!"

She looked around and we ran toward each other. "What are you doing here?" I asked as I hugged her tight. "I thought you were in Fiuggi or Ravenna or somewhere else."

"If you let me breathe, I'll tell you," she gasped. "I was in Ravenna but then I was asked to be a driver for some of the top brass who came here today."

"Hooray for the women drivers of the ATS!" I grinned and hugged and kissed her again.

As we pulled apart I noticed a few soldiers smiling and making remarks. "Ignore them," I said. "They're only jealous."

That night, between a quick meal in the mess hall and going out on patrol, we went for a walk and caught up with each other's news. I told her a little more about some of the missions I had taken part in, but left out the more gory details. She told me where she had been driving and how she had learned to deal with certain mechanical problems.

"So now I can change spark plugs and oil and air filters," she said proudly. "And yesterday I learned how to replace fan belts and how to check if the dynamo is working properly."

"That's great," I said. "So when I have my own garage in Tel Aviv after the war, you'll be my chief mechanic."

She looked at me strangely for a moment and then gave me a long kiss. It was the first time I had said anything about our being together after the war.

Between duties we managed to see each other a few times over the next three days. Sometimes Danny and Esty would join us and make up a foursome. However, the best time was when I took a lorry and we all drove into Brissighella to have coffee and pastries. Like tourists, we walked around the ancient town and made our way up to the ramparts of the castle. As we were standing up there admiring the view, Danny and Esty told us that they were planning to get married after the war. Tamar and I looked at each other and then said "*Mazal tov*" together.

On the following day, Tamar left, leaving me with mixed feelings. I was glad we had met up again and talked about our future. But I was also feeling rather low, as I did not know when and where we would see each other again. However, I was not allowed to feel this way for long. The following morning we were ordered to take part in a breakthrough as part of a major Allied campaign to push the Nazi forces back into Germany. The Jewish Infantry Brigade Group, as we were officially known, was to cross the River Senio and then occupy the strategically important Mount Ghebbio.

Before our ground attack started, a thousand American bombers flew over in ten waves and began pounding the enemy positions below. The noise was tremendous as the sound of the high explosive bombs rumbled and echoed around the hills and the River Senio valley.

"The recent bombing of Dresden must have sounded like this," remarked Danny as we crouched down, covering our ears in a trench.

"Well, I'm glad we're not on the German side," I replied. "It must be absolute hell over there."

Suddenly there was a weird silence as the bombers, having finished "softening up" the enemy lines, flew back to their bases. With a sigh of relief, Danny and I stood up, but then a few second later we threw ourselves down again into our trench. Our heavy artillery guns had started firing salvo after salvo in the direction of the German lines. Again our ears were assaulted by the sounds of high explosives and destruction. The shelling stopped as suddenly as it began, again leaving us in a strange silence. This was soon broken, though this time more gently by the chirping and twittering of the birds in the nearby woods. On the other side of the Senio tall columns of thick, dirty smoke could be seen rising from where the bombers and the artillery had left their black, scorched marks of destruction.

We knew that in a few moments we would be given the order to charge the German positions. Of course we all hoped that our forces had done a great job blasting the enemy's defenses to smithereens, and that our charge would be a cakewalk.

I looked down the line. Danny was a few yards away to my right, and beyond him I could see Yossi, Baruch, David Goldsmith and Heinrich Grunwald. They too were all separated from each other by a few yards and they all looked keyed up and ready to go. Danny returned my quick smile and thumbs-up and then immediately turned to face the enemy lines again. This was the moment we had been waiting for: to smash the German lines once and for all. To make them retreat into Germany and to bring about the end of this terrible war. Crouching on full alert, it was unnerving to wait there in the trenches. And for a moment, images of the Great War with its soldiers lined up to go "over the top" flashed through my mind.

Suddenly the order "Forward!" was shouted and we all climbed up out of our trenches. Gripping our rifles and screaming, we ran across the bridges the engineers had laid across the Senio. I expected to be hit by a German bullet at any moment, but, keeping my head down and looking ahead, I kept on charging with the others.

Out of the corner of my eye I saw one of our men stumble and fall as he dropped his rifle and rolled over on the wet grass. Nobody else stopped and we continued to charge up the north bank toward the enemy pillboxes.

I saw a few muzzle flashes as the Germans fired back at us but nothing else seemed to be happening on their side. I could not see or hear any enemy shelling and wondered when it would start. Had our "softening up" been so successful? For men defending such an important position, their resistance to our attack seemed to be very feeble.

CHAPTER FIFTEEN: TRAGEDY AT MOUNT GHEBBIO

By the time I realized why, I had already reached the pillboxes on the hill. They were now silent. A few enemy soldiers were sprawled inside, dead, the results of our earlier hand grenade assault. Outside, some of our men were taking the remaining enemy soldiers prisoner.

"Where are they all?" I called out, looking at a half dozen shellshocked Germans in their dirty uniforms.

"That's all there is," Yossi shouted back. "Looks like most of them got away yesterday and this lot were supposed to hold us off."

"Well, thank goodness they did a lousy job," I said. "And now we've crossed the Senio. It's in our hands now."

Yossi smiled and then looked serious. "I know, but it cost us a couple of men. I saw Baruch's friend, Avi, go down and I think Yigal got hit as well."

Later as names were called out we heard that Avi had been killed but Yigal had suffered only a flesh wound in the shoulder. We had gotten off lightly and we were all thankful for that. But however pleased we were feeling, we knew that this was just the opening stage of the attack. We still had to continue pushing the enemy further back. We still had to capture Mount Ghebbio, a steep green hill that commanded a wide view over the surrounding countryside. Taking this position would allow the American Fifth and the British Eighth armies to continue chasing the Germans back to Bologna and even further north.

We dug into our new positions. Fortunately the weather was fine so we had no problems sleeping outside in our two-man tents. The problems we did have were that the tents were really too cramped to hold us along with all our gear and our rifles. Although we heard the occasional crack of a rifle or burst of machine-gun fire in the distance, nothing disturbed our stay as final plans were laid for the attack, led by Major Kahan, on Mount Ghebbio. We were up and ready early the next day.

As with the other attacks I had taken part in, my nerves were taut, and when someone accidentally fired a single shot into the air, I jumped and spilled my mug of coffee over the table. And while we were approaching the hill, Baruch's tin mug fell out of his pack and hit the stony track with a metallic clang; I reacted with a sharp jump. The tension became even greater as we could see no sign of the enemy. Had they retreated? Were we walking into an ambush? Was I being picked out in the cross hairs of an enemy sniper's rifle? It was very unnerving. As I looked around, I could see that Danny, Yossi and the others were also looking around nervously – all expecting a sudden hail of shells and bullets to explode all around us.

We marched on. Our heavy army boots made crunching noises on the stones below. At a given signal we left the track and started climbing the lower slopes of Mount Ghebbio, and a tense quiet surrounded us. We moved up in a box formation. At the head was the commander of one platoon and several officers, and following them were two other platoons, each led by its own officers. By now I was feeling really jumpy because we knew that the Germans had buried anti-personnel mines all around the area. A dead cow to our right, its bloody guts spilling out staining the green grass red, showed what lethal damage these simple wooden box mines could do.

Perhaps to relieve my nerves, I turned round and shouted, "Mines!" to Danny, who was about thirty yards behind me. He returned my thumbs-up but suddenly there was a roar and a blinding flash and I was thrown to the ground by a hot, stinging blast. I was lying there trying to recover my breath when I heard someone cry, "Oh, no, not Danny!" and I turned around to see that Danny's body and uniform were a mess of blood and khaki. He had stepped on a mine and was now lying there on the bloody grass, his face pale gray and his eyes half-closed. He was moaning something in English and Hebrew but I could not make out what he was trying to say. Suddenly his body jerked and he tried to sit up. He could not and he fell back and lay still. His eyes were shut and he was not moving; there were no signs of life.

"He's gone," Yossi choked.

"No, look. He's opened his eyes," I whispered. And it was true. Danny was looking around, but it was clear he could not focus on anything. A medic pushed his way through and took over from me to try to staunch the flow of blood, but it did not help. Danny's moaning stopped and his gasping for air grew weaker.

"Danny! Danny! Stay with it!" I cried. "Don't leave us now! Stay! Stay! Danny, open your eyes!"

He turned his head toward me, opened his eyes and tried to concentrate on my face. He half opened his mouth to say something, but the effort was too much. No words came out, just a bloody gurgle.

"Danny! Danny!" I pleaded. "Don't die on us now! Stay with us! Think of Esty! Come on, man, try. Try!"

He opened his eyes again and looked at me like a drunk trying to fix his sight on something. "My guts," he whispered. "Killing me. Benny, I want…" But clearly the effort was too much. His eyes rolled back and his head slumped to the right. His body jerked again and he was dead.

Some of the men took their final look at their fellow soldier and then rushed up the hill to catch up with the others. I stayed behind with Yossi, the medic and an officer. As the medic pulled a blanket over Danny's face, Yossi and I could do nothing but look at each other. We were helpless. We did not know what to say. What can you say when your best friend has been blown up? What can you say when the guy who has been your best buddy all through high school and the army – the guy you have been so close to for over ten years, from Tel Aviv to Egypt, North Africa and now Italy – is no more? Just a mangled wreck lying under a blanket one yard away from you.

Words cannot help. They are inadequate. There is nothing glorious in dying on a battlefield. The writers and filmmakers have got it all wrong. Death on a battlefield is dirty and brutal. It is also pointless. No one gained from Danny's death, but many people, including his family and friends, lost. I decided that the Nazis would not have an easier battle now that they had killed him, and I was sure that Yossi felt the same. The enemy would pay for this. Somewhere in the Bible it is written, "Vengeance is mine, saith the Lord." That may be so, but it would be Yossi's and mine too; we would avenge the death of our best friend.

And with such murderous thoughts in mind, Yossi and I stood up, took our last look at where Danny lay and ran up the hill to where the sounds of rifles, machine guns and hand grenades were growing louder and more urgent. Glancing behind me, I saw the officer and two medics carrying my best friend's bloody remains on a stretcher. I could not cry now, but knew I would do so later.

Looking out for where our platoons had gone ahead up the hill, Yossi and I climbed as fast as we could. We ran up to Captain Peltz and reported Danny's death. He wrote something down and then with a thin-lipped expression put his hand on my shoulder and swore the brigade would avenge his death. He then motioned us to fall in line and prepare for the final charge. We were only a few hundred yards below the hilltop where the enemy was concentrated.

Suddenly there was a lull in the firing. All the noise and shooting stopped as though someone had thrown a switch. Now I could hear the wind blowing through the long grass, and a few birds were chirping to my left. It was not fair. Here I was, on a hillside in Italy. The scenery was green, lush and beautiful, and all I wanted to do was to have revenge, to kill the enemy. And the more dead, the better.

As I crouched down with such black thoughts whirling through my brain, ready to charge, Captain Peltz yelled, "Forward!" Without thinking of the danger, I got up and, keeping in line with the rest of our men, charged up to the top of the hill yelling and shooting. The Germans started raining bullets and hand grenades down on us but I did not care. I was completely oblivious to it all. All I wanted to do was kill. My bayonet thrust forward and my finger on the trigger, I ran and screamed. I did not hear the bullets and explosions. All I wanted to do was avenge Danny's death. Nothing else mattered. Suddenly I saw an enemy sniper crouched on the roof of a low, smashed-up building higher up on the hill about to take aim at Yossi. Without thinking, I stopped for a second, took aim, fired and smiled. "Got 'im," I said to myself as I saw him fall, along with his helmet and rifle, off the roof, and roll over as he hit the muddy ground below.

We had now reached the area where most of the enemy's fire had been coming from. That did not bother us as we laid down such a heavy field of fire that it blasted anything we saw moving on their side. From the church and the cluster of buildings that made up their command post they tried to fire back, and even threw some grenades, but nothing could stop us. "Remember Danny!" I kept yelling as I fired and reloaded, fired and reloaded.

Then, over the sounds of bullets and explosives, I heard Major Kahan shouting for us to retreat. I did not want to go; I was intent on killing as many of the enemy as possible. Yossi grabbed me by the shoulder. "We've got to get out of here – pull back. We're going to blast them out of there. Rifles and grenades aren't enough."

"We're going to shell them?"

"Yes, now let's go."

Crouching down low, we ran back along the hilltop until we could take cover behind some trees. Just as we did so, we heard our forty-millimeter shells crashing into the German headquarters. Fragments of roof tiles, walls and military equipment went flying in all directions. I was so happy to see this that I forgot the orders to keep down and shouted, "And another shell for Danny!" It came, but it did not hit the German command post. It landed in the copse of trees behind me and the sharp metal shards split some of the trees wide open. I was flung to the ground as I felt the hot air of the blast and the earth and stones rain down over me. The noise stopped as quickly as it started. As I lay there wiping the dirt out of my eyes, I could smell cordite mixed with the sweet smell of the newly ruined trees. I crawled over to Yossi. He was not moving, but I could not see any blood. "Yossi! Yossi!" I said, fearing the worst.

"I'm OK," he replied groggily. "I'm OK. But I've got this terrible ringing noise in my ears."

Then as we lay there, we heard the signal to meet up with Major Kahan for the next stage. Keeping out of rifle range of the now smoking command post, we made our way over to our commander.

"This is what we are going to do next," he said, holding a detailed map of the area. "I am going to divide you up into three separate assault groups. One will move in from here, from the right," he said, indicating on the map before pointing to a spot on the hill. "The second group will move in from the left, and the rest of you will charge in from the center. The third group will move in but only after the first two have secured their positions. Is that clear?" He again pointed to the different places on the hill and checked that we all understood our orders.

"Now remember, this is a dangerous movement and I don't want anyone to shoot any of our own men by mistake. Especially the first two groups, and also later when the third group moves in. You'll all be firing on top of one another, but just make sure you hit the enemy and not each other. Is that clear?"

I did not like this plan. I thought it was weak and that the enemy might have a chance of fighting us off and maybe make some sort of retreat over the other side of the hill. "Why can't all three groups attack at the same time? Surely we'll have a better chance of success if we all rush them together?" I asked. I saw two or three others nod their heads in agreement.

"You have a point there, Benny, but as you can see, our target is not very big. All of the enemy are in that central building over there. If too many of you rush in together, it is more likely that there'll be more of you shooting each other than the enemy. I prefer for us to take a bit longer and have more of you alive. OK?"

He looked around at our grim and grimy faces and continued. "I know you're all determined to finish off the job, especially after they killed Danny and Moshe, but we've got to do this carefully. I don't want any accidental deaths. So look and think before you fire. *B'hatzlachah*, good luck."

He divided us up into three groups; Yossi and I were in the central one, which would rush the enemy after the opening attack. We all moved stealthily into position and waited for the signal. It came, and the first two groups quickly rushed the shattered building, firing machine guns and throwing hand grenades. From where I was crouching down, I could see one of our men fly through the air as he stepped on a mine. But luckily for him, unlike Danny, he was not killed. He lay there, rolling on the grass, screaming and rolling about and clutching his bloody leg. The next thing I saw were two medics lifting him onto a stretcher and carrying him off to safety behind the trees.

Another signal and we charged at full speed toward the smoking remains of the enemy headquarters. Only a few bullets seemed to be fired at us and I could make out only a single muzzle flash or two. As we reached the almost silent building, I could see why. Almost all of the enemy soldiers were dead. The shelling had done its work – and how! A few soldiers in field gray had their arms high up as they surrendered, their faces showing shock and fear. Three of our men were herding them together as they staggered out of what had been their communications center. Smashed radios and transmitters lay everywhere. Useless lengths of wire dangled from the walls and shelves. Rifles and bullets were scattered haphazardly, and muddied documents all bearing German military insignia and swastikas littered the floor.

"Get over there, 'master race,'" Grunwald taunted the half dozen prisoners in German as he pushed them into the corner with his hands. One of them moved too slowly and Grunwald poked him in the back with his rifle butt. He was about to spit at the man when Yossi laid a restraining hand on his shoulder. "Later, Grunwald, later. You'll have time for revenge then."

"He's right," I added. "Just show him your shoulder flash and tell him they've been captured by Jews. That will hurt them more."

Grunwald stopped for a moment, thought and then thrust his brigade badge under the nose of the nearest German. Like Corporal Grossman, Grunwald was consumed with hate for the enemy. Before setting out on this assault he had told me that his parents, who had lived in Munich, had been sent to the nearby concentration camp at Dachau. He had not heard from them since the war had started.

We tied up our prisoners using some of the radio wires, and Grunwald said he would remain behind to stand guard over them. I was not sure this was a good idea, but just then we were told to come outside and comb the area for any enemy soldiers who may have escaped. As I was looking around I said to Yossi that I would not be surprised if Grunwald gave some of his prisoners a chance to escape.

"Why? He hates the Germans."

"I know, but then he'll have an excuse to shoot them."

"No chance of that," Yossi said. "They're in such a state of shock. They're probably too happy to know they're still alive to try something dumb like that. Look around, Benny. See how many we've killed."

We looked around and saw a couple of our sergeants ordering some of the prisoners to lift up the bodies of their dead comrades and lay them out in lines. They would be collected later for burial.

It had been a vicious and accurate shelling. Seeing all the bloody bodies there, my mind went back to my last sight of Danny. But before I could dwell on that, I heard some cheering and ran to where some of the men with field glasses were shouting and pointing toward the bottom of the hill.

"Look, look over there, Benny. Can you see? They're heading north." And through the field glasses I could see disorderly groups of field-gray lorries, halftracks and *Kübelwagen*s retreating, leaving large clouds of dust and smoke in their wake.

"We did it!" I yelled. "Danny! We did it! We crushed them! Mount Ghebbio is ours!"

It was true. We had beaten the enemy and we could see them making their way north toward Forli, Imola and Bologna. But we were not allowed to sit back and enjoy our victory. Thirty minutes later an order came through that we were to chase them and do all we could to prevent them from regrouping. All the Allies needed at this stage was for the enemy to mount a last-ditch firefight. Our victory had to be complete.

We continued harrying the Germans as they retreated northward for the next few days until we reached Bologna and the southern edge of the Po Valley. There, we were ordered to come to a halt.

"What's up?" Yossi asked when he heard the order. "What have we done wrong?"

"Nothing," I said. "Probably the opposite. We've done everything right. Maybe too right. Maybe the Brits don't want a Jewish rigade that is too successful."

"Why not?"

"They're probably scared that we might take revenge on the Nazis for what they've done to us," I said.

"You're right there," added Grunwald as he joined us. "I have a feeling that the fighting may be over for us as a brigade. Our success at Mount Ghebbio may have been recognized by the Brits, but we haven't finished with the Nazis yet. Oh, no. They've still got to pay for what they've done to our people. The day of reckoning isn't over yet."

"What do you mean?" I asked.

I had never seen anyone look so serious. "Some of us," Grunwald said very quietly, "some of us, including Corporal Grossman, have decided that the Germans are not going to get away with what they've done. Whether there's a ceasefire soon or not, those thugs are going to pay for it. Benny, you can be sure about that."

I looked at his intense face.

"If you're interested," he continued, "meet me by my lorry at seven o'clock this evening. If not, forget this conversation. It never took place."

PART TWO

REVENGE

CHAPTER SIXTEEN
Revenge Is Mine

Two weeks later, on May 2, 1945, the Germans surrendered in Italy. The war in Europe came to an end five days after that, when General Jodl and Admiral Freideburg signed the unconditional German surrender documents at General Eisenhower's headquarters. Although we were very happy to hear the war was ending, this period for the brigade was very difficult. It was a period when we were transformed from being an active combat unit to being one of the reserve units of the British Tenth Corps, and it was one of the most annoying times of my army career. All we could do was fume and kick our heels in frustration as we were shunted aside and watched the other units pushing ahead. We felt cheated. We had a good reputation and had done a good job and yet we were not allowed to play our part in the final defeat of the murderous Nazi occupation of Europe. Fifty-seven of our men had been killed in action and nearly three times that number had been seriously wounded. Now with the end in sight, the British were insulting us by being patronizingly kind and considerate. Their attitude could be compared to a parent dealing with an impatient child. "Don't you worry. You did a great job and soon you'll be needed again. So sit tight for the moment and be patient."

None of this helped our morale. What did help, at least for my own personal morale, was the meeting I had with Grunwald that evening near Bologna. As arranged, we met by his lorry at seven o'clock, and when I got there, I found Yossi waiting there as well.

"What's with all the secrecy?" I asked. "I didn't know you were also in this."

He shrugged. "Let's just see what Grunwald wants. He's been acting a little strangely recently. I wonder what – Ah, here he is."

Grunwald appeared from behind another lorry and seemed to be acting very oddly. He kept looking around furtively like a hunted animal.

"Are you sure you weren't followed?" he asked us. "Are you sure no one saw you come here?"

"Sure, sure. Who wants to follow me? Come on, man, what's all this secrecy about?"

He did not answer, but signaled for Yossi and me to follow him into a shady corner at the far end of the perimeter fence. There he eased up and looked us straight in the eyes.

"Benny, Yossi, what I'm going to tell you now is top secret. You must promise me you won't repeat a word of it to anyone. Not to anyone. Do you promise?"

Yossi and I looked at each other for a moment, shrugged and nodded. "OK, Grunwald. Spill the beans," I said. "We promise we won't tell anyone. But make it quick. I'm on guard duty soon."

"OK, then, this is the story. Several men in the brigade have organized some revenge squads – special squads to kill off any Nazis we find in this area. Between here and the Austrian border."

I looked at him. His eyes were sharp and shining. His thin lips were pressed together tightly.

"Then this is true," I said. "It's not just one of those rumors you hear floating around here every day."

"Yes, Benny. It's true. It's very true. These squads are highly organized and they've already killed quite a few Nazi high-ups in this area."

Yossi and I looked at each other. We were not completely convinced. Was this story true or was it merely Grunwald's wishful thinking?

"Are you sure about this?" Yossi asked. "It's not just stories?"

"Yossi, believe me, what I'm telling you is very true. There are several squads doing this now and each one is independent of the other."

"That doesn't sound very efficient," I said. "Maybe two squads are planning to kill the same person."

"Yes," added Yossi. "And if you're all in independent groups, then you can't share information with each other."

Grunwald shrugged. "Maybe you two are right. But this way if one group is caught by the Brits or anyone else, then they can't squeal on the other ones. That is more important than sharing information or anything else. It's been decided that this is the safest way to run this thing."

"But isn't there some sort of guiding hand at the top, like an officer or maybe someone from the Jewish Agency?"

"Yes, Benny, there is. But I'll only tell you more if you swear that you'll never tell a soul. Nobody. And that goes for you too, Yossi."

I immediately had a flashback of Danny. My best friend sprawled on the ground, his body bloody and broken.

"Grunwald, in memory of Danny Schwartz, I swear I will never tell another soul. And I'm sure Yossi will do the same, won't you?"

Yossi nodded quickly in agreement.

"Then let's all shake on it," Grunwald said. In what I thought was a bit of a melodramatic gesture he took our hands and we all shook on an oath of silence.

"So this is what's happening," Grunwald explained. "We are organizing a new squad that will go out at night and do what I've just been telling you about."

"Who's 'we'?" I asked.

"Me and the other men. Especially those who speak German."

"But who's organizing this thing? Who's at the top?"

Suddenly a twig snapped somewhere and Grunwald jumped like a startled cat. "It's all right," I said. "It was probably a fox or something. There," I pointed. "I was right. It was a fox. You can see it running away."

Grunwald calmed down. "There are several men and officers running this thing. First, there's Second Lieutenant Meir Zorea who organizes the actual killings. Sergeant Carmi is responsible for intelligence, and Haim Laskov is in charge of the logistics and planning."

Yossi and I looked impressed. These men were known as professional soldiers who carried out their duties very seriously. Too seriously, some said.

"And does this revenge squad have a name?" I asked.

"Yes it does. It's called DIN."

"Din? Noise? That's a strange name. I thought you'd have wanted to bump these Nazis off as quietly as possible."

"No, not 'din' in English, the acronym DIN, in Hebrew," Grunwald explained. "*Dalet, yud, nun.*"

"What do those letters stand for?" Yossi asked.

"*Dam Yisrael nokem.*"

"The blood of Israel will have revenge," I translated.

Grunwald nodded. "That's right, and of course *din* is also Hebrew for – "

"Judgment," I said, completing the explanation.

Grunwald nodded again.

"And is this the only organization carrying out these, er, exploits?" I asked.

"No, Benny. There are others. One is called the *Nokmim*, the Avengers, and I've heard of others who don't call themselves anything. There are revenge squads all over the place: here in Italy, in other places in Europe and also in Russia and the Ukraine. But whoever they are and wherever they are, they've all got the same aim."

"To kill off as many Nazis as possible before they can escape," I said.

"Right," Grunwald said. "We know we don't have too much time on our hands so it must be done as quickly as possible. We have to exploit the chaotic situation that's going on around here. You know what I'm talking about: roads crowded with refugees and DPs wanting to return home and all sorts of people looking for their families. As you know, it's a mess out there and that will work in our favor."

"So what do we do now?" I asked. Now that I knew about this squad I was impatient to join. I could see Yossi was as well.

Grunwald looked at his watch. "Meet me back here tomorrow night at the same time. And remember, not a word – not even half a word – to anyone. Understood? Now you two go and I'll follow you in a few minutes. We don't all want to be seen together."

"Grunwald," I said. "Aren't you exaggerating the cloak-and-dagger bit a little?"

"No, Benny. I know the Brits and the Americans have heard something about what we're doing, so we must be as careful as possible. Believe me. I know what I'm saying and I'm deadly serious."

I was sure he was.

"And besides," he added as we turned to leave. "Let's be honest. I'm not known around here as one of the most forgiving types, am I?"

And with that remark in our ears, Yossi and I made our way back to the base to get ready for guard duty.

Twenty-four hours later we met up with Grunwald again. This time he was not alone. Haim Laskov was with him. We recognized the tousle-haired officer immediately. He was well known, especially as he had been a member of the Haganah paramilitary organization as well as Captain Wingate's Special Night Squads.

He began by asking us a few questions about our backgrounds: where we had served, what action we had seen and who our friends were. After we told him, he said that our answers matched what he had read about us in our files.

"OK," he said at last. "You seem *kosher* enough to me. I'll report back to a couple of the others and I want you to report to me in my office tomorrow evening at six o'clock. And remember – "

"Yes, we know," I said. "Not a word to anyone." I was impatient to get started.

He half smiled. "That's right. Now you two get back to what you were doing and I'll see you tomorrow. *Shalom.*"

If I had been nervous after the first meeting with Grunwald, I was even more so now. The time could not pass quickly enough. You can be sure that when it was six o'clock Yossi and I were waiting there outside Laskov's office. It looked like any other army office. Notices were tacked onto various boards everywhere; stacks of papers covered the central table next to an old black typewriter, and a pile of beige army files lay on top of a khaki metal filing cabinet. A helmet and a belt full of pouches were hanging behind the door. The only personal items, a few photographs of what I assumed were family and friends, were pinned on a small board behind the desk. A corporal came out and asked us who we were waiting for. When we said we had a meeting with Laskov, he told us to wait outside until he came.

I asked, "How long will that be?"

The corporal shrugged and went back to filing various papers and documents, but we did not have to wait long for Laskov to appear. Without a word, he motioned for us to enter.

"Brandt," he said to the corporal. "Drop what you're doing and disappear for half an hour. I have to talk to these two about a private matter. Be back here at seven."

As soon as Brandt left, Laskov turned to us. He went straight to the point.

"I take it that Grunwald told you something about what we are doing here?"

"Yes, but not much," I said guardedly.

"Good. He wasn't supposed to. Now this is the situation – which, of course, is top secret. Is that fully understood?"

We nodded. Despite having spent several years in the army, I felt like a schoolboy standing in the principal's office.

"Most nights we go out in small groups to where we know a Nazi officer or two are hiding. We then make them disappear. Forever. It is as simple as that."

"Excuse me, sir," I began.

"Benny, you can drop the 'sir' while we're on this business. Now what's your question?"

"How do you know where these Nazis are hiding?"

"Our intelligence boys have found out from other Nazis."

"But why should they tell you? You're the enemy."

"Because they think that if they snitch on their fellow officers, it will save their own miserable lives."

"And does it?" Yossi asked.

"No, not usually. We have handed one or two over to the intelligence boys, but not many. Usually we get rid of those we catch and that's it," he said, rubbing his hands.

"Doesn't anybody, say wives and family, ask questions if a certain officer goes missing for more than a day or so?" I asked. It all sounded too simple to me.

"Not so far. They're all so busy trying to save their own skins that they don't want to make any fuss. Remember, it's not a good thing to be associated with the Nazis these days. Besides," he added, "during this chaotic period, who cares what's happened to Captain Schmidt, or whoever, if he goes missing?"

"And what do you do with the bodies, sir?" I asked, forgetting his words about not having to say "sir."

"You'll find out soon enough," Laskov replied. "Now are you two on any kind of duty tomorrow night?"

"No," we replied.

"Good. Then report back here at nine o'clock sharp and make sure you're wearing jackets that don't have brigade flashes on them. Just bring yourselves, your rifles and fifty rounds of ammo. And no papers either."

CHAPTER SIXTEEN: REVENGE IS MINE

I was about to ask if we should at least bring our driving licenses but Laskov continued. "We'll give you any papers you'll need. Now, do either of you have a pistol or revolver?"

"Yes," I said. "I've got a Luger. I took it off a dead German when we were at Tobruk."

"And I got one as a souvenir from Mount Ghebbio," Yossi added.

"Good. Then bring them with you tomorrow and make sure you've got extra ammo for them as well. Any more questions? No? Good. Now remember…"

"Not a word to anyone," we said.

Laskov smiled and we all shook hands and left just as Brandt returned.

I did not sleep well that night. All I could dream about was dead Nazis in gray uniforms rolling on the ground as I kept shooting them and they begged for mercy. Was this really me? I know I had killed some enemy soldiers before, but that was in battle. What we were being asked to do now was to kill the enemy in cold blood. Once they were in our hands they would not stand a chance. Could I do this? This was a new side to my life. Would I be able to tell anyone about it in the future? Would I be able to tell Tamar? No wonder I tossed and turned all night.

As soon as the morning parade was over I took Yossi aside. "Come over to my lorry now. There's something I have to tell you."

We started off to where the Bedfords and Dodges were parked and someone asked us where we were going. I muttered something about having to replace a worn fan belt and check out a faulty dynamo.

"Do you need any help? I've got a couple of spare dynamos in the back of my vehicle."

"No, thanks," I said. "We'll be OK. Thanks for the offer, though." And we walked off as quickly as possible.

"Listen, Yossi," I began as soon as we were out of sight. "I didn't sleep much last night. All I could do was think about that revenge squad thing."

"Me, too. I was wondering all night if we had the right to take the law into our own hands like that. I mean, do we have the right to bump these Nazis off without giving them a fair trial?"

"Exactly," I continued. "Just because we've won, does this mean we can now do with them what we want? I know Grunwald and Corporal Grossman are burning to take revenge because of what the Nazis did to their families, and maybe they do have some sort of justification, but what about you and me? Our families spent the war in Palestine; the Nazis didn't get there and none of our families or friends back home suffered directly from Nazi persecution. So what I'm saying is, in a way we don't have any personal reasons to kill them in cold blood, but I must confess I am also thinking that it *was* the Germans who killed Danny…"

Yossi hesitated for a second and then said, "You're right, Benny, and I've been thinking more or less along the same lines. But there's something very important you haven't mentioned."

"What's that?"

"We're not just British soldiers. We're also Jewish ones in our own Jewish brigade. Now knowing what we do about the Nazis and what they've done – and I'm sure there's lots more that we don't know – doesn't that give us the right to take revenge, first as Jews and then as soldiers? Remember, Benny, if what we've heard is right, the Nazis have murdered thousands of our people, if not millions. Doesn't *that* justify killing the Nazis that DIN finds?"

I was silent. I had to think this one out.

"But aren't we going down to their level – the Nazi level?" I asked after a while. "Killing people we hate. And not for personal reasons either, but just because of who they are and what they stand for? They killed us because we were Jews, and now we are being asked to kill them just because they're Nazis. Isn't that the same thing?"

Yossi was silent. He stood there, leaning on the door of his lorry, looking at the ground as if the answer were buried there. He was measuring and balancing what I had just said. At last he lifted his head and looked straight at me.

"Benny, you're right. We are going down to their level in a way and we are carrying out the biblical idea of 'an eye for an eye.' But, my friend," he said slowly, "one word has given us the right to join Laskov's revenge squad and kill these Nazis."

"Which word is that?"

"Scale."

"Scale? What scale?"

"The scale of what the Nazis have done to us. Even if only half the stories we've heard are true, and I'm sure many of them are, then that means that since Hitler came to power in '33, he and his Nazis have killed hundreds of thousands of our people. That, the sheer *scale* of this murderous regime, gives us the right to take revenge."

What Yossi was saying made sense to me. I was just about to say something when he continued.

"Just think about this, Benny. Everywhere we've been since we arrived here in Italy, and even when we were in North Africa, all we've heard about is Nazis killing Jews and other terrible stories. Why are all the Jewish civilians we meet refugees and DPs? No one voluntarily leaves their homes and their loved ones for no reason. All these people knew what would happen to them if they stayed behind. Am I right?"

Of course he was right. He had cleared the murky clouds in my brain. From now on I would have no more pangs of conscience when it came to killing Nazis. The opposite was now true.

"But, Yossi," I said, "let's say we kill only a hundred or so Nazis and SS men – what difference will that make? There will still be hundreds if not thousands of them out there still running around scot-free."

Yossi shrugged his shoulders. "I've also thought about that, but you know, we can't right all the wrongs in the world. We can only try to do our part."

I agreed with him and then added, "At least we know that some of the Jews fought back. I mean, we did our part at Mount Ghebbio and at La Giorgetta, right?"

"Yes, Benny, and some of the partisan stories we've been hearing about, like the Warsaw Ghetto and what happened in the Ukraine, show that we did put up some resistance. The trouble is that we weren't able to do more."

"And so," I said, "there's also a question of national pride involved."

"Of course there is. Isn't that one of the reasons you and I joined the army? To show the Brits we Jews could fight as well?"

"That's right, Yossi. That and revenge. And now the time has come for revenge. We can't let them get away with what they've done. As Laskov said last night, it's as simple as that."

The next night, dressed as ordinary British soldiers with no insignia, Yossi and I made our way over to Laskov's office.

Israel Carmi and Meir Zorea were also sitting there. Laskov introduced us to them and it was clear that military rank was not important here. Only the job that we were going to do mattered. We all had a mission to carry out and that mission's importance overruled any other consideration. Besides, we all knew who Laskov, Carmi and Zorea were. We did not have to be reminded.

Laskov sat down behind his desk and told Grunwald to pull down the blinds. He then told us to pull up a chair and Carmi locked the door. Laskov then rolled up a large map of Italy on the wall to show a similar one underneath. This one had black circles marked on it. I noticed that they stretched from Bologna and the southern side of the Po Valley up to Pontebba, Tarvisio and the Italian-Austrian border to the north.

"These circles," he said, pointing to several of them, "are where we know certain middle rank and high-up Nazis are hiding – those with ranks such as SS *Obersturmbannführer*, SS *Sturmbannführer* and SS *Hauptsturmführer*, that is, lieutenant colonel, major and captain. But whatever their ranks, we know that they have been responsible for killing, torturing and sending many of our people to death camps. For that, they must pay."

There was something about this that I had to know. "Excuse me," I asked, "but how reliable is your information about these men? After all, we don't have any spies in the German army."

Carmi looked at me. "You're right, Benny. We don't have any spies in their accursed army, but we have collected many reports together from all sorts of DPs and refugees and we have built up a solid bank of information about these particular Nazis. I can assure you we are as knowledgeable about them as we will ever be. Does that satisfy you?"

It did.

The next half hour was spent poring over maps, checking weapons and papers and other important final details. We were divided into three groups. Yossi, Grunwald and I were separated, as we would be doing all the driving. After locking away any incriminating DIN documents and lists, we went outside to the jeeps we would be using. They were marked with British military police insignia, as were our helmets and our red and black MP armbands.

Meir Zorea, who was in charge of this operation, looked around from where he was standing next to the lead jeep.

"Everyone ready? Benny will be my driver. The rest of you will follow. Yossi will take the second jeep, and Grunwald, you'll follow him. OK? So let's go."

He climbed into the seat next to me, I let out the clutch and we were off. After Zorea had snapped a smart salute to the sentry at the gate, the gate was opened and we headed north over the flat plain. The sky was cloudy and every so often the full moon would poke through, lighting up the nighttime scenery. Zorea gave me directions quietly, and apart from asking me a few quick questions about my family and where I had served in the army, we did not talk. I guessed we were all thinking of our mission. I was aware of my pistol pressing into my hip, a strange feeling since I did not wear it often.

We drove in silence for an hour, and every so often I looked behind me to see whether the others were with us. Most of the time we drove along quiet country roads. Sometimes Allied military convoys passed us coming from the opposite direction, while at other times we overtook long convoys carrying men and supplies on their way to the northern front.

As we continued, I started to get used to driving a light jeep instead of a heavy Dodge or Bedford. Suddenly a soldier loomed up out of the darkness on the road in front of us. He indicated that we should stop. I looked at Zorea and he said we should. No point in arousing any suspicion. Standing by the side of the road was a British army staff car. The soldier who had flagged us down was the driver to the colonel sitting in the back. They were lost and wanted to know the way to Verona. Zorea whispered to me, "Do you know?"

"More or less."

"Then you tell him. I don't want him to hear my accent. And be quick about it."

I walked over to the driver, who told me he was new and had never driven around these parts before. I gave him the necessary directions as quickly as I could and just as I turned to get into my jeep he asked me which unit I was in.

Without thinking I said, "The 178th. I have to go, we're late." I ran back to the jeep and took off immediately. I saw Zorea smile. He had heard everything.

"Good work," he said. "I hope that's the only problem we have tonight."

After that we continued driving for another half hour. As we passed a sign saying "Venice," Zorea tapped me on the arm. "Slow down here and turn right, and drive along this track for about ten minutes. Turn off your lights and take it carefully. When you come to a fork, take the left track and then I'll give you more directions. Now keep your eyes open as there are potholes everywhere. Let's go."

We continued along the shady track through the trees in tense silence for ten minutes. Following Zorea's instructions, I took the left fork and stopped.

"You see that light ahead of us?"

"Yes, but it's not very bright."

"Doesn't matter. That's where two SS captains and a major are hiding."

"The ones that ran the camp you told us about?"

"Yes. Now drive up to where those trees are on the right and wait there while we bring them out. Keep the engine running and be ready to drive off immediately."

I drove up quietly to the trees and I could hardly hear the other two jeeps as a light wind rustled the branches around us. I presumed Yossi and Grunwald had been given the same instructions, as I saw them waiting in their jeeps. Zorea and the others got out and, taking their rifles, walked over to the small farmhouse. Through the windows I could just about make out two or three men. It looked as though they were playing cards. A few wisps of smoke were coming out of the chimney. I turned to Yossi and Grunwald and gave them a thumbs-up, which they returned. Then I heard footsteps on the muddy path by the farmhouse and I saw our men walking toward us with four Nazi officers. With their hands tied behind their backs, they were pushed into the backs of the jeeps and Zorea, who was smiling, told me to start driving.

"We were lucky," he said. "Our information was wrong. Instead of getting three of them, we got four."

"Where are we taking them?"

"You'll see where soon. Now stay on this track for another five minutes but be careful. There's a reservoir at the end of it."

CHAPTER SIXTEEN: REVENGE IS MINE

We drove on in silence. I could hear one of the Germans making strange muffled sounds behind me. It sounded like he was trying to call out for help. But it was no use. One of our men had stuffed a rag into his mouth and gagged him afterwards. Zorea turned around and hit him on the arm and the German was silent. Within a few minutes we arrived at the water's edge and I stopped. The moon was shining on the reservoir and apart from the small waves on its surface everything was very calm. Zorea got out of the jeep and ordered the now silent officer to do the same. Trying to use his arms tied behind his back he did so with difficulty. No one helped him. Two of our men pushed him toward a large tree and everyone stopped there. I got out of the jeep and joined the others. I could see the German's eyes were wet and shining with fear.

"Do you speak English?" Carmi asked him.

The SS major nodded his head up and down and gave a muffled reply.

"Benny, take that gag off him."

"Now, you swine, you make one sound and I'll shoot you. Understand?"

"*Ja, ja.*"

"Do you know who we are?"

"*Ja*, British soldiers."

"Wrong. *Wir sind Juden.* We are Jewish soldiers. We are Jews that you swine didn't kill. But now we are going to shoot you for what you did to our people. Understand?"

The major began to cry out and Carmi slapped him and he fell silent.

"Tell me, are you a Christian and do you know your New Testament?"

"*Ja, ja.*"

"Then you should know that in the Book of Romans it says, 'Revenge is mine, saith the Lord.' That is not quite right. Revenge is *ours*, and we Jews will pay you back for what you have done."

Carmi stepped aside and Zorea moved in and faced the shaking German. He took out his pistol, the major's eyes following every movement he made.

"In the name of the Jewish people, in the name of the thousands you Nazis have killed, you have been condemned to die. The Jews will have their revenge."

Just as he finished saying this, a single shot echoed among the trees, and some birds flew off, squawking. The German lay on the ground, writhed for a few moments and was still. I looked at the other three. They had witnessed it all. That was part of the plan. Zorea rolled the dead officer out of the way with his boot and Laskov pushed the second SS major forward. He tried to resist but a blow to the back put a stop to that. As before, Zorea asked him if he spoke English. He moved his head from side to side and Zorea asked Grunwald to step forward.

"Grunwald, take off his gag and ask him about the ten men on this list. Are these their real names and are they hiding in the places next to their names? Tell him that if he helps us, we may let him live."

Grunwald yanked the gag off the major's face. He interrogated him for a few minutes and scribbled down a few more details on the list, which he then handed over to Laskov.

"*Vielen Dank*, thank you very much," Zorea said sarcastically. "But as you Nazis used to say, you cannot trust the Jews. You are right. In the name of the Jews who suffered at your hands, you are going to die." And once again he shot him with a single bullet. The Nazi fell and landed on the ground next to the first one.

Carmi pushed the third German into position by the tree and as he stood there we suddenly smelled something.

"What's that smell?" Yossi asked.

"He's wet himself. Look." And we could see a large stain spreading all over the front of the captain's trousers. He was shaking uncontrollably and two of us tied him to the tree. This time Carmi told him he was to die and he shot him just as he finished the sentence. Carmi also shot the last officer. He had tried to be brave, but as he was dragged to the tree, he broke down. As we tied him to the tree, we could hear him whimpering through his gag like a little kitten.

Then we all went back to the jeeps and took out some small sacks of rocks. We tied these to the dead men's belts and stuffed a few more rocks into their pockets. A few minutes later, four splashes and some ripples on the otherwise calm surface of the reservoir signaled their watery funeral. We waited for a few minutes to see that there were no more bubbles and then we walked back to the waiting jeeps.

Before leaving, we picked up the four bullet casings and ropes, and apart from our tire tracks and footprints, there was no evidence of our visit. As we drove back through the forest I thought that I was glad I had not been asked to pull the trigger. However, I knew that if I had been asked, I would have done so. We drove back in silence. Everyone was sunk in his own thoughts. It was only when we were a few minutes from the base that Carmi and Zorea started talking about everyday matters such as supplies and timetables, as if nothing special had happened an hour earlier.

After parking my jeep and removing the MP insignia I walked back to Zorea's office. Carmi was standing outside on his own. I went up to him and asked him was there anything special that drove him to do what he did.

"It's like this, Benny. Like you, I wasn't sure all these stories about the Nazis were really true. As you know, in wartime you hear all sorts of propaganda that tends to exaggerate the bad things that you hear about your enemy. Well, recently, Captain Peltz and I, for our own personal reasons, went to a concentration camp in Austria. That was very soon after it had been liberated by the Americans. It was far worse than we had ever imagined. The people who were there, the lucky ones, the survivors, were like walking sticks. No flesh on them at all. And their eyes, Benny. Their eyes told everything. The beatings, the suffering, the hunger – no, the starvation. Everything.

"And then they saw our gold *Magen David* badges on our uniforms and they just couldn't believe it. "Are you Jews? Are you really Jews?" they kept asking. And they kept touching us to see whether we were real or not. And you know what? When Peltz and I walked out of that camp later in the day we couldn't help crying. The whole thing had been so moving that we knew we had to do something to try to set things right. Those responsible for the suffering we saw would have to pay. And that's my answer to you. I know we won't get them all, but we must do something to regain our national pride. That and revenge. Very human, very simple."

I shook hands with him and saw his eyes were wet at the memory of what he had just described. "Good night," he said quietly, "and I hope you'll join us again."

I said I would.

CHAPTER SEVENTEEN
Further Acts of Revenge

Despite what I had seen and done the previous night, I was able to carry out my regular duties without any problems. I even managed to snatch an hour's sleep in the afternoon. Later I spoke to Yossi and told him that I had been affected less by the previous night's events than I had expected. "Thinking about avenging Danny's death kept me focused," I added. "I didn't join this squad for nothing. I did it especially for him."

"I know how you feel, because I feel the same way," Yossi nodded.

That night we set out again with the same teams, Yossi, Grunwald and me driving as before. This time I was less tense, as I had some idea of what was going to happen.

We drove to a small house in a village north of Bologna. The village consisted of a few houses near a crossroads. There was also a café and a small church. We pulled up in the small cobbled square in front of the café. Several groups of people were sitting around drinking and gossiping. Apart from a few casual glances, nobody paid us any attention. I guessed that by now they were used to seeing British and American army vehicles driving around at all times of the day and night. Zorea told the others to wait in the jeeps while he took Caspi, Laskov, Grunwald and me to a tall, narrow building about fifty yards off the square. We split up into two groups. Laskov and Carmi went around the back and I stood by the front door with Grunwald and Zorea. Grunwald knocked on the door and a pretty little girl of about eight years opened it.

She was wearing a flowered nightdress and holding a stuffed toy puppy in her hands.

"Does Captain Runstedt live here?" Grunwald asked pleasantly in German.

"*Ja*," the girl answered. "I'll call him." And she disappeared into the house as Zorea and I kept our hands ready on our hidden pistols. We heard the little girl inside the house tell her papa that there was a nice man at the door who wanted to talk to him.

"Did he say who he was?"

"No, papa, but he had a funny smile."

"Hooray for childhood innocence," Grunwald whispered to me.

A few seconds later, the SS captain appeared at the door. As soon as he saw us and our MP insignia, his face dropped and he tried to move back into the house. He couldn't. I was standing behind him and I had quietly closed the door.

"M-M-Maybe you've got the wrong house?" he stammered.

"Captain Runstedt? Captain Erich Runstedt?" Grunwald asked.

"*Ja, ja. Ich –*"

"Then come with us. Now."

"But I must tell my wife first."

"No need. You'll be back soon." And before he could protest any more, Grunwald and I gagged him and signaled for Yossi to bring his jeep over to us. As we were expecting a struggle we quickly bound his arms and bundled him into the back of the jeep. As soon as he was in, we drove off, and fifteen minutes later we stopped in a wood by the side of a canal. We all got out. Grunwald and Corporal Grossman removed the German's gag, but only after warning him that if he cried out, we would shoot him on the spot.

In addition to Grunwald and Grossmann asking him questions about other Nazi officers in the area, they also asked him to confirm some of the details on the list they showed him. When the captain faltered, Grunwald tapped him with his rifle butt, which caused the captain to cooperate. Then Zorea gave Grunwald another list.

"Ask him about the names and details on this one."

Grunwald did, and after each question Captain Runstedt nodded his head and said, "*Ja, ja,*" as Grunwald pointed out the names. Only at the bottom of the list did he say, "*Nein,*" and shake his head.

"It's a good thing he said that," Zorea said to me in Hebrew. "We put that name on the list just to see if he was telling the truth. That last guy doesn't really exist. We just made up his name and rank."

Then Zorea took over.

"Do you speak any English?"

"*Ja, ja.* A little. *Ein bisschen etwas.*"

"Good. Then listen to me carefully. We know you are an SS officer and that you were personally responsible for the deaths of hundreds of Jews in Italy and – "

"*Nein, nein,*" he replied, suddenly shaking. "I was just filling in *Papiere*, papers. I was in the *Büro*, the office with the *Dokumente*, the documents. Those men on your lists killed all the – "

Zorea stopped his protests with a slap and he was silent.

"Now listen, you scum. You have been found guilty by the Jewish people for your murderous crimes and you are going to pay for them. Do you understand?"

Captain Runstedt stopped shaking. It was as though had suddenly realized what was about to happen. The only thing he could do was protest his innocence. He opened his mouth to do so but Zorea rammed a piece of rag into it. The German tried to cough it out but Carmi had tied another rag around his head. Runstedt's eyes moved wildly from side to side as if he were expecting some help. None came. We were the only people there. Zorea moved in and stood opposite his prisoner, who had started shaking again.

"Now know this. In a few seconds you are going to die for what you have done to my people, the Jewish people. Our only regret is that we cannot have revenge on all of you."

Runstedt still kept looking around wildly as Zorea told Grunwald to tell the German why he was about to die. "I'm not sure he fully understands what is happening here. Tell him in German. No man deserves to die without knowing why. Even this swine."

In a calm tone, Grunwald told Runstedt, and it was clear that he enjoyed doing so. He finished translating Zorea's words and then suddenly hit Runstedt in the face with his rifle butt. "And that was for what you did to my family," he added. He was about to hit him again, but Laskov and Carmi held him back. "Enough, Grunwald. This man is dead anyway," Carmi said. "It's just a pity that his death won't bring any of our people back to life."

By now Runstedt was a shaking wreck with a bloody face. Zorea gave a quick nod to Grunwald, who stepped in and faced our prisoner. One shot to the head, and the SS captain collapsed like a sack of potatoes. He lay there, face down, in a muddy puddle. He did not move or even twitch. He was dead by the time he hit the ground.

Seeing him lying there made me think of Danny for a second, but then I brushed this thought out of my mind. Danny was a proud Jewish fighter. This man was one of the worst scum on earth.

We quickly weighted the dead Nazi's body with rocks and pushed it over into the canal. It sank immediately and the bubbles stopped after a couple of minutes. We got back into our jeeps and headed back to the base. Another small act of revenge had been carried out. DIN had struck again.

Over the next three weeks I joined another half dozen such missions. Sometimes Zorea, Caspi and Laskov came with us, and sometimes only two of them did. But whoever came, each mission followed the same pattern: driving to where the holed-up Nazis were hiding or trying to lead a normal life, showing them our false British Military Police documents, taking them to a deserted spot in a forest or farm building for a quick interrogation, telling them who we were and then obtaining more information or confirming what we already knew. After that we would tell them that they had been condemned to death by the Jewish people, and then shoot them before dumping the body into a reservoir, lake or canal.

Once, when there was no water nearby, we threw the body into the corner of a disused farm building and covered it up with several layers of bricks and rubble. On almost all of these occasions either Grunwald or Grossman was detailed to shoot the condemned men.

Then one night, Yossi and I were told to carry out the shooting. To my surprise, it was easier than I had thought. I did not hesitate, even when the SS major's gag slipped and he started pleading for his life. I had learned that Major Baumann had been responsible for the deaths of over eight hundred Jews near the Italian-Austrian border. Many of them had been women and small children at the labor camp where he had worked.

As usual, the whole operation went like clockwork, and we found the wanted SS men exactly where we were told they would be hiding. The information that DIN received from the refugees we were helping and from our victims' final words was always thoroughly checked before we shot our SS captives. We did not want to be responsible for the deaths of innocent people.

As time passed, our lists of future targets grew. Each one was told that if he could supply us with more names, or confirm the details that we had on their fellow SS officers, then perhaps we would let them go. Of course, this would have been out of the question. We knew that if we let them go, they would have found some way of warning their comrades. There was also the risk that they might inform the British army authorities about our activities. And so, for our revenge squad to succeed in its self-imposed task, we did our best to leave no evidence behind. We left no bodies by the roadside as examples, and we provided no printed explanations of any sort. We kept no records of who took part or whom we killed. Nothing. The only documents we used were the false ones recording the use of His Majesty's Army's jeeps.

The only time we thought we were about to be found out was late one cloudy night while we were on our last operation. Driving near Pordenone, we were signaled to halt by a fat-bellied MP sergeant.

"Show me your papers," he said, leaning into the jeep, "and please step outside."

Managing to look both unconcerned and impatient, Zorea remained calm and did what he was told. The sergeant sent one of his men, a bored-looking corporal, to check that the number on the jeep matched the one on the travel pass. It did.

"Right, Captain Zorea, why are you going to Udine at this time of night?"

Playing his part well, Zorea looked around and beckoned the sergeant to come over to him, away from the corporal. "Ssh, don't speak too loudly, sergeant, but we've just received some information that there's a top Nazi hiding out there. So let us get on our way before he escapes. I wouldn't like to tell my superiors that our plan was ruined because of you, now would I?"

"No, sir, certainly not, sir. But just tell me, how come you have a foreign accent," he said, returning Zorea's travel pass. "You don't sound very British, sir, if you don't mind my saying so."

"I was born in Romania and escaped and joined the army to fight the Nazis. So lift your barrier and let us go."

"Yes, sir. Just doing my duty, sir. You know, there's all sorts of funny characters running around these days: smugglers, refugees and even people out to get revenge on the Germans, sir, in the middle of the night." He then called to one of his men to lift the barrier and waved us on. As he did so, he saluted and said, "I hope you get him, sir," and we were off.

The following day, after morning parade, I looked for Yossi and found him sitting on the running board of his lorry, cleaning his rifle.

"Yossi," I said, as I pulled up a toolbox and sat down. "I'm beginning to have problems with this revenge squad thing."

"Why? Because you shot that lieutenant the other night? Remember, Benny, we had solid proof that he was directly responsible for killing hundreds of Jews, and most of them were women and children."

"No, no. It's not that. He deserved to die. I have no pangs of conscience about that. It's just a question of the efficiency of what we've been doing that's bothering me."

"What do you mean?"

"Well, according to my figures, our squad has shot between fifty and ninety men, about half of whom were killed before we joined."

Yossi leaned forward. He was listening carefully to what I had to say.

"My problem is that this is only a drop in the ocean. For the Nazis to have carried out their program, they must have had thousands of people helping them. Germans, Austrians, French, Hungarians, everybody. Haven't you heard the stories that all the refugees have told us? And see how quickly it's taken us to build up our lists. Every time we've told a Nazi officer to give us names, they've been able to give us tens of names without any problems. I'm telling you, Yossi, there must be hundreds if not thousands of Nazis out there. What we're doing is just the tip of the iceberg."

Yossi sat there, still. He had stopped poking a piece of flannel down the barrel of his rifle.

"You're right," he said, looking up. "But what can we, I mean the Jews who've survived, do about it? We can't do any more, can we? We can't kill *all* the Nazis, because we don't know who they all are. And I'm sure many have escaped and are now claiming they were innocent civilians or that they were just simple soldiers, you know, privates and corporals just carrying out orders."

There was a lot of truth in what he was saying. He continued.

"For example, what about that weedy-looking officer I shot last week? If you'd seen him in civilian clothes, you wouldn't have guessed that he was responsible for killing two hundred Jews and for sending another three hundred to death camps in Poland, would you? I mean, what did he look like? An old retired schoolteacher or bank clerk. And anyway, Benny, I gather that some of our people have been talking about some more efficient ways of carrying out revenge."

"Like what?"

"While we were waiting in the jeeps last week, someone told me that some of the top brass in one of the revenge squads were cooking up a plan – yes, cooking is a good word – to bake poisoned bread and have it sent to the prison camps where the Americans are holding hundreds of captured Nazi and SS men."

"Like that big camp at Nuremberg?"

"Yes. And I heard about another plan to poison the drinking water of certain German towns. That would certainly kill thousands of people before it was discovered and stopped."

"But Yossi, are these just ideas or are they going to be carried out?"

He shrugged. "I don't know. All I know is that a guy called Abba Kovner, who is or was an important partisan leader in Vilna, Lithuania, was involved in these plans. I believe the poisoned bread idea, for which they used cyanide, was actually carried out already, and a lot of SS men died as a result of it."

"Well, I'm not happy with what *we're* doing. Not because of the shooting, but because thousands of Nazis have literally gotten away with murder. It's not fair. Where is the justice of it all? Thousands of our people have been killed by these thugs, and they're escaping any form of punishment. And on top of that, here we are, stuck up in the north of Italy and not allowed to do anything about it – officially, that is. I'm telling you, Yossi, I'm really sick of the whole situation."

"Well, don't worry, Benny," he said, laying a friendly hand on my shoulder. "There's another, more positive side to this coin."

"What's that?"

"More and more of us in the brigade are now helping with the refugees. You know, collecting and distributing food and clothing and making sure that they have some sort of shelter."

"But that's not new, Yossi. We've been doing that ever since we arrived in Italy."

"I know, but now that the Germans have been forced out of Italy, this helping the refugee business has been stepped up. And there's more to it than just giving them food and clothing. We're also using our lorries to transport these refugees to the ports."

"To ship them over to Palestine? Yes, I've also heard about that. It's a great idea, but it's crazy, too. Shipping them to Palestine right under the noses of the Brits."

"So listen, Benny. If you're interested, come with me tonight after the parade and I'll take you to someone who's really involved in this thing and knows a lot more about it than I do. And apart from anything else, it should give you more satisfaction than just brooding over the impossibility of killing off thousands of Nazis."

"I'll think about it. And now, Yossi, you can go back to cleaning your rifle."

PART THREE

HOPE

CHAPTER EIGHTEEN
From Tarvisio to Belgium

That night we were informed that the brigade was being transferred from our base in the Po Valley to Tarvisio, a small town near where the Italian, Austrian and Yugoslav borders met. We would spend the next two days packing up all our personal and brigade equipment, loading it into the lorries and then driving 150 miles north. The first part of the journey would cross the flat Po Valley; the second would include driving through the mountain ranges in the north of Italy. During this period of feverish activity, I took time out to write a letter to Tamar telling her about the move, and that I missed her a lot and hoped to see her somehow, somewhere soon. I was thinking about scribbling a few lines about DIN in a vague sort of way, but then I decided against it. Military censorship was still in operation and anyway, I would tell her when we next met up – wherever and whenever that would be.

The next morning when I walked up to my overloaded lorry, a surprise greeted me. Large white slogans were chalked on the sides: *Kein Reich, Kein Volk, Kein Führer* – which meant, "No Reich, No German People, No Hitler." When I looked at Yossi's lorry I read, *Die Juden kommen!* The Jews are coming! Some of the more artistically minded men had added swastikas painted over by the brigade badges and *Magen David*s, while Yossi's lorry had a picture of a large boot with a blue star on it kicking a broken swastika. In addition, most of the lorries, including mine, had a large blue and white flag attached to the front fender.

The war may have been over, but now we were going to drive through Austria. We would show the Nazis there that despite the murders and the massacres that they had carried out, we Jews were still around and a force to be reckoned with.

We made good speed, and Baruch, sitting next to me, compared this journey with the one pushing Rommel's Afrika Corps westward along the North African coastal road. We agreed that a lot had happened since then: the Nazis had been crushed; the Jewish Brigade had come into existence; we had taken an active part in the fighting and Danny and a few other friends had been killed in action. Then, as we were comparing our British Bedfords with the American Dodges, our convoy came to an unexpected halt. "What's up?" I asked. "Can you see ahead? We've been making good time so far."

"I can't see anything from here. I'll go and have a look."

Five minutes later he was back, grinning from ear to ear. "It seems there was a convoy of German prisoners coming toward us and some of our men saw red."

"So what happened?"

"They forced the convoy to stop and then started pelting the Germans with anything that came to hand: cans of food, tools, bits of wood, everything. Then the British officers in charge tried to stop our men."

"And?"

"They started quoting the Geneva Convention rules about how to treat prisoners, but our men weren't having any of it."

"I bet they weren't. By the way," I asked. "Were Grunwald and Grossman involved?"

"Involved? They were leading it."

Just then I heard the engines start and soon we were moving again.

"Baruch, how did that incident up ahead end?" I asked, as I changed gears.

"Our officers stood in a line between the two convoys and in that way they protected the Germans."

"I hope they didn't do that too quickly."

Baruch grinned. "Don't worry. They took their time."

Just as he was saying this, the first lorries carrying the German prisoners passed us on the other side of the road, and I could see that many of the Germans were trying to clean up their bloody wounds; none of them were talking or smiling. I smiled at the irony of the situation. To have been a German soldier, attacked and injured by a Jewish soldier! It was too much. And to have been hurt by a flying can of beans or bully beef. So much for the thousand-year *Reich* that Hitler had promised the German nation. Thinking about the Nazis being pelted by cans of food, I wished that DIN could have killed off more of them, especially the SS officers – the worst of them all.

We had an overnight stop at Udine and early the following morning set out for Tarvisio to the north. Some fifteen miles outside Udine, Baruch pointed at the jagged gray Julian Alps that stretched threateningly ahead of us.

"You see those mountains over there? Well, that's the border between Italy and Austria. You'll have to be very careful driving over there. I've heard the roads are twisting and narrow, and there are some really frightening hairpin turns. They say that in the winter it's almost impossible to drive around there."

"Don't worry, Baruch. It's May now, so sit back and enjoy the view. And anyway, I like driving in tough conditions. It's a challenge. You remember some of those roads we used to drive through in Egypt and North Africa? Weren't they a challenge?"

But Baruch was right. The road did become more treacherous as we drove north, but the magnificent scenery made it worth it. The high, rocky mountains with their snow-covered peaks – even in May – contrasted with the dark green forests and lighter green pasture land below. From time to time we could see a few people, but most of the movement came from the innumerable small rivers and streams rushing down from the heights and flowing out to the Po Valley we had left behind.

We had a short stop in Pontebba and then turned east and drove the last twelve miles to Tarvisio. If I had thought the scenery was impressive down below, up here in the Alps it was truly inspiring. More than once I found myself almost driving off the road as I could not help but look at the breathtaking mountains instead of concentrating on my driving!

We arrived at Tarvisio in the afternoon. This border town dates back to Roman times, and since then has exploited its position as a local route center in the Alps. I was not really interested in the town's distant past, but more in its recent history. Tarvisio had been one of the enemy's centers in northern Italy and as we drove into the town's square I noticed an anti-Semitic Nazi poster showing a hunchbacked, unshaven Jew next to a picture of Uncle Sam. I was tempted to rip it off the wall but I had more important things to do. I hoped that we would be able to rid the town of this foul propaganda as soon as possible.

"How long are we staying here?" Baruch asked me that night.

"Not long, I hope. I'm looking forward to driving into Germany with our "*Die Juden kommen*" signs on our lorries. That'll show them who won in the end."

But it was not to be. It seems that a report of the pelting of the enemy prisoners had reached some of the high-ups, and an official recommendation was issued saying that "in view of the many and complex problems that have arisen in connection with this occupation we do NOT consider it advisable to add to them by employing the Jewish Brigade Group there in the initial stages."

This meant that we would be staying in Tarvisio until further notice. When I heard this I was very disappointed. We were told to guard the hospital, although no one told us from what, and we were also told to guard the ammunitions dump the Germans had built as part of their last-ditch defense system.

One evening, as I was sitting in the mess complaining about our situation to Yossi and Baruch, a smiling Gabi Ben-Zvi came over to join us.

"What are you so happy about?" I asked.

"You know the hospital we're guarding, the one that was used for wounded German soldiers? Well, I've heard we're going to take over all the supplies, which we will then be able to use for any Jewish DPs who arrive in Tarvisio."

"But who's going to come here?" Yossi asked. "It's miles away from anywhere. That's probably why the Brits sent us here in the first place."

"No, Yossi. You're wrong," I said. "I can see what Gabi is saying. Tarvisio is at the junction of the Italian, Austrian and Yugoslav borders. Many of our people who want to head south will have to come this way and I'm beginning to wonder if it wasn't a blessing in disguise that we were sent here in the first place."

I was right. A few days later a group of Jewish DPs from Yugoslavia arrived and we were able to give them food, medicine and clothing. All of this was supplied by the defeated German army's convalescent center.

This was the good side to the story, but there was also a very bad side: we were hearing more and more terrible reports of what these refugees had suffered. I noticed that as we learned more and more details, Captain Peltz became increasingly angry. He decided to exploit his officer's rank and the general chaotic situation, and see what was happening firsthand. Taking a jeep, he went first to the Nazi camp at Mauthausen and then continued to where his family had lived in Zabiec, Poland.

Soon after he arrived there, he learned that the Nazis had wiped out his entire family. His father had been sent to Auschwitz and his mother had died in the Treblinka death camp. He heard that his grandfather had succeeded in escaping to the surrounding forest but a local Pole had betrayed him to the Germans, who had then shot him. Peltz now knew there was no reason to stay in Zabiec any longer. He took the brass door handle from the smashed-in remains of his family's house as a keepsake, and returned to our base.

In the meantime, news of the brigade's presence in Tarvisio was spreading. Soon after we arrived, four gaunt, hungry-looking Jewish youths walked into the base. As if by instinct, they immediately headed for the kitchen, where they were given a good meal. It was only afterwards that they told us their story and what was happening in Poland now that the war was over.

"There are about fifty thousand Jews still there," said Motke, the oldest of the four. "Many of them are still living in the groups that they organized as partisans, but now they want to leave and go to Palestine. The trouble is, they don't know how to get there."

"So why did you come here?" I asked.

"We'd heard stories about you and wanted to see if they were true. Believe me, I am so happy to see that you really do exist and are not just a rumor."

"That's right," added curly-haired Yankel. "Now we can go back and tell all the others. No Jew wants to stay in Poland one day longer than necessary."

"Why not?" Yossi asked. "The Allies have promised to help all the refugees return to their own country of origin. That sounds like the natural solution to this refugee problem, doesn't it?"

"No, Mister British Jewish soldier. That is *not* the answer," Motke said. "That idea may be good for the other refugees, but not for the Jews."

"Why not?"

"Because there are many Poles who want to finish off the job that Hitler started. And besides, there's been more than one very unpleasant incident when a Jewish family that survived the camps returned to their own house, and when they got there, they found that the people who were now living in it refused to give it back."

"Yes," Yankel added. "And some of our people were beaten up and even killed over things like that. So you see, it's no wonder we want to leave Poland. The place is a death trap for Jews, whatever the Allies may say about returning refugees."

"And how did you get here, to Tarvisio?" I asked.

"Once we decided to leave Poland, we chose to avoid the big towns and cities and travel only on the side roads. Sometimes we were lucky and got lifts with trucks and farm carts, and at other times we walked. All in all, it took us three weeks to get here."

"What did you do for food and shelter?"

The youngest-looking one, who had been sitting there silently, suddenly joined in. "We stole what we needed to eat from fields and markets. I was the best at stealing food in the markets because I was the smallest and the quickest. I never got caught," he added proudly. "And as for shelter, sometimes we slept out in the open and sometimes we slept in barns and abandoned buildings. That was never really a problem."

"And what about crossing borders?" I asked. "Didn't you need any passports?"

Now it was Motke's turn to grin. "Over there," he said, pointing in the direction of Austria, "there is such chaos on the roads. There, and in Poland, there are thousands and thousands of refugees on the move, and not just us Jews. Everyone – Poles, Jews, Czechs, Slavs, Hungarians, Germans – *everyone* is on the move. There is such pushing and confusion at the borders that it's really very easy to slip across."

"Yes, especially at night, like we did."

Yankel took over. "And then a few days ago, after we got to Klagenfurt in Austria, we saw a truck with a *Magen David* painted on it. At first we were too scared to ask, but then we heard the soldiers next to it talking in Yiddish. Do you know what that means? To hear British soldiers talking Yiddish? That was a fantastic moment! We went up to them and asked them who they were. They told us about the brigade, and here we are."

This was not the only group of Polish Jews who succeeded in finding us at Tarvisio. A few days later, three refugees were seen hanging around near the entrance to the base.

I was on guard duty at the time, thinking about when I would see Tamar again. Suddenly, these three, seeing the brigade shoulder flash on my uniform, ran up to me shouting, "*Shalom!*" Then one of them thrust a letter in my hand, which they insisted I read right then and there. At first I thought it might be in Polish, but then I realized that it was in English, and written on a piece of paper headed "MGO, GS Office, HQ 11th United States Armored Division, Ebensee, Salzburg, Austria." The letter was a request from the American camp commander asking that the Jewish Brigade accept 1,600 Jewish refugees who had refused to be sent back to Poland. He wrote that the Division was planning to close the camp and that he did not know what to do with these Jewish refugees, but he was prepared to transport them to Villach, an Austrian town just over the border.

I took the letter to Chaplain Caspar. He contacted a higher official, who refused to help out. Caspar then got in touch with the United Nations relief authorities, who agreed to accept the refugees. A few days later the 1,600 refugees were taken to two large camps south of Tarvisio.

The following day Chaplain Caspar came up to Yossi and me in the mess hall.

"You two are drivers, right?"

"Yes."

"Are you on duty now?"

"No, we're free until tomorrow."

"Good. So get ahold of another driver and three more men and meet me at the main gate with your lorries in half an hour. Make sure the backs of your lorries are clean and empty and that your tanks are full."

"Why? Where are we going?"

"To somewhere near Villach."

"But that's in Austria."

"I know, but I've been given special papers and permission to go there. I'll tell you more on the way."

As Yossi, Baruch and I made our way from Italy to Austria, crossing the border at the mountain pass near Unterthörl, Chaplain Caspar told me the reason for our journey.

"Early this morning, two British MPs turned up at the base asking if we could supply them with a good mechanic. They needed him to help them repair one of their vehicles. One of their lorries had broken down in Austria near where we're going now. Sergeant Major Sanitt and a corporal went with the MPs and began to work on the broken lorry. Suddenly there was a lot of shouting, and the MPs and our two men saw two soldiers in German uniforms approaching them. The MPs drew their revolvers ready to fire and then the two Germans started shouting, *Shalom! Shalom!*"

"You've got to be kidding!"

"I'm not, I assure you. Anyway, Sergeant Major Sanitt shouted '*Shalom*' back to them and told the MPs to put their guns away. The Germans were actually Jewish refugees in stolen German uniforms. It seems that they had seen the *Magen David* on our jeep and had rushed over to our men. They then told their story, in Yiddish, to the corporal and Sergeant Major Sanitt."

"It must have been some story," I said, as I negotiated a tight hairpin turn.

"It was, and a pretty grim one, too. Three weeks earlier, these two men had been prisoners in an SS camp just as the war was ending. Some of the guards had selected the healthiest men and women there, lined them up and shot them. Just like that."

"What for?"

"For no apparent reason. Just so that these people would not be able to enjoy any freedom, I think. The two men I'm talking about were then forced to dig a pit for the dead bodies, and then the SS men drove away, leaving the people there to fend for themselves. They left the camp gates open and the two men raided the stores and changed their prison camp rags for some German uniforms. Before leaving to find help, they made sure that they ripped all the Nazi insignia off them. Then they found our men repairing the MPs lorry and that's where we're going now."

"To the SS camp?"

"That's right. The MPs went back to the camp and saw the state of the people there, and as a result, we've been given permission to cross the border and bring the survivors back to Tarvisio."

A short time later, we reached the old mansion that had been the camp's central administration building, and there we were greeted by one of the strangest sights I would see during my time in the brigade. Sitting around in the courtyard and not doing anything special were a hundred thin, emaciated survivors, all wearing German army uniforms. Scattered around in the dust were the various badges and insignia the prisoners had ripped off their new clothes. We gave them the food and drink we had brought with us, and we also found some more supplies in the camp's stores. After that, we got the stronger ones to help us lift the weaker ones into the backs of our lorries and then we returned to our base at Tarvisio.

This was the largest group of Jews we had rescued so far and I felt very proud that I had taken part in this operation. Another result of this action – apart from having rescued these people – was that we had shown the British an example of how our people had suffered at the hands of the Nazis. Soon after this the MPs gave permission for Jewish refugees to cross the border from Austria into Italy without any problems.

From then on, what had begun as a trickle of refugees making their way to Tarvisio now became a flood. Jews began crossing the nearby border from Austria and Bavaria. It was from them that we began to learn firsthand about the scope and meaning of Hitler's "Final Solution to the Jewish Problem." Their stories of persecution, imprisonment, torture and murder were the terrible side of the coin; the good side was that we were saving these people and giving them hope and self-respect again. Many of their stories were truly shocking, complete with details of rapes and massacres, but some did have happy endings as people discovered that their friends and families had somehow survived. We even had a few family reunions that took place at our base, and when this happened, no one could remain dry-eyed.

I cannot say how many Jews we saved. Yossi said he heard it was somewhere between ten and twenty thousand. However impressive that number sounded, though, it was nothing in comparison to the millions the Nazis had killed. However, I was not given too much time to think these grim thoughts because soon after this, at the end of July 1945, the brigade was ordered to leave Tarvisio.

"Where now?" Yossi asked me.

"Belgium. I've heard that the Brits, that is, the high-ups in London, don't like us being here in Italy. They say we're too close to the Mediterranean ports."

"You mean, shipping our Jews on to Palestine?"

"That's right. The Brits don't want to make the Arabs angry by bringing in all these refugees."

"But we still have so much work to do here," Yossi said. "But I guess, if we can't help our people from here, then we'll have to do it in Belgium."

And that's what happened. At the end of July 1945, a convoy of six hundred vehicles left Tarvisio and started out on the long journey through Europe to Belgium.

Naturally, it was not easy for us to cross the Brenner Pass from Italy into Austria knowing that while we were looking at the wonderful scenery below, many of our people had been killed in this country. As the day wore on and we crossed from Austria into Germany in the direction of Munich, many of us became silent and thoughtful. This is where Hitler had started. This is where his terrible dreams had become a reality, and this is where our nightmare had begun. However, I was glad that now several thousand Jews were returning to a defeated Germany, Hitler and many of his supporters were dead and we had *"Die Juden kommen"* painted on the sides of our lorries.

Soon after we crossed the border we were ordered to halt and our officers reminded us how to behave. They wanted no further repetitions of the earlier can-pelting incidents.

The journey through Germany was some of the worst driving I had to do. This was not because of the poor roads – they were, in fact, in good condition. It was bad because of the looks we received from the local people as we drove by. They could not believe, after living through a dozen years of

Nazi propaganda, that Jewish soldiers were driving through their defeated country in a massive convoy. It simply did not make sense to them. Of course, the large signs saying "*Deutschland Kaput*" and "*Kein Führer*" painted on the sides of our lorries rubbed even more salt into their open wounds. Although we had been ordered to behave in a civilized and disciplined way, it was not unusual for some of our drivers to veer deliberately to the side of the road and, with their heavy iron fenders, smash a parked car or send a crowd of civilians scuttling for cover like frightened rats.

At night we slept in our vehicles or in the fields by the roadside. Some of our men would use this opportunity to sneak off into nearby villages and take out their revenge on the German people by setting fire to farm buildings and haystacks. In addition, some other Germans paid an even higher price when, on more than one occasion, Nazi prisoners of war were blown up while clearing minefields. During a break soon after we had driven west of Munich, Chaplain Caspar called me over. "You know, Benny, now that the war is over, the brigade's main aim is to rescue as many of our people as possible."

"I know that," I replied. "And then we have to try to ship them over to Palestine."

"Right. Now, I've obtained permission for you and a few others to leave the convoy for a while and take me over to a DP camp at Landsberg. It's only a few miles away and I have a report saying that there are four thousand Jews there. Now, what I want to do is to take over some basic supplies – food, clothes and medicine – and see for myself what the conditions of the camp are like. So if you are willing, we'll set out in half an hour."

It did not take us long to reach the camp and, to my surprise, when we arrived we were greeted by a huge crowd who had hung up a large "Welcome" sign above the main gate. Next to it a large blue and white flag was flying proudly in the wind.

"How did they know we were coming?" I asked the chaplain.

"One of my men first discovered this camp a few days ago and they've been waiting for us to return ever since."

It was hard for us to drive into the camp as hundreds of the DPs surrounded our convoy. It seemed that they all wanted to touch our vehicles and to make sure that we were real, and that they were not dreaming. Although, as a Jewish Brigade driver, I had driven through happy crowds of Jews before, this crowd was something special. They had survived the war. They had lived through the Holocaust, and for them to see Jewish drivers in lorries decorated with *Magen David* badges on the front mudguards was solid proof that the Nazi reign of terror was well and truly over.

"Look," they kept pointing at the *"Deutschland Kaput"* sign on the sides of my lorry. "We never thought we would live to see this day."

We spent two hours in the camp. The chaplain and his men checked out the camp's conditions and we, the drivers, distributed the supplies we had brought with us. Chaplain Caspar also made another list of supplies that would be needed for the future. Leaving the camp was just as hard, if not harder, than entering had been. The people surrounded us at the main gate; they did not want us to leave. Some of them shouted, "Take us with you! Take us to Palestine! Get us out of here!" Eventually we were able to get moving, and we returned to the main road knowing we had brought hope as well as much-needed supplies to the DPs there in Landsberg.

From the camp we continued driving north, and it was while we were approaching Cologne that Baruch, my co-driver, and I smelled a terrible stench.

"What's that smell?" he asked.

"Bergen-Belsen."

"The concentration camp? That's the most terrible smell I've ever smelled. I wish you could put your foot down on the gas and just get out of here."

"So do I."

Fortunately the winds were westerly so we did not have to suffer for long, but that did not stop Baruch and me from brooding over the fact that the Jews who had lived in the camp had had to suffer this terrible smell of death for years, while we were complaining about it after just a few minutes.

Soon after this our convoy turned west and we were very happy to read the border post signs near Aachen saying we were about to cross the border from Germany into Belgium. We continued driving westward into France and entered the country near Valenciennes. Here, as at Landsberg, the Jews of Valenciennes received us like conquering heroes and it took us two hours to thread our way through this old historic French town. We did not stay long in France and soon crossed the twisting border back into Belgium.

CHAPTER NINETEEN
Belgium, Tamar and Home

We stayed in Belgium for ten months, from August 1945 until June 1946. During this period I was involved in many of the brigade's activities, which ranged from transporting food and medicine to taking DPs to various European ports where they could be shipped to Palestine. This usually meant driving through Belgium, Holland and France to the ports of Antwerp, Rotterdam and Marseilles. Much of this driving was done in cooperation with the two Jewish DP organizations, *Brichah* (Flight) and *Reshet* (Network). I found that helping Jews escape Europe was an exciting and satisfying job even though it involved a lot of driving over all sorts of roads.

Usually these missions went pretty smoothly, as each country wanted to get rid of as many DPs as they could, as quickly as possible. However, sometimes overzealous or officious border guards would give us problems, especially when it came to having the correct travel passes.

One of the officers who often traveled with me was a cheery soul called Memie de Shalit. He was very good at charming the various border guards and officials, who would then let us continue on our way without any unnecessary interruptions.

"What did you say to that guard just now?" I asked him as he clambered back into the cab holding a handful of stamped documents. "He looked as though he was going to give us a lot of problems."

"Oh, nothing, really," he smiled. "I just told him we had a whole lot of German prisoners in the back and that we were returning them to Germany. He said, 'Good riddance to the lot of them,' and that was it."

"But didn't he want to see them?"

"Yes, but I told him that we had received orders to keep the back flaps tightly closed at all times. And you know what, orders are orders."

"And he, being an official, accepted that."

"Of course he did. But you know what? When he saw the *Magen David* on the front mudguard, he raised his eyebrows and grinned. I'm sure he knew we were transporting our DPs in the back."

Later I told Yossi about this de Shalit guy and he said he had used the same trick a week earlier. From then on, the pair of us decided to copy him, and this saved us a lot of problems at the borders.

While Yossi and I were at a Jewish DP camp in France, he told me that David Ben-Gurion, the head of the Jewish Agency, was going to talk to us that evening.

"What's he doing here?" I asked. "Shouldn't he be in Tel Aviv or Jerusalem?"

Yossi shrugged. "I guess he's come to see us like when Moshe Shertock came to see us in Egypt. You know, to boost morale. Anyway, I want to go hear him speak, and if you want to join me, be in the big hall at six o'clock tonight."

The big hall, usually used as a dining room, was packed. There was standing room only and, as I was late, I had to squeeze my way in and stand at the back next to Yossi and Baruch. I did not expect to hear much, but I was wrong. Ben-Gurion's voice penetrated through the excited buzz of sound in the hall and there was immediate silence after his first few words.

He did not speak for long and he also spoke using different languages, but this was his main message: "The Jewish people will have their national home. It will be a struggle. We will confront the enemy intent on destroying us. But we will win. Have no doubt about that. The Jewish flag will fly over the Land of Israel, and no one will stop this from happening."

That night I wrote to Tamar. I told her about my work and listening to Ben-Gurion, and I asked her if there was any way we could meet up. One week later I received a reply saying that she had volunteered to go to Brussels at the end of the month for a few days as an ATS driver, and asking if I would meet her by the Mannekin Pis statue by the Grand Place. Would I! What a question! I wrote back immediately, and ten days later we met at the foot of Belgium's most famous statue.

After kissing and hugging for a few minutes we walked hand in hand to a nearby café to sit and talk. Not having seen each other for many months, we had a lot of catching up to do. As we faced each other over coffee and cakes I saw that she was as pretty as ever, her eyes were shining and her black curly hair threatened to completely cover her ATS peaked hat.

This was the first time I had seen her since the brigade had left Italy, and now we were able to tell each other all our news without fear of the army censor's blue pencil. I told her some more details of how Danny had been killed and Tamar told me how Esty had been devastated when she had heard the news of her fiancé's death. I then told Tamar how the men and I had felt at the time and how I had taken part in various offensives around the River Senio. I hesitated before telling her about my activities with DIN. She said that she had heard rumors about the Jewish revenge squads but thought they were just that, rumors. Reaching over the table she took hold of both of my hands. "And did *you* shoot any of these SS men?"

"Yes, one of them."

After a long pause, she asked, "Was it hard?"

"No, not really," I said quietly. "I knew why I was doing it. I knew that the two men we confronted that night, a major and a captain, had been responsible for killing hundreds of Jews, mostly women and children, as well as sending many more people to Auschwitz. I felt that they had to pay for that. I felt it then and I feel it now. I shot one of them and I don't regret it at all."

"But, Benny, by shooting him, you couldn't bring these people back, could you?"

"I know that, and we all talked about this a lot at the time. But I felt I had to do something. And that was what I did."

We sat there quietly for a few minutes, each thinking of the past and what we had gone through, and then suddenly she perked up.

"Come," she said, smiling. "We didn't come here to be sad. I want to tell you my news. I'm being discharged soon and I'm going to live in Tel Aviv."

"Tel Aviv," I repeated, hardly believing my luck. I had already planned on persuading her to leave Egypt. "Why Tel Aviv? And when are you moving there?"

"In about two months. I've decided that when I get my discharge papers I'll move to Tel Aviv and not go back to Alexandria, to my horrible Uncle Obadiah."

"But that's great! And where will you live? Who do you know in Tel Aviv?"

"My aunt Hannah."

"Aunt Hannah? I've never heard you mention her before."

"That's because I didn't know much about her until six months ago. Then I learned she lives on Gordon Street and I got in touch with her. She's not my real aunt, but someone related to a cousin on my mother's side, and her husband died a couple of years ago."

"But Gordon Street! That's fantastic! It's only about ten minutes away from my house."

"Here, let me show you a photo of her. Maybe you know her. She sent it to me when I was at the ATS base in Rome." Tamar took out a photo showing a smiling, round-faced lady with twinkling eyes and curly hair.

"Just like yours," I said, running my fingers through her curls.

"Thanks," she said. "Except that her hair is gray. And yes, Esty wants to come with me, too. So I won't be lonely either, or at least until you come home. It will also be good for her. Naturally she's been feeling depressed since Danny was killed but she's slowly beginning to move on."

This was getting serious. This was talk about the two of us together after the war back in Tel Aviv. "Ah, that's right," I said. "You'll be my chief mechanic when I open my garage in Tel Aviv."

"Oh, no," she replied. "I've had enough of greasy hands and broken fingernails. I'd like to be a teacher or go and study languages at the university."

"But that's in Jerusalem," I said. "And I want to live in Tel Aviv. It's the most exciting city in Palestine, and on top of that, it's got the sea as well."

"Well, we don't have to decide now, do we? Besides, who said we'll be together then?"

"You're joking," I replied. "Of course we'll be together. Tamar, I want to marry you."

There, I'd blurted it out. No romance, no ring, no engagement party. Just the bare facts. Good old Benny, I thought to myself. You and your big mouth. You've just blown it.

Tamar suddenly got up, rushed around the table and threw her arms around me. "And I want to marry you." And she gave me a long kiss on the lips.

The rest of the afternoon passed in a dream. I don't remember much apart from walking around the Grand Place with our arms around each other. I seem to remember that at some point we stopped at a small café near the Palais de Justice for another round of coffee and cakes. I don't think either of us took much notice of the fine old buildings we passed, as we were so intent on discussing our future plans.

That evening I took her back to her base and then returned to mine. We promised to write to each other as much as possible, and Tamar would tell me when she got to Tel Aviv.

When I thought about that I became slightly jealous. Tamar would be a civilian again before me and then live in Tel Aviv, *my* town. But then again, when I got discharged I would have her there to go home to. No, life wasn't that bad after all. It was pretty good. And besides, I was enjoying myself as a soldier in the brigade.

So apart from having to put up with Yossi and Baruch mocking me for being "an old married man," the opening months of 1946 continued smoothly in routine fashion. I spent a lot of time driving, sometimes did guard duty and also played football or took part in interunit athletics competitions. I also wrote tons of letters to Tamar and she faithfully answered each and every one.

She told me how everything had gone according to plan: she and Esty had been discharged, collected all their back pay and were now settling down in her aunt's apartment. She wrote that she was trying to learn Hebrew, which wasn't too difficult as there were many words that were similar to spoken Arabic.

One day I was sitting on my bed reading her most recent letter when Yossi entered the room. He was grinning from ear to ear.

"What's up with you?" I asked, looking up. "Have you just heard that joke that's going around the base, the one about the sergeant and the broken lorry? Or have you been discharged?"

"I've heard the joke and I haven't been discharged – though there are rumors that the Brits want to disband the brigade in June."

"I know. I've heard them, too. There are always rumors in the army. But tell me, what's so funny?"

"Doubles. It's all about doubles."

"What's all about doubles?" I asked. "Have you been drinking a double whisky?"

"No, no. Listen. You know the Brits are against us shipping our DPs back home because of pressure from the Arabs? Well, it seems that there's talk of disbanding the brigade so that we won't have the means to help our Jewish DPs."

"That's not news. There's been talk of that for some time now."

"I know, but this time it's more serious. And as a result, some of our men have been looking for DPs who look like them and who speak some English, and they are teaching them to act as doubles for our own men."

"What for?"

"The idea is that when we're discharged, we'll send the doubles home and we'll stay here in Europe."

"To carry on the good work here?"

"That's right. Don't you see? It's a great plan. The DPs get to Palestine despite the British, and we stay here. And not only that, we'll now be here as civilians without having to worry about the army. This way, everyone's happy."

"Except the British."

"No, Benny, they'll be happy as well. There'll be no brigade and they won't know the difference anyway between the real brigade soldiers and their doubles."

"And are we all going to be included in this plan?"

"No, it's for about only a hundred to two hundred men."

"So that means that when it's my turn to be discharged and I want to go home, I'll be able to do so?"

"That's right. Why? Don't you want to take part in this double thing?"

"No, Yossi, I don't. I want to go home. I've been away for over five years now and the last time I saw my home was when we went back from Egypt for that big recruiting parade. Do you remember?"

"Of course I do. That was when Danny dropped his rifle in front of that fat sergeant major when we were on inspection parade."

We stopped for a minute and thought about Danny. Danny, my best friend – the friend who had gone through so much with me, first in school and then later in the army – Danny would never be going home again.

"Listen, Yossi," I finally said. "I want to go home. I've had enough of the army, and besides, I've got Tamar there now and my parents have written to say they'll help me start a garage in Tel Aviv. I'd be a fool to throw all that away now, wouldn't I?"

"You're right, Benny. If I were in your shoes I'd say the same thing. But if they offer me the chance to stay on, I'm going to take it."

The brigade did find a double for Yossi, as well as for over one hundred thirty other men. Our brigade officers took the doubles to a large house outside Ghent, an old medieval town northwest of Brussels, and there, as though they were preparing to be spies, the doubles learned all the details about the soldiers' families and girlfriends, how to behave like British soldiers and how to answer any questions about their newly forged identities and travel documents.

In the meantime, Yossi and the others were given new papers, and Yossi was even given a cross to wear instead of his *Magen David*. Baruch refused to wear one but was issued two photos of his new blonde girlfriend, each picture with "To Barry, with all my love, Christine" written on the back.

In the first week of June 1946, we all – both those who were to remain in Europe and those who were to go home – learned that the Jewish Brigade, which had become a thorn in the side of the British army, was to be disbanded. Most of the men and the doubles were to be shipped home to Palestine, or given rail passes to travel to wherever they wanted in Europe.

Since I had been one of the first to enlist, I was in the first batch of five hundred men to return to Palestine. This time I crossed Europe in a train and was put aboard a British army transport ship in Marseilles. As the ship pulled out of the bustling harbor I looked back, but only for a few moments. I was looking forward to going home – to being with my family and Tamar once again.

Now, as our ugly transport ship sailed into Haifa Bay and I could see some of the old ships that our DPs had arrived in earlier, I thought about having been away from home for over five years. I had left as an excited schoolboy on the threshold of an adventure and was now returning as a discharged soldier who had driven lorries all over Europe, Egypt, Libya and other parts of North Africa. I had seen some action at Tobruk and had fought in northern Italy. I had been on patrols and had killed enemy soldiers, but best of all, I had helped my fellow Jews in all sorts of ways and had given them hope for the future. Now, as my ship was being tied up at the quayside, I thought about my own future and the future of the country I had come home to. Would we ever have our own independent state? If so, when? Would the British acknowledge the help they had received from the Jewish Brigade and the other Jewish soldiers? And how would my new life be with Tamar? Only time would tell, but I was already impatient to learn the answers.

Afterword

Although the Jewish Brigade officially lasted for only two years, from 1944 to 1946, well over thirty thousand Palestinian Jews served as combat soldiers in the British army during the whole of the Second World War. This happened even before the 5,500-strong Jewish Brigade Group was formally established in September 1944. The Brigade consisted of a combination of various Palestine Regiments and others, and its dedicated fighters were later recognized as an important military force that fought the Nazis in northern Italy.

Apart from the brigade's major military role in fighting various *Wehrmacht* and SS units along the River Senio and other places, the brigade also had a civilian part to play, rescuing many thousands of concentration camp survivors and transporting them to Mandatory Palestine.

One of the most important long-term aspects of the brigade's history is that many of the future State of Israel's military and civilian leaders, as well as its writers, civil servants and businessmen, gained their first military and civilian organizational skills and experiences while fighting and working within this framework. Several of these men are listed below:

Yehuda Amichai (1924–2000) is often considered to be Israel's greatest modern poet. He was born in Germany and came to Palestine in 1935. He fought with the Jewish Brigade, and during Israel's War of Independence he took part in the fighting in the Negev Desert. He then went on to study Bible and Hebrew literature at the Hebrew University of Jerusalem, and had his first book of poetry published in 1955. This was followed by a novel in 1963. Amichai's writing was well received and he was awarded several prestigious literary prizes, including the Shlonsky and Bialik Prizes in Israel, as well as several literary prizes from France, the United States and Norway. He fought in the 1973 Yom Kippur War and later became a visiting professor at the University of California, Berkeley. Toward the end of his teaching career, he taught literature at the Hebrew University of Jerusalem.

Ted Arison (1924–1999) became one of Israel's most famous and successful businessmen. He was born in Romania, and after serving in the Jewish Brigade he went to Beirut, Lebanon, to study commerce at the American University. He moved to the United States in the early 1950s and made a fortune as the founder of Carnival Cruise Lines. He established the National Foundation for Advancement in the Arts in Miami, and brought professional basketball – the Miami Heat – to South Florida in 1988. He set up the Arison Foundation in Israel and the United States and later bought Bank Hapoalim, Israel's largest bank.

Hanoch Bartov (1926–) is a journalist and author and, unlike many of the people listed here, was born in Israel. He served three years with the British army and the Jewish Brigade in Palestine, Italy and the Netherlands. He became very involved in looking after concentration camp survivors at various European DP camps. After the war he studied Jewish and general history at the Hebrew University of Jerusalem and then fought in Israel's War of Independence. When the war ended in 1949, he moved to a kibbutz and became a farmer and a teacher. Later he worked at the Israeli embassy in London. After this, he recorded his wartime experiences in *The Brigade*, and he also wrote four other books. These earned him the Bialik, Agnon and Israel prizes for literature. In the 1998 documentary film *In Our Own Hands*, he said of his time in the Jewish Brigade, "We were neither saints nor knights. We were simple Israeli boys who understood that we stand for the Jewish people.... Soldiers are supposed to fight, kill or be killed. And what we did as soldiers, we found dead people [concentration camp survivors] and we helped them to go back to life."

Israel Carmi (1915–2008) was born in Poland and arrived in Israel in 1934. A year later he began a three-year period with the British Mandatory Police. He then transferred to Wingate's Special Night Squads (SNS), where he was promoted to become one of this unit's commanders. During this period he was also awarded a medal for bravery. He volunteered to serve in the British army (the Buffs) in 1940 and in 1943. Disguised as a German soldier in Egypt, he led a unit behind the enemy lines and "relieved" the Nazis of five tons of weapons and ammunition. These were later transferred to the Jewish Palestinian Haganah forces. In 1944 Carmi fought with the Jewish Brigade and played an active part in the revenge squads after having helped many concentration camp survivors move on to their new homeland in Palestine. He served in the newly created Israeli army as a commander in the south of the country in the War of Independence. A few years later he was promoted to command the Armored Corps training center. During the Suez Campaign of 1956, Carmi was second-in-command and served under Dado Elazar (later chief of staff of the Israeli army). From 1962 to 1971 he headed the military police, and in 1960 he wrote a book about his military career.

Dov Gruner (1912–1947) was born in Hungary and was the son of an army rabbi. He studied engineering and became a leader in a local youth group. He came to Palestine in 1940, was arrested for entering the country illegally and was imprisoned for six months. He was then released after going on a long hunger strike. He joined the British army in 1941 as a paratrooper and then fought with the Jewish Brigade until it was disbanded. He also worked with many concentration camp survivors and even donated his own clothes and shoes to help them. Back in Palestine he was severely wounded in an action fighting the British Mandatory authorities. Later he was caught and tried by the British for his subversive anti-British activities. He was condemned to death and was hanged in April 1947. Today, Gruner Square in Ramat Gan, Moshav Misgat Dov and many streets in Israel are named in his honor.

Haim Laskov (1919–1983), the fifth chief of staff of the Israeli army, was born in Barysaw, USSR (now Belarus), and moved to Palestine when he was six years old. His father was killed by Arab fighters in 1930. Later Laskov joined the Palestinian Jewish paramilitary Haganah and the Special Night Squads, and afterward used these experiences to become a Jewish Brigade commander during the Second World War. He took an active part in the revenge squads, and on his return to Palestine in 1946 he became the head of security of the country's electric company. In 1948 he was made responsible for training the Israeli army's new recruits, and even though he had never been a pilot, he was appointed the commander of the Israeli Air Force in 1953, a post he held until he went to the United States to study. He became the deputy chief of staff in 1955 and in January 1958 replaced Moshe Dayan as the next chief of staff. After leaving the army Laskov was appointed director-general of the Israeli Ports Authority and oversaw the building of Israel's new Ashdod seaport. He also served as the country's first military ombudsman, and in 1973 was appointed to serve on the controversial Agranat Commission, which investigated various problematic aspects of the Israeli army's actions during the Yom Kippur War.

Nataniel Lorch (1925–1997) was the son of a lawyer father and linguist mother. He came to Israel in 1935 and studied education, then joined the Haganah in 1941 and the Jewish Brigade in 1944. After the war he worked for military intelligence, and during the 1948–1949 War of Independence he was part of the forces that broke into the Old City of Jerusalem. In 1957 he was appointed the Israeli consul in Los Angeles and five years later became the Israeli ambassador in Peru and Bolivia. On his return to Israel he took up the position as the first secretary-general of the Knesset, the Israeli Parliament, and held this position for eleven years, until 1983. He also worked for the Truman Institute at the Hebrew University of Jerusalem, and wrote several books about Israel's military history as well as about various important debates in the Knesset. He was also the founder of the Israeli army's historical division.

Mordechai Makleff (1920–1978) became the Israeli army's third chief of staff in 1952. When he was only nine years old, his parents were killed by Arab marauders in their home in a small village near Jerusalem. Makleff managed to escape by jumping out of a second-story window and was later raised by other members of his family in Haifa and Jerusalem. He became chief of staff after having served in the Haganah and the Special Night Squads in Palestine before the war, and in the Jewish Brigade and the British army during the war, when he fought in North Africa and Italy. He finished the war with the rank of major and then helped to smuggle weapons into Palestine for the Haganah. He also was responsible for sending concentration camp survivors to Palestine to begin new lives there. Toward the end of his life he took on two important civilian positions: director-general of the Dead Sea Works and director-general of the Israeli Citrus Marketing Board. Today, one of the most important of the Israeli army's bases is named after him.

Shlomo Shamir (1915–2009) was born in Russia, arrived in Israel in 1925 and four years later joined the Haganah. In 1940 he passed the first course for civilian pilots and then joined the British army and the Jewish Brigade. Ben-Gurion appointed him responsible for all the Jewish soldiers in the British army. After the brigade was disbanded in 1946, Shamir was sent to the United States to represent the Israeli army there. He was recalled in 1948 and took an active part in the War of Independence, including raising the siege of Jerusalem. He was appointed commander of the navy and was then given a similar position a year later as commander of the air force. After leaving the military he was responsible for establishing the important Negev Phosphates company, a position he held for eleven years. He then moved on to manage Pazgas, Israel's largest gas company, and later headed the Civil Aviation Authority. Toward the end of his life he left Israel for the United States to study business management at Harvard.

Meir Zorea (1923–1995) was born in Romania, moved to Palestine in 1926 and joined the Haganah in 1939. He was awarded the Military Cross for bravery by the British, and he fought with the Jewish Brigade and was an active member of the revenge squads at the end of the war. Back in Palestine, he participated in the War of Independence, taking part in the battles around Jerusalem. After the war, he commanded the officers' school and was then appointed to command the armored corps. He left the army in 1962 and after spending some time working on a kibbutz, he became the army's ombudsman before being asked to manage the Israel Ports Authority. He was recalled to the army in 1967 and fought with distinction against the Egyptians in Sinai during the Six-Day War. He then worked for several commercial companies before Prime Minister Yitzhak Rabin appointed him as comptroller of the Israeli army. Zorea entered politics in 1976 and served in the Knesset for two years as a representative of the short-lived "Dash" party.

Acknowledgments

Although this book is a work of historical fiction, it is based on events that really happened in Palestine, Egypt, North Africa, Malta, Italy and Belgium during the Second World War. In addition to consulting the books and other sources listed below, I also talked to several past members of the Jewish Brigade whom I met in Jerusalem, as well as to several others at the opening of the new, impressive exhibition dedicated to this same brigade. This moving event took place in the summer of 2009 at Moshav Avihail, near Netanya, Israel. It was also during this period that I traveled to Italy to check out various facts and to see the area where the brigade had played their part in the final defeat of the Nazi army in Europe.

You can imagine how proud I felt. Standing there under that almost cloudless Italian sky in the calm atmosphere and under the shady trees in the British War Cemetery at Mezzano, just north of Ravenna, I thought of the brave deeds that the soldiers of the Jewish Brigade had carried out. The neat lines of over thirty white gravestones, these silent witnesses, all standing there like soldiers drawn up on parade. These memorial headstones, all carefully inscribed with the fallen soldiers' names and ranks, the *Magen David* and the military badges of the Palestine and Royal East Kent Regiments, were, and still are, a permanent and moving reminder to us of how we Jews fought the Nazis on the European battlefield and, despite great odds, took part in their final defeat.

Next to the main entrance to the cemetery, on an impressive commemorative plaque in English, Hebrew and Italian, and accompanied by the Jewish Brigade Group's regimental badge in blue, white and gold, is the following inscription:

> In this cemetery alongside many other soldiers repose thirty-three Jewish fighters who fell in the Battle of the Senio. They were soldiers of the Jewish Brigade – Palestine Regiment – a part of the thirty-five thousand Palestinian Jews who enlisted voluntarily in the British Armed Forces when scarcely half a million Jews lived in Palestine. The ardent desire of those volunteers was to take an active part in the fight against the Nazi enemy. Here in the Romagna their wish became true.

I would like to thank my Jerusalem friends Barry and Barbara Zinn, who let me use their flat in Pontebba, Italy, while I was carrying out my research in Italy and Austria. I would also like to thank Kezia Raffel Pride, Rebecca Maybaum and Smadar Belilty from Gefen Publishing for their continuous and cheerful help with the editing and production of this book. Finally I must thank two important ladies: my ever-patient editor, Marion Lupu, for making sense out of a sometimes confused manuscript, and also to my wife, Beverley Stock, who cheerfully shared our house with the Jewish Brigade for well over a year.

However, despite my careful reading of the books and other sources mentioned here, if any military or historical mistakes come to light, then I alone am responsible. I would be very pleased to hear from readers through my e-mail: dlwhy08@gmail.com or my website: www.dly-books.weebly.com.

D. Lawrence-Young
Jerusalem, Israel,
February 2011

Bibliography

Aron, Wellesley. *Wheels in the Storm*. Canberra, Australia: Roebuck, 1974.

Bauer, Yehuda. *Flight and Rescue: Brichah; The Organized Escape of Jewish Survivors of Eastern Europe, 1944-1948*. New York: Random House, 1970.

Beckman, Morris. *The Jewish Brigade: An Army with Two Masters 1944-45*. Staplehurst, UK: Spellmount, 1998.

Blum, Howard. *The Brigade*. London: Simon & Schuster, 2002.

Bradley, John. *The Illustrated History of the Third Reich*. New York: Exeter Books, 1984.

Brayley, Martin J. *The British Army, 1939-1945: Middle East and Mediterranean*. Oxford: Osprey Publishing, 2002.

Caspar, Bernard M. *With the Jewish Brigade*. London: Edward Goldstone, 1947.

Kimche, Jon and David Kimche. *The Secret Roads: The Illegal Migration of a People*. London: Secker & Warburg, 1955.

Linklater, Eric. *The Campaign in Italy, 1939-1945*. London: HMSO, 1959.

Naor, Mordechai, ed. *HaHaganah*. Tel Aviv: Ministry of Defense Publishing House, 1985.

Zuccotti, Susan. *The Italians and the Holocaust: Persecution, Rescue and Survival*. London: Peter Halban, 1987.

Other Sources

Lidor, Lisa. "Hope, Humanity and Honor: The Jewish Brigade and the Meeting with the DPs (*She'erit Hapletah*)." Unpublished thesis, Hebrew University of Jerusalem, 2009.

Shamir, Aharon, ed. "Habrigadah Yotzet Lekrav" [The brigade goes to war]. *Niv Ahim*, [*Journal of the Israeli War Veterans' League*], May 1994.

Commonwealth War Graves Commission: *The Commonwealth Cemeteries and Memorials in Italy. The War in Italy 1943–1945*. (Undated explanatory booklet).

About the Author

Born and educated in England, D. Lawrence-Young arrived in Israel in 1968. Since then he has spent most of his time teaching English and history in high schools and universities, as well as lecturing for organizations such as the Association of Americans and Canadians in Israel (AACI). He loves researching and writing about military history and Shakespeare. In addition to writing historical novels, he is a regular contributor to *Skirmish*, a military history journal, and also to *Forum*, a magazine for English teachers. He also served eighteen years in the armored infantry reserves in the Israeli army. A published (USA) and exhibited (UK and Jerusalem) photographer, he also plays the clarinet (badly) and lives in Jerusalem. He is married and has three children.